This Too, To

£1.60

Also by Jonathan Ross

The Blood Running Cold (1968)
Diminshed By Death (1968)
Dead at First Hand (1969)
The Deadest Thing You Ever Saw (1969)
Here Lies Nancy Frail (1972)
The Burning of Billy Toober (1974)
I Know What It's Like To Die (1976)
A Rattling of Old Bones (1979)
Dark Blue and Dangerous (1981)
Death's Head (1982)
Dead Eye (1983)
Dropped Dead (1984)
Burial Deferred (1985)
Fate Accomplished (1987)
Sudden Departures (1988)
A Time for Dying (1989)
Daphne Dead and Done For (1990)
Murder be Hanged (1992)
The Body of a Woman (1994)
Murder! Murder! Burning Bright (1996)

Under the name of John Rossiter

The Murder Makers (1970)
The Deadly Green (1970)
The Victims (1971)
A Rope for General Dietz (1972)
The Manipulators (1973)
The Villains (1974)
The Golden Virgin (1975)
The Man Who Came Back (1978)
Dark Flight (1981)

THIS TOO, TOO SULLIED FLESH

Jonathan Ross

Constable · London

First published in Great Britain 1997 by Constable & Company Ltd
3 The Lanchesters, 162 Fulham Palace Road, London W6 9ER
Copyright © 1997 by Jonathan Ross
The right of Jonathan Ross to be identified as the author
of this work has been asserted by him in accordance with
the Copyright, Designs and Patents Act 1988
ISBN 0 09 477680 6
Set in Palatino 10pt by SetSystems Ltd, Saffron Walden, Essex
Printed and bound in Great Britain by Hartnolls Ltd, Bodmin

A CIP catalogue record for this book
is available from the British Library

1

His mind surfaced from the unremembered dark of unconsciousness to a nightmarish recognition of choking smoke and the taste of vomit in his mouth. Lying face downwards on the hard flooring – held helpless it seemed by the weakness of his body – sick and wretched with a thudding pain in the back of his skull, he felt movement beneath him, the lurch and sideways shifting of the boat.

He could see from the grey streaks of daylight entering through the shuttered portlights that he was in the cabin, feeling that he was held from rolling with the movement of the boat by the metal legs of the fixed table. Groaning his anguish, burning spasms tearing pain in his stomach, he thought of her and what had gone wrong. Where was she? The bitch! She had done this to him. He tried to call out, but he heard only croaking sounds. Like a bloody frog he told himself unhappily, not thinking it very funny.

Where was the smoke coming from? Christ! Was the boat on fire? With him seemingly nerveless and unable to move? Befuddled in the torment of his pain there was a growing fear. He couldn't remember how he had come to be lying here. He wasn't able to turn his head, but she was certainly not in what he could see of the smoke-filled cabin's interior.

In his suffering there was a physical languor, a feeling that this was something he couldn't struggle against. He groaned. He was going to burn to death if he didn't get out. He coughed harshly, drily, tasting the smoke, feeling it in his lungs and panic gripping him. 'Oh, God,' he whimpered in his mind. 'Help me. Please help me.'

Raising himself painfully on his elbows, he shuffled his body, his legs dragging behind him, towards where he could see dimly the two steps leading to the cockpit hatch. Hauling himself up them, still on his elbows, he balanced on one for long hurtful moments, fumbling for the hatch's handle, reaching it and pulling the hatch open to an incandescent blast of red flame that sent withering heat into his face, scorching down into his lungs and toppling him backwards to the blackness awaiting him.

*

Detective Superintendent George Rogers, operational head of the Criminal Investigation Department at Police Headquarters, in the extremely ancient town of Abbotsburn, was, with some ifs and buts, at peace with himself and, for the moment, with the society in which he lived and worked. He was, in fact, on a rest day and playing golf with a fellow member of his club.

In his forties – his very early forties he would insist – his hair was still a glossy black, his out-thrusting inquisitorial nose, which he occasionally regretted having, was still sniffing for guilt in crimes of unlawful violence and man's apparently built-in dishonesty. Six feet and two inches of a dark amiability which just brushed the edge of sardonicism, he was without a middle-age paunch and in good breeding condition – sometimes not being overly grateful for that – and was attracted by and to women who were within a decade or so either side of his own age. He carried within himself his own brand of cynicism having dealt with too many killings, too many cruelties and much too much corruption for him to believe that *Homo sapiens* could be God's most important or most cherished creation. There were times when he was embarrassed and sad at having to accept that he was one of them.

He was in that unusual state of finding life quite satisfying – a rare condition – because he had no murder case under investigation and his ex-wife, to whom he had been paying fifty per cent of his salary for years, had finally kicked out her 250 pound primitive and unemployed rugby-playing live-in lover and married a so-called captain of industry, wealthy enough for her to beat Rogers to the punch and to tell him scornfully what he could do with his always unwilling maintenance payments with all the gall and wormwood of their failed marriage.

That he didn't now know quite what to do with it was something he believed he could overcome; to spend it for a start – were she to permit him – on his engagingly attractive sexual partner, Angharad Rhys Pritchard, widow of a retired Royal Naval Commander and now the owner of his yacht, *Lady Pink Gin II*. That he didn't go overboard in an enthusiasm for sailing was matched by Angharad's indifference to his playing golf.

It was this that he was doing at nine in the morning on a pleasantly autumnal day and about to pitch his ball on to the eleventh green some thirty feet away when a police patrol car, approaching him along the almost hallowed turf of the fairway, froze him into holding for a moment the club at the top of his swing.

Knowing what the arrival of the car foreshadowed, knowing that his game was to be ended, he swung the club down in a spasm of irritation, topping the ball and sending it scuttling yards past the green. His face said it all and his partner looked ostentatiously elsewhere as the PC driver climbed from the car and approached them.

'Sir,' he said, lowering his voice, being obviously unwitting of his heinous offence in driving a car on the closely shaven turf, 'a man's body has been found at Farquharson's Folly and I've been ordered by the Assistant Chief to tell you.'

'How long ago?' Rogers was trying to be gracefully philosophical about losing his rest day.

'About quarter to nine, sir, and he's been shot with an arrow.'

'An arrow!' Rogers echoed frowning. 'You mean by a bow and arrow? A crossbow?'

'I don't know, sir. The Assistant Chief didn't say.'

'Do we know who he is?'

The PC shook his head, not being expected to anyway.

'Do you know who's at the scene then?'

'Inspector Blanshard, and I think he's been told to wait for you before doing anything.'

'Tell the ACC and Mr Blanshard that I'm on the way. And do it while you're taking me back to the clubhouse.' Apologizing and leaving his opponent – who wasn't worrying too much, having been in serious danger of losing a fiver – he allowed the PC to load his trolley and bag of clubs in the boot of the car before driving him off.

Having hurriedly showered and changed and climbed rather damply into his almost new dark-green shark-nosed Citroen, bought to celebrate his financial disunion from his wife, he turned it on to the coastal road leading to Little Rygg Sands and the Farquharson Folly.

Pointing the Citroen's nose at his destination, seventeen miles of undeveloped countryside away, he called on that part of his mind not involved in driving to remind him of what he knew about the folly and its conversion to a club and entertainment centre. It wasn't a lot, for he had had no occasion to visit it either before or after its metamorphosis from being a long neglected folly into being the uniqueness of the Farquharson Country Club Resort Plc. What he did know of its origin was part of the local folklore, a part reading of a local history of the area and a high-up view of the restructured building and grounds from a police helicopter engaged otherwise in a search for an escaped prisoner.

Lord Farquharson had been an early nineteenth-century eccentric – Mad Farquharson he'd been called in his youth – being later notorious for badly wounding a one-eyed Major Gotz von Ranke in a duel with flash-pan pistols. That von Ranke was an Hanoverian second cousin to the Prince Regent necessitated Farquharson's immediate disappearance to Italy, returning to his estate in England, having married a wealthy Signorina Falcucci, only after the death of George IV the former Prince Regent in 1830.

To honour his wife he had built – with her money – an extravagantly Italianate baroque building on his coastal estate, this huge multi-towered and domed building set inappropriately at the sea's edge, and abandoned almost immediately on her death in childbirth. Unlived in, it was kept from disintegration in its uselessness by the estate's successive managements, serving now as a commodious and well-equipped Leisure Club.

Four years prior to Rogers's now official interest in it, it had been bought by an hotel tycoon and reconstituted as it now stood. Its apparently most important feature as a country club was a quite massive glazed dome connected to the frontage of the main building and containing in it a subtropical climate supporting palm trees, exotic flowering bushes and creepers; and a warm-water lagoon with its own mechanically induced waves. With this was a breezeless sandy beach and an adjacent Mediterranean-style village of bars and shops together with facilities for indoor sports and games. Outside the building and its dome was an expanse of the estate's wooded countryside and, on the sea side a long sandy spit known as Little Rygg Sands curved around the bay which, together with many tons of limestone blocks, formed a harbour mooring for the club's modest fleet of small sailing yachts and motor cruisers.

Rogers had heard from the Abbotsburn salacious that this was not a club for the local community, nor for any of the too-sober-suited citizenry outside its own ambit. Its advertising in the broadsheets and better magazines was aimed at an international clientele; at whom it called the *bons vivants* and the frankly hedonistic singles, who were by implication able to afford the accommodation and tariff, referred to only as extravagant and for the gourmet.

Out of Rogers's reach by virtue of his profession, he knew he could stand on the sidelines and suffer the denial to him of its amenities fairly happily. Apart from a late remembering that his golf trolley and bag of clubs were still in the boot of the patrol car and now only God and the car's driver knew where, and not having the time to change into one of his dark-grey business suits he wore on duty, he was facing the unwelcome, possibly embarrassing, calling out of the Home Office appointed pathologist. And that pathologist wasn't going to be his gourmandising friend Dr Wilfred Twite, now hospitalized with a justly earned duodenal ulcer, but Bridget Hunter, Doctor of Medicine and Graduate in Morbid Pathology, the neighbouring county's loaned stand-in; and, to Rogers's regret and unjustified irritation, his past lover. This fact, as he steered the car with one hand and stuffed tobacco into his pipe with the other, his smoking frowned on by Angharad anyway, gave him no uplifting of the spirit. He felt about this that Fate was being rather unkind to him.

2

Rogers, unusually wearing off-white trousers and a cream linen jacket, found that his climbing approach to the Club Farquharson was through an electrically operated gate manned by a character who appeared to be a guard and who had apparently been warned of his coming, not actually reading Rogers's warrant card outstretched to him from the car's window, but passing him through without question.

Passing a large flat-fronted and very civilized Georgian house in coffee-coloured stone a thousand or so yards to his right and assuming it was the old Farquharson family home – now occupied by a different unrelated family – he descended steeply a sanded road running down into what he knew to be Blackthorn Forest. After a seemingly interminable series of acute bends, it dropped into a sunken ravine flanked by huge pine and deciduous trees growing through a fern and fallen leaf carpet and closing in on him from both sides of the road. Being well into the morning, shafts of brilliant sunlight lanced down through its foliage, illuminating dancing summer insects.

Breaking out from the forest on to a civilized half-acre or so of sloping mown grass and ornamental garden, he was confronted by the huge house which had been named a folly. To Rogers it was a monument to sheer inelegance, having among other grotesqueries two tall and slim square towers, each with improbably arched and balustered windows reaching to its pinnacle and to the central lead-covered cathedral-like dome.

From below, it appeared enormous and, even with its back in shadow as it now was, its extravagantly white-painted and grotesque exterior made it resemble an exuberantly iced wedding cake. The access to what was obviously the rear of the building was a wide yellow gravelled drive on which stood a police patrol car and two dark-blue hatchback saloons. To the right was a covered-in car park – architecturally intrusive, he thought, even against this curious building – probably packed wheel-to-wheel with Jaguars, Mercedes and BMWs with only a few of the lesser breeds. Rogers, dismounting from his car, had no difficulty in appreciating why the folly's builder had been called Mad Farquharson.

The thickset uniformed PC who had been standing on the steps leading to an oversized solid-looking door discreetly labelled *Reception* in gold leaf, approached Rogers, saluting and indicating the beginning of a path leading into the adjacent forest on the far side of the house.

'The jogging track, sir,' he said. 'I was ordered by Mr Blanshard to point it out to you. He's down there with the body.'

'What are you here for?' Rogers asked. 'To make sure I don't get lost?'

'Nothing like that.' The constable smiled. 'Nobody's to leave the premises or the grounds other than for the most urgent of reasons and then only when they've been identified and cleared to my satisfaction and Mr Blanshard's.' He tapped a thick finger on the mobile radio he carried.

'And has anybody asked to leave? Or actually left?' He was becoming impressed with Blanshard, until now just another uniformed body to him.

'No, sir, and I don't believe Mr Blanshard is likely to let them anyway.'

Matters were so far going to an approved pattern and Rogers was thinking ironically that he probably wouldn't have been missed overmuch had he taken the time to finish his game of golf. Skirting the building and a planting of tall cigar-shaped conifers in what looked like an Italian-type cemetery, he saw through them the top of a vast glittering dome from which, it seemed, the hedonistic delights were on offer to the members. The track he entered was leaf-covered earth overshadowed by the trees; and he walked briskly down the slope of a shallow ravine which must lead to the sea. Walking through the dusty bars of hot sunlight slanting dappled light on the spongy ground he trod, he could smell it and hear the waves breaking on the beach.

It was the best of a half-mile of soundless walking before he came upon the three men standing on the path. Blanshard, tall and solid in his uniform, possessed in himself an ex-guardsman's self-assurance. The youthful sergeant – Rogers could put the name Traughton to him – was similarly uniformed and looked to Rogers as if he had only recently left his school's sixth-form. The harassed-looking dark-haired man with them, sporting a black moustache like a thick inverted V, was of obvious executive stuff, formal in a dark chalk-striped suit with a crimson tie. A white four-seater buggy, identified with the letters FCCR, was parked off-path behind them.

The suit man's name was given as Charles Jarvis, his reason for being there that he was the General Manager of the club and its facilities. Rogers told him that while he needed to speak to him about this most unpleasant happening, he would prefer to do so later in the manager's office when he had decided what action should be taken about the dead man whose body he could now see yards off the path and partially concealed in shrubbery.

With Jarvis having driven off in his buggy and Blanshard having ordered the sergeant to continue blocking off the path to stray joggers, Rogers said, 'Right, Mr Blanshard, to the body, please.' So far he had a wholly unwarranted feeling that the coming investigation was one that should go well.

Standing over the body and pointing his investigative nose at it, he accepted in a brief moment of pity that the man who had lived in it had died unhappily, though this was understandable and usual with the violently dead. Dressed in a patently new blue tracksuit which was partly unzipped and similarly new trainer shoes, the dead man lay on his back. With his head arched backward, his widely opened mouth showed his teeth and tongue in the rictus of death, flies already settling in on the kill. Slimly built and apparently somewhere in his thirties, he sported a close-cut dark-brown beard and moustache on a narrow face that even in death seemed to reflect a meanness of spirit. His death had come to him by a miniature aluminium arrow, one and a half inches of its thin shaft, flighted with red plastic feathers, protruding at an angle from the left side of the bloodstained throat. The tracksuit below it was copiously bloodied, as was the leaf-covered soil on which the head rested. His hands were clenched, the left being badly bloodstained.

'Searched?' Rogers asked Blanshard, indicating the opened tracksuit.

'No, sir. It'd already been opened.'

Reading the signs, Rogers could accept that the man had been up on his feet when shot and had bled in that position for a short time before toppling over on to his back to bleed the remainder of his life away.

Bending his knees, the sun hot on his back, Rogers crouched over the body, examining closely the arrow penetrating the throat and the source of the bleeding. He put a finger on the end of the shaft and moved it gently back and forth.

'It seems to be in fairly deeply,' he observed to Blanshard, 'and only God knows what it hit inside to bleed him so much.' He frowned his puzzlement. 'Have you seen as small an arrow as this before? Surely much too small for a crossbow?'

Blanshard shook his head. 'It's a new one on me.'

'Small, but big enough to kill and I've no doubt I'll be told,' Rogers said, not too optimistically. The sun was warm on his back and some of the flies were disengaging their unpleasant attentions from the dead man's face to the light sweat on his forehead. 'We seem to be fatally vulnerable to small pointed things. Especially as it's probably not an arrow at all, and only by a stretch of the imagination a crossbow bolt.'

Smoothing his hand over the pockets and feeling little but a possible bunch of keys and a handkerchief, he grimaced his distaste and slipped his hand through the neck of the tracksuit and under a body vest to feel the dead flesh. 'A couple of hours or so?' he said. 'He's still warm. Does that fit in with what you know? And doesn't getting himself killed before breakfast seem to you a mite uncivilized?'

Accepting the inspector's nod and approving his apparent taciturnity he rose from his crouch, fishing his pipe and tobacco from his jacket pocket and starting to fill it. 'Of course,' he said, almost to himself, 'it could have hit an artery and he wouldn't have been long in the going.' But he wasn't yet prepared to expend too much pity on an unknown man who might, in the event, have deserved to die as he had.

Putting a match to his pipe, he said, 'Tell me how it happened – if you know – and what you've done about it?'

Blanshard, competence crisp in his voice and now not so taciturn, said, 'So far as the finding of the body is concerned, I've been through to Headquarters and I've notified the Assistant Chief, instructed that you and the coroner be informed, asked for the pathologist to be advised of a probable request for her attendance at the scene of a suspected murder and ordered a standby for the Coroner's Officer and the Scenes of Crime department. I also asked for the Murder Wagon to be readied and personnel allocated for a possible search of the missing weapon; also for Chief Inspector Lingard to be located and advised in case you hadn't been located yourself.' He seemed to be hunting for detail, saying after a brief pause, 'Then I sent for a couple of my own PCs to act as stoppers at the entrance to this part of the forest and at the Folly's back door.'

'I imagine not much chance of sealing shut the forest part?'

'No, though in view of what Jarvis told me later and if I'd had more men, at least I'd have had it checked. It's wide open until you get to the boundary fence, though I don't know of any fence that can't eventually be climbed.'

Rogers grunted. 'Nor I. What did Jarvis say?'

'Nothing positive other than he couldn't recognize the dead man as a member. It was the beard, I think.'

'I see, though not very clearly. How far are we from the fence you're talking about?'

'A hundred, a hundred and fifty yards or so. And it's back behind us.'

'It's a damned sight nearer than the way I came in. How far from here to the clubhouse, or whatever it is?'

'The Club Farquharson?' Blanshard wasn't quite sure what Rogers was getting at. 'Eight hundred to a thousand yards? It'd easily be that.'

'As I've to walk it, it'll probably be more,' Rogers grunted. 'Now fill me in with how the body came to be here and with whatever else you've happened on.'

The inspector pulled a face. 'There isn't much of that I'm afraid. What I have, I've got from the manager, and he knew practically sod all.' He took out his notebook and flipped pages. 'I received notification of the finding of the body at eight-fifteen from Jarvis himself. He was very, very agitated; saying that he thought there'd been a serious accident and that there was a dead man found in the trees. He thought at first, though he didn't seem to want to admit it, that it could be the body of one of the members who'd been out jogging before breakfast.' Blanshard wagged his head in disapproval over something. 'He wouldn't say more and as I was anxious to get on with it I didn't press him.'

He referred to his notebook again, then said, 'I got here with

Sergeant Traughton at eight twenty-five, was met by Jarvis and we were brought here in golf carts by him and his lady PA. When I saw the body I knew what would be wanted and got moving on it.' He cleared his throat. 'When Jarvis's PA pointed out to him that the dead man had a beard – he was looking sick about it by then – he cheered up a bit and said he was now almost certain he couldn't be one of the members because he thought he knew only two here who wore beards and he didn't think this chap was one of them. When I said, Well, all right, then, what was he doing here on private property in running gear? he couldn't say. Nor in fact could his PA and I should think she's bright enough for two or three.' He paused then, probably sparing a moment or two to think about the probable delectability of Jarvis's personal assistant. 'I then told him,' he continued, 'that when you got here you'd certainly want to know about the bearded members and who he might or might not be and suggested that the young woman should get on back to whatever office dealt with the inmates and find out for certain.'

'And?' Rogers said. 'What was the result?'

'Nothing yet. I think there're quite a lot of them to check on.'

'Panic stations not helping either, eh?'

The inspector smiled. 'Not at all, I imagine. While Jarvis was here I asked him who'd found the dead chap and he said one of the members called Toplis – Peter Toplis – an apparently mad bugger who was climbing on the rock face: it's called Butters Rock Climb by the way.' He paused to point to a sheer expanse of blackish-grey rock visible to Rogers at an angle only in fragments seen through the upper foliage of the tallest trees and appearing to be about fifty or so yards behind him. 'This Toplis chap heard voices coming from below him – well, more or less below – though he couldn't see them. That's not surprising really when you see where he was and how his attention would be all on what was happening on the rock in front of his nose. It was quiet though and he could hear them quarrelling – at least that's what he thought was happening – and that the voices were those of two men, though Jarvis said that he didn't appear to be too sure about this. Then, Jarvis said, Toplis told him that one of them screamed, a pretty fearful scream it seems to have been and enough to persuade Toplis that he ought to get down on the ground and find out what was happening. When he couldn't see anything or anybody he was still shaken enough to run back to the hotel to report to Jarvis what he had heard.'

'Do we know the time of all this?'

'Toplis told Jarvis about eight.'

'Go on.'

'It's only that a couple of the waiters, or whoever came here on the trot with Jarvis, found chummy where he is now, almost certainly being dead. Dead enough anyway to decide Jarvis against getting in a doctor from the village which is three or four miles away and to call me instead.'

Blanshard paused again, obviously wondering whether he was being explicit enough for Rogers. Then, forging on, he said, 'That's about all that Jarvis told me other than that this chap Toplis had come barging panic-stricken into the staff restaurant where he was getting outside his grapefruit juice and bacon and eggs – he told me that – and in telling him about this dreadful screaming he'd heard was also succeeding in telling everybody else in the restaurant. Not to Jarvis's pleasure, as he made it plain to me. He seemed to believe that if this got abroad in the rough so to speak then his seniority might be put on the line with his future in jeopardy.' The inspector pushed his notebook back into his tunic pocket as if that was that.

'Ah,' Rogers said, his expression reflecting his disappointment, together with a touch of irritation with the little he had to work with. 'This climbing chap saw nothing then?'

'Nothing. He'd be more concerned with not falling off the rock face, I'd imagine, even though there're belaying ropes. I've had a look at it and it's a pretty tricky climb. Dangerous if you happened to put a foot wrong or started to think about something else but where you were.'

This, Rogers knew, was as far as he could go here without seeing people and having his back-up specialists and a searching team here to do things. His first need was to have the dead man identified and this he couldn't have done in a wilderness of trees, attractive as it was.

'Is this the track used by the joggers?' he asked Blanshard. 'Or by anyone else daft enough to chase around the place before breakfast, whenever that is?'

'A few, I'm told.'

'H'm.' Rogers couldn't think of anything further except to instruct Blanshard to send the sergeant, not at present wholly earning his keep, to the boundary fence on the, as yet unproved, assumption that the dead man had entered through or over it, and to see whether or not there was any evidence to support it. Having thought about that, he then asked if that part of the forest was anywhere near civilization. On Blanshard assuring him that it was not, Rogers said it might be that the dead man – if indeed he wasn't a club member – could have left some means of transport outside the fence or, possibly, somebody who had brought him here and could now be anxiously waiting his return. It was a long shot, but it reinforced his decision to have Sergeant Traughton go there and do what a sergeant had to do in whatever circumstances arose. He said Blanshard himself might be happy to remain at the scene and to notify Rogers of the attendance of the pathologist and any of the back-ups as they arrived.

As he strode below the arch of summer-smelling trees to the Club Farquharson which, according to Blanshard who hadn't to do it, was a little less than three-quarters of a mile away, his mind was already dictating to him the overly familiar routines consequent on slipping loose the dogs of a culpable and bloody homicide committed.

3

It was a lordly wood, Rogers thought, as he strode the track to Farquharson House; in places as dark and secret as hidden sin. After half a mile of rapid walking, already having startled a horrified pygmy deer to fleeing back into the shadows, he was beginning to sweat in the growing heat of the advancing day. Worried about the time he was taking in walking this wilderness of trees – albeit an attractive wilderness – he was relieved when a silently moving buggy, driven by a slender young woman, rounded the bend he was about to negotiate.

Braking to a halt only a foot or two from him, she stared at him appraisingly, it seemed with a cool arrogance, through the large windscreen. 'Good morning,' she said, sticking her head around it, 'I take it you're the police superintendent I've been sent to collect?'

She was a woman somewhere in the maturity of her thirties, irresistibly suggesting to him a tawny-haired greyhound bitch of impeccable pedigree. Not classically beautiful, she was leanly and coolly attractive with an Australian-type nose that looked to have been handed down to her by a blood relative of the first Duke of Wellington, and what he considered to be down-putting blue-grey eyes. Her mouth – he approved that it was without lipstick – looked as if it could curve into an occasional smile. She wore elegantly a country-style oatmeal-coloured costume with an orange shirt and with an absence of visible jewellery.

After he had said yes, that he thought he was, she put out her hand to be shaken, looking at him searchingly as he took it. 'Nancy Duval,' she said, in what was probably a Roedean Girls School accent. 'Just Duval will do until we know each other better. I'm known here as a "Mrs", though that mightn't be terribly accurate, and I'm Charles Jarvis's personal assistant.'

'And Rogers for me,' he replied amiably, wondering, what the hell? He was already tagging her – admiringly so – as one of those super self-confident and efficient women who could wreak psychological damage to over-assertive males, and to be able to surf the Internet almost in her sleep.

Cutting short the thought that he might warm to her in something less than a decade and disciplining his mind to his investigation, he asked, 'Could we be definite about the dead man being a member here or not?'

'I've been briefed by Charles to say that it's not one of ours,' she said crisply. Shifting on the bench to make room for him, she added, 'For myself, I'm positive too that it isn't.' She tapped a polished fingernail on the bench beside her. 'Now would you hop in and I'll turn around. You wish to come to Farquharson House?'

'It'd help,' he said, stepping into the low-on-the-ground buggy – he thought clumsily – and sitting almost in contact with her splendid body. 'I do need to question Toplis the rock climber.'

'I've anticipated you,' she told him while she was doing a neat three-point turn in the narrow track and charging noiselessly off at about ten miles an hour in what must be the direction of the club's headquarters. 'He'll be waiting for you at the administration side of the House.' She added an almost inaudible, 'I hope,' for a Rogers not too sure that he had heard it.

'I'm obliged,' he said, preparing to dig in on the developing investigation. 'It seems that friend Toplis disturbed Mr Jarvis's breakfast with his news of the death of our so far unknown man. That possibly makes breakfast time and those being there – or not being there – of significant interest.' She was making him nervous with her driving, rounding blind bends without seemingly caring a damn for any approaching unfortunate. 'Could I ask you about this? Or do I wait for Jarvis?'

She was almost derisively facetious. 'Charles isn't available, I'm afraid. He's gone to eat dirt at Head Office, to explain, if he can, how he has apparently allowed a dead man to be left on their property.' She smiled then, said drily, 'I think you'll find I'm accustomed to taking breakfast here every morning and being a mine of useless information about it.'

'Astonishing,' he said as drily. 'What time is breakfast served? And where?'

She had been speaking without turning her head, for which Rogers, in view of the narrowness and the steepening gradient of the ground, full of unyielding tree trunks on each side, was thankful.

'Assuming that the dead man was killed by a club member,' he said, 'would his absence from breakfast be noticed?'

'Yes, it would. The waiters would know even were the fellow diners at the same table to decide not to remember.' She braked the buggy to a standstill, taking no more than a couple of yards to do it, the air immediately smelling of pine needles.

She turned to him, almost fully frontal, her closer knee in a no doubt unintended contact with his and staying there. 'Is that what you want?' she demanded. 'A list of possible suspects?'

'Indeed it is.' He was getting there carefully. 'Would the staff be included in that?'

She looked surprised. 'The staff? You would include them?'

'Yes. They bleed too, don't they? And they are subject to the same emotions as the members.' He smiled, his brown eyes seeking her agreement, keeping it amiable. 'Even you.' He flapped a hand at the flies seeking to use his face as a landing strip, believing that they had followed him from feeding on the dead man's moistures.

'Point taken,' she accepted, smiling back at him and removing her knee from its contact with his. 'I think I can say that you could be told who the late comers or absentees were this morning.'

'Tell me how you can be so happily certain,' he said. Unobserved, he had slid his pipe halfway from a pocket on his leeward side, thought about it in an unfamiliarly negative way, then poking it back in a fit of a smoker's newfound cowardice.

Holding the steering wheel and squeezing it as if still driving, she told him, 'A waiter is given two tables of eight members as his personal responsibility. Being briefed beforehand on their names and needs, he would obviously know who was, or wasn't, served breakfast this morning. And, naturally, who had arrived substantially late for it.'

She smiled briefly, as though some thought had amused her. 'I should also say that none of the members would necessarily be doing or not doing what they are perfectly entitled to do.'

'Of course not,' Rogers agreed. 'What are the arrangements for the staff?'

'Difficult. For you, I mean. There's a separate dining-room for us. Some take breakfast between seven and eight, some between eight and nine and some after nine. Nevertheless, we would know who attended and who did not, and who were significantly late. Or covered in blood,' she added, either in irony or humorously.

'I'm grateful, and I'll stick to the earlier breakfasts,' he said as he and his accompanying flies were again set in motion; so near to her, even though so seemingly untouchable. Nancy Duval was certainly a woman about whom even strong men could fantasize. 'Tediously,' he said over the whining of the battery-driven motor beneath their seats, and returning to the more serious subject of violent death, 'how many members have you now staying here? And how are they accommodated?'

'Sixty-eight,' she replied promptly. 'We are, for reasons unknown this late summer, suffering one of our lows. Our accommodation? We have two wings in the House with the use of forty double rooms and twenty single.'

'Might I see the register for the names of those staying here now?'

'I imagine so, though I'd better check with higher command first.'

'And the names of the staff, please? You never know, do you?' he said ambiguously.

She nodded her head, not looking from the track on which they were silently riding. 'You shall have them, of course.'

'How do the members come? As singles and doubles? As unmarried, divorced or of ambiguous status?'

She turned her head and stared at him. 'You mustn't encourage me to discuss our members,' she said, not quite reprovingly, but near enough to be taken as a warning.

A widening of the now gravelled track, a salute from the second of Blanshard's uniformed PCs in his role as guardian of the gate, and Rogers, abruptly out from the restrictive surround of the forest trees, could view both the immensity of the crystal dome rising above them and behind it the glittering sunlit green of the sea breaking its rather gentle waves on the sandy foreshore.

Nancy Duval braked the buggy to another halt and smiled at the expression on his face. 'You hadn't seen it before?' she asked.

'Not from ground level, and not so close. I'm impressed.'

The dome with its sheer glittering walls was a spider's web frame of thin metal and glass panels. Out-thrusting metal buttresses like a giant spider's legs appeared to be holding the whole structure from subsiding and flattening itself out in a momentous crashing of glass. It was, Rogers estimated, well over a hundred feet in height with a glazed nipple-shaped cupola on its summit and with an inside acreage enough to accommodate easily a football pitch and a half, and two or three tennis courts.

The sun, now overhead, splintered its eye-dazzling glare from the multiplicity of the dome's skylights. Despite this, Rogers could see by squinting his eyes an interior panorama of a lush jungle of palm trees and subtropical flowering shrubbery. Through it, obstructed somewhat by the green fronds of palm, he could glimpse the foreshortened blue water of an interior lagoon with its gentle heaving of slow waves and its shore of yellow sand. Even more obscured, he thought he could see the white walls and red-tiled roofs of Mediterranean-style lodges and shops. Members were in there, mostly, he could briefly see, undressed for swimming or sunbathing. He wasn't certain, but he thought that he had glimpsed two or three bare-breasted women. His mind, escaping briefly from his control, took a mini-holiday from thoughts of murder.

'It's not its proper name,' Nancy Duval told him as she put the buggy in motion again, 'but our members – even our staff – persist in calling it Shangri-la, which I must admit is perhaps more descriptive of it than the Solarium or Pleasure Dome.'

The track, now paved and civilized with kerbing, led them behind the dome to bring them on to a parking area below the towering ornate walls of a glaring white Farquharson House. While Mrs Duval – dammit, he thought, but he did have to think of her sometimes as a married woman – parked the buggy in a space marked GENERAL MANAGER and joined a rank of similar white carts, Rogers unloaded himself and stood looking up at the front of the folly. To his architecturally blinkered mind, it appeared to be an incestuous amalgam of what he thought to be white-painted Byzantine and Italian Baroque, containing in it the same grotesquenesses and improbabilities. And why not? he thought, for he had seen much the same at its rear.

Being led by Duval into it, Rogers found himself in a heavily carpeted circular foyer, its ceiling two floors high with a massive crystal chandelier hanging from an iron gantry. Two mahogany and brass bannistered stairways led up to two overhanging left and right open passages. Near the door by which they had entered was an unmanned bulky mahogany counter with rows of door keys hanging at its rear. Opposite it was a door – also mahogany – with a sign OFFICES at its side. Twenty or so feet of expensive carpeting from it was a similar door signboarded MEMBERS ONLY. There was a palpable odour of much money about the place, making Rogers feel somewhat deprived.

As if anticipating his unspoken query, she said, 'The members' breakfast room is where you see it.' She was looking at him in what had to be her familiar milieu as if wondering, was he going to fit in with whatever it was she had in her mind? 'You may use my office for the time being,' she said, peering at her tiny wristwatch, her attitude somehow different from what it had been. 'Mr Toplis will be with you in ten minutes.'

Following her through the door marked OFFICES into a spacious windowed corridor, Rogers could see out into the dome and through it to the sea beyond. There, heaving slightly in a fairly quiet sea, was a pontoon boom harbouring a line of shoulder-to-shoulder sailing boats and powered cruisers.

Reaching her office, it was the end one of three, she waved him into it. 'Feel free,' she said. It was a room large enough for her to be able to sit at her leather-topped desk and wait for her callers to traverse the long yards of blue carpet. Before he had arrived at the desk he had noted on it a set of red calf-leather bound books, virtually empty trays, an elaborate blotting-pad, two brass *fin de siècle* tubular telephones and a fax machine. There were two executive chairs, the larger one at her desk, and a glass-door bookcase contained rows of legal-looking books. Stood near one of the telephones was a small white card with unreadable small print on it, arousing his curiosity. The sun shone through the two tall and narrow windows, enhancing, it seemed, the scented air in the office.

'You are kind,' he said cheerfully, looking around admiringly. 'What high-powered investigations am I to be permitted to run from here?'

'Only one: that for your seeing Peter Toplis.' She smiled back at him. 'Then I shall organize a takeover.'

'Our Murder Wagon should be outside your rear entrance at any time now. I shall be doing my stuff from there as soon as I can.' He felt happy with her and had no trouble in showing it. 'In the meantime, could I ask you to get me the names of the waiters on duty this morning and have them available for interview by one of my staff? That should be short and painless and not at all time-wasting.'

He took his personal radio from his inside pocket – it was a new model, no larger than a packet of twenty cigarettes – and, extending its aerial, stood it on the desk. 'I've been out of touch with my office for too long,' he told her, not unhappily. 'There must have been somebody having to get in touch with me by now.'

She turned as she was leaving him. 'I'll chase up Toplis for you,' she promised. At the open door she paused again. 'You know, Rogers,' she said with, he thought, amusement in her voice, 'you are not at all as I thought you might be,' the door closing silently on her enigmatic words.

And that was a statement Rogers would find difficult to question or interpret. Seated at the desk he satisfied his curiosity about the small card by reaching for it and reading it. In small print it read, *Too Much Marriage Can Seriously Damage Your Health*. Rogers managed a wry grin. He had suffered too, though more in his wallet than in his emotions. He could now suppose that there might be a lot more to Nancy Duval than an aristocratic nose, an interesting body structure. He was blessed, he knew, with having been born an admirer of women with slim bodies, small breasts and beautifully white teeth.

The call sound of his radio disturbed what could have been an inner contemplation of a temporary transfer of one of his basic needs from a not over-possessive Angharad – she had always insisted that they should not each walk in the other's shadow – for whom he had a deep affection, to, perhaps, an interested and apparently available – he hoped – Nancy Duval.

It was Blanshard, shuttled to him through Headquarters Control, telling him that a woman, Sarah Gadd, had been intercepted by Sergeant Traughton where she had been waiting in her car outside the forest fence; she had said, for her friend Frank Ward. He, she had explained, was meeting a woman who owed him a large amount of money. Traughton climbed over the fence – it seemed not to be much of a fence in fact – and, without disclosing that her friend was undoubtedly dead, told her that there was a serious matter to be resolved concerning his unauthorized entry into the grounds of Farquharson House. First obtaining her name and address from the driving licence shown to him – she apparently came from an out of county town Amborum-on-Sea – he had ordered her to drive him to the house for an interview with a senior officer.

She was, Blanshard said, now being held in the Major Incident coach which had since arrived under the supervision of Woman Sergeant Sturton – Rogers had whispered, 'Oh, my God!' on hearing that – together with the Scenes of Crime officers and other troops urgently needed.

Blanshard added that there was one other thing. Dr Hunter, the stand-in pathologist, had only just been located at Rooksby Castle and, on being informed of the finding of the dead man, had said that she would be at Farquharson House – should she ever happen to find where it was – in about forty-five minutes. That she was coming, although expected and necessary, didn't add to Rogers's happiness.

With the possibly dead-end business of the absentees from the killing-before-breakfast theory to be dealt with, he asked Blanshard to put a call out for Detective Inspector Hagbourne – at present dealing with what must be the overpowering tedium of investigating a falsification of company accounts complaint – to report to him at the House with a spare DPS as soon as possible, this to be interpreted as of now.

He was making a note or two in his pocket-book when he heard footsteps – quick confident ones, he recognized – approaching. With his thoughts about Nancy Duval fled – he rarely permitted the contemplation of a woman's unsettling attractiveness to override his commitment to unmask villainy – he prepared himself to meet the madman Toplis who apparently climbed slabs of rock for pleasure, in preference to having breakfast.

4

Peter Toplis was a biggish man in his thirties, his features preset to being friendly, though his grey eyes somewhat militated against any ready acceptance of that. His lips were full, showed a humour of a sort and were no doubt attractive to women. His brown hair had been carefully set and Rogers could smell on him a good aftershave lotion, his initial impression of Toplis indexing him as *Homo erotica*. He wore a tailored white shirt and trousers with leather sandals, his wrist trappings a gold watch and chunky gold bracelet. He wasn't Rogers's idea of a climber; climbers he had met being usually lean and sinewy.

Rogers, shaking his hand and telling him to take a seat, said he was pleased to meet him and thanked him for coming; having done his quick evaluation of him at close range and believing him to be a man he wouldn't normally wish to know, adding as he did so that Mrs Duval had probably told him the reason for his being interviewed.

Toplis said, 'Exactly. I understand I'm the only witness – if you can call me that – to what I'm told by Jarvis to be a nasty murder.'

'You're a rock climber, I'm told,' Rogers said with a put-on amiability, placing his pocket-book on the blotting-pad, ready for the notes he might take. 'Doesn't that come under the description of a dangerous sport?' He didn't wish to start Toplis on the fact of murder too soon.

'Is it? I suppose it is if you don't know anything about it.' When the detective made no reply to that, he said, surprisingly modestly, 'I'm not all that good, just adequate really, and I haven't been at it all that long. What you have there is a slab climb of no great shakes, a lump of flattish rock just a slight slope off the vertical, fitted with belay ropes for us less experienced climbers.'

He cocked an eyebrow at Rogers, gaping slightly as if wondering what the hell. 'You want me to go on?' he asked, getting an amiable nod from Rogers who knew exactly what he wanted. 'I do a climb most mornings I'm here to keep myself in trim. I should explain, I suppose, that I'm aiming to be a free-style no-rope climber, though that's for the future. For the moment I use the belaying ropes so you can't call it dangerous.' He cocked his head. 'Is that what you want?'

'I'm with you,' Rogers said equably, though he still thought him eccentric if not mad, and decided to get to the point, now that he'd more or less summed him up. 'What time was it when you started your climbing this morning?'

Toplis scratched at his chin. 'Getting down to brass tacks are we?' he muttered. 'I've been waiting all bloody morning to get out to my boat.' Then he smiled. It wasn't wholly pleasant, but still a smile. 'Mustn't moan at you, must I? Got your job to do and all that.'

'You'd be surprised how often I've had that said to me,' Rogers murmured, mostly to himself. To Toplis, he smiled, encouragingly he thought.

Toplis was patently thinking things over, twisting his gold bracelet around his wrist. 'It was near enough half-past seven. Do you want me to go on? I can string a sentence or two together without coming to a halt if you leave me to do it in my own way.'

'I'm happy if you are, Mr Toplis.' Rogers wasn't about to fight the man. 'I'll only butt in when and if I want you to clarify.'

'Right,' Toplis grunted, looking at his watch which now appeared to the detective to be both a timekeeper and an astronaut's navigational computer. 'I've somebody waiting for me at the boat, so I won't waste your time or my own.' He cleared his throat. 'I started the climb at half-past seven as near as dammit; on my own and with nobody visible to me for miles. It was crack climbing, you know. Pushing your hand in a vertical crack and making a fist of it, using it as a handhold while your spare foot's looking for a smear, a support to give you balance.'

He looked at Rogers's face for some sort of understanding in the non-expression of his listening, then said resignedly, 'That's single-pitch climbing for you and it doesn't matter, I suppose, how I do it except that after twenty minutes or so I was approaching the top of the slab – it's somewhere about a reasonably easy vertical hundred and twenty footer – and facing the rock, which you have to be of course. That's when I heard voices coming up from below me in the wood.'

Toplis frowned, looked at his watch again, then scratched again at his chin while Rogers tried to visualize him being flattened lizard-like with his face averted against the high rock. 'I'm not sure about this,' he continued with something of authority in his voice, 'because other people's conversations are none of my bloody business or of interest to me and normally I wouldn't have cared less. I could hear some man's voice sort of floating up to me. Then there seemed to be two men arguing the toss. I could be mistaken about that, for I was concentrating on making the pitch and certainly not giving a damn what was going on with some silly buggers down on the ground.'

He paused as they both heard footfalls approaching, then passing and fading away. 'I didn't hear what was being said,' he continued, 'but one man's voice was beginning to sound a wee bit angry, though keeping it down to what I thought was under control.' He frowned. 'Don't ask me even then what was being said because I don't know from Adam. Then, in between whatever the man was saying, I thought I heard the second man, a harder-voiced one, though it could have been the first getting angry with the other.'

Shaking his head he thought about it. 'Damned if I know,' he admitted irritably, 'but I still can't understand exactly what happened. By this time I must admit I was getting more or less interested in what was going on though still concentrating on my climb, for it's all concentration if you don't want to do a faller or get trapped on a non-access pitch. Well, this man – or one of them – was really winding it up, getting angry you know, with the other not saying much at all.' He scowled, seemingly an easy thing for him to do. 'Then suddenly, I heard a sharp chuffing noise and I'm sure it was the first man who cried out ... you know? Bloody awful, it was.' His face showed nothing of any emotion. 'I've heard it once before from a man who was falling from a high pitch and banging his head on the way down.'

Rogers asked, 'The sound, Mr Toplis. What do you think made it?'

'God knows,' Toplis said. 'It was like this.' He pursed his lips and made a noise as if pronouncing a breathy *cha*! 'Something like that,' he explained, 'but I was too far away from them and there were trees in between us. It was him, of course, doing his dying, and while I clung on to the slab with my fingertips and toes wondering for Christ's sake what was going on I could hear the bushes being pushed through, and then there was nothing.'

He looked at his watch once again, though fairly absently, and to Rogers he seemed in the recalling of the tragedy to have forgotten he was supposed to be in a hurry. 'I came down then,' he continued, 'to have a look-see. Not fast, for that's an easy way of falling, and when I was down I went into the trees where I thought the voices had come from and that's where I found him.'

He swallowed. 'He was lying on his back and looking up to the sky and there was a lot of blood on his neck and on the ground. Also, there was an arrow sticking in his neck and I could see that he was dead, though I did feel his wrist for a pulse to make sure.'

He moved uneasily in his chair, an expression in his face as if he were brooding unhappily on what he had seen; a man not, apparently, going much on the handling of dead bodies. 'I ran then,' he said, 'looking for Jarvis who I knew would be having his breakfast in the staff restaurant. I'm afraid I panicked a little, but it isn't every day you hear a murder being committed and then finding the body, is it?' He gave a short laugh. 'God knows, it isn't anything I wish to be involved in either. Or hear again that terrible cry when he died.' He checked his wrist-watch again, frowning at it, his body making jerking movements as if he were about to rise from his chair.

'How long did it take you to climb down, Mr Toplis?' Rogers asked.

'For God's sake, man,' he said in a sudden gust of irritation, staring hard at him. 'What does that matter? And how much bloody longer have I to sit here answering stupid bloody questions? I've told you everything I know and I'm losing some very expensive sailing time.'

'Not much more,' Rogers said placatingly against his wish to chop Toplis off at the knees. He considered it a possibility that there was a somebody female waiting for him and, if there were, she would almost certainly be a large-ish armful of bulky femininity, probably somebody on whom he could practise his climbing. Less amiably, he said, 'I'd want to know how long in order to fix more precisely the time of the man's death.'

Toplis shrugged, even that done irritably. 'Not as fast as it may take to climb up.'

'More than twenty minutes then?'

'It could be.' Toplis had obviously stopped being talkative.

Rogers beamed at him, suspecting that it would irritate him further. 'Thank you for your assistance, Mr Toplis. I'll have an officer see you for a written statement after you've finished your sailing.'

When the sometimes tetchy Toplis had left him, Rogers used

his radio to get through to Sergeant Sturton, cooped up in the Murder Wagon, asking her had she been genned up fully on why she was there? When she replied tartly that she most certainly had been – he felt he deserved the rebuke – he detailed her to advise the woman Sarah Gadd of the death – though not letting her know by what murderous means – of the man believed to be Frank Ward, he, presumably, being someone other than her husband. 'Do it gently, sergeant,' he had added, knowing of Sturton's sharp-tongued tendency to bossiness in dealing with the public and her fellow police officers alike.

'There's something else,' she told him as if it were somehow his fault. 'PC Cummins on the rear door here has let two guests leave the house; contrary to your orders I understand. He was absent for some time, though he says only for a few minutes, while visiting a lavatory in Reception. When he returned he saw the back of the car – it was a dark green TVR Chimaera he says, being only able to read PMB and R of the registration number – taking the estate road from here and he's now finding out from Reception who it could have been.'

She added, before he could contrive to say anything, 'I didn't see it myself from the coach and I hadn't been told you'd put a stop on guests leaving. Nor had ...'

He broke in then. 'I know, sergeant, but we can't properly prevent anybody leaving if they wish to. Have you put a stop and check on it?' He was a bit peeved, but dammit, a man couldn't hold out indefinitely against his body's internal demands.

'I did,' Sturton told him tersely, for somehow he had obviously failed her. 'I notified Headquarters as I'd be expected to.'

'Well,' a slightly chastened Rogers told her, 'try not to worry too much about it. It's probably a prominent somebody who doesn't wish to be caught trousers-down with another man's wife; not a man who's recently murdered someone. We shall know soon, I hope. In the meantime, get on to Miss Gadd will you. Gently, please, and make notes of her reaction to the bad news.'

As he was switching off from the sergeant, Nancy Duval entered the office, her reappearance doing nothing to diminish the physical attraction she had left implanted in the lower reaches of his mind.

She carried papers and she said, smiling friendlily at him, 'Your time's up, I'm afraid. Charles is on his way back and he'll need my informed presence – which it isn't at the moment.'

She handed him a small key and a folded sheet of paper, her blue-grey eyes creased with humour. 'Apart from any temporary withdrawal from you, I am to give you all the assistance and co-operation you require – that'll be nice, won't it? – together with the use of any one of the two-seater buggies parked outside. The list you hold relates to the relevant on-duty waiters at breakfast this morning.' She smiled at him again. 'I'm apparently all yours to do with as you want, Charles having sold me into temporary slavery.'

'That,' he said with more intensity than perhaps her light-hearted words justified, 'is wonderful, and I'm grateful.' He hesitated, lost for suitable words. 'I'll be in touch,' he said, not finding anything else to say to this bewitching and bedazzling woman he had known only for about thirty minutes of what he could now think to be a hell of a lot of wasted years.

With his hand twisting on the oversized door knob, she added to his bewitchment by saying softly, 'And I think you've quite an attractive nose, Rogers.' At least he thought that was what she had said.

Without having a notion of an answer to that and finding himself outside the door, he realized that he didn't know how to get to the rear of the building and the Murder Wagon. Unwilling to return and admit to idiocy, he navigated his way by instinct through the entrance foyer and two lengths of picture-hung passages with unidentifiable closed doors. It was as he walked the passages that he pondered on the apparent trivialities of a man's physical attractions – such as, improbably, his own nose – which could seemingly stir a woman's passions. The curl of a man's lip, the fashion in which he wore his hair; even, he had read, the neatness and tightness of his buttocks. And, not to be onesided about it, he had to take into his consideration that women were sometimes, if not too occasionally, as disgusting in their sexual appetites as were men. His quite unnecessary contemplation of the frailties of *Homo genitalis* were cut short on finding himself at the reception office and with the hapless PC Cummins guarding the rear door.

'Bloody stupid twit,' he said in his mind, referring to himself and not to Cummins and determined to get his mind fully back with the investigation.

5

The acidulous Sergeant Sturton, hovering somewhere about the thirty years mark and weighing in at about one hundred pounds in full uniform and handcuffs, was doing her collating of incoming information at her tiny desk in the compartmented coach dubbed the Murder Wagon when Rogers entered.

She had, he knew, much to be acidulous about. Having a few years back been married to a rapidly disappearing bigamist, she was then callously discarded after a short engagement to a constable colleague known to almost every serving officer but her to be the force's Lothario. Understandably and subsequently, anything apparently male approaching her wounded pride was in dire peril of being transfixed by her suspicion and dislike. That Rogers was one of the foremost in commiserating with her misfortunes didn't help him at all, as any person familiar with the feminine temperament could have told him.

Rogers smiled at her with no return, feeling himself accursed of women. 'How did she take the bad news, sergeant?' he asked in a low voice; low because he could see an unknown and visibly unhappy or angry woman sitting at the far end of the coach's narrow corridor.

Sturton shrugged blank-faced. 'Badly, as you might expect. She keeps asking why and I've not been allowed to tell her.'

'That's as I wanted it,' he said affably. 'Is there a policewoman available?' He didn't want to interview the woman – any woman – with Sturton in forbidding attendance.

'Detective Constable Bunting's at the scene,' she said. 'You want her here?'

'If she's the only one; and at once, please,' he told her. 'Very definitely at once and I'll be in my office with a coffee until she comes.'

Drawing himself a frothy coffee from a token-clunking machine with the complicated choice of drinks system, he sat in the kiosk-sized off-white painted office allocated for his deep thinking and the issuing of instructions, scratching at his memory and his notebook for what he had done so far. Occasionally, he found it necessary to dismiss from his recall fleeting fragments, sometimes illustrated in colour, of the apparently generous-with-her-affections Nancy Duval.

DC Bunting, a bubbly, happy and plump twenty-year-old, entered Rogers's office – she made it full almost to being overcrowded – having arrived with a satisfying promptness. He knew her only professionally, though he knew too what she hadn't yet realized – as Sergeant Sturton had – how, with a smidgen or two of ill-luck, life could be so bloody awful and wicked to bubbly, happy and innocent young girls. She was, he considered, probably too gentle a soul to be an effective policewoman.

He was genial with her, telling her exactly what she was to do in what would amount to be an interrogation. Then, with her in tow, he went to the woman, Sarah Gadd, still sitting in the corridor, and introduced himself and Bunting, both grave-faced like a couple of undertakers, asking her to step into the claustrophobic and starkly furnished interviewing room.

Seating her with Bunting at the other side of the flap-down table, he took in her appearance which he initially saw as being thin-bodied with a long stalk of a neck. Undeniably, she made an immediate feminine impact with her short wheat-coloured hair, her crimson over-lipsticked mouth and her charcoal-rimmed eyes with lashes which she flapped like a black butterfly's wings. Holding a faux crocodile-skin clutchbag and giving off the perfume of a high-powered scent, she wore a tight-fitting powder-blue costume, the skirt of which was – in Rogers's view before she sat – immodestly short, leaving much of the upper thighs and a white lacy something to feed a man's erotic imagination. Fortunately Rogers was, for the moment, relatively indifferent to naked female thighs, and he had, unforgivingly he thought, already assessed her as one of those happily available women the French would call, without disrespect, *les horizontales*.

Her face, presumably the mirror of her inner persona, showed a barely-contained anger. 'Where the hell have you been?' she snapped at him without preamble. 'I want to know what's happened to have Frank die like this. And what's it got to do with you, a policeman? And me being kept here for bloody hours?'

'I'm sorry, Miss Gadd,' Rogers apologized. 'It was impossible for me to get here earlier. It *is* Miss Gadd, is it?'

'It is. I'm not married to him, if that's any concern of yours,' she spat out, making Bunting at her side blink. 'You *are* going to tell me who killed him, aren't you?' Apparently reading it in his face, she said, apparently less hostile, 'He was killed then, wasn't he? And by her it sounds to me, the poor man.' She wrinkled her forehead. 'How did she do that to Frank who definitely wasn't a softie?'

'Ah,' Rogers murmured, holding back on agreeing with anything. 'You're not too surprised by the fact of his murder apparently? You did know?'

'How could I not,' she said, still snappishly, 'what with you lot being so shut-faced about him being dead.'

'Would you bear with me for a few questions, Miss Gadd? I'd be grateful.' He put on a less solemn expression – even a brief pacifying smile – for she appeared not to be too grief-stricken. 'You came here with Mr Ward it seems, intending that he should enter the Club Farquharson's grounds more or less illicitly to speak to a woman in here. Would you care to tell me about that?'

'I don't care to tell you about anything. Neither do I want to be involved in something I know nothing about.' She was only simmering now, not being at an alarming boil.

'Your Frank was murdered, Miss Gadd, while you were waiting on the other side of the fence he had climbed. And that, no doubt, with your connivance if not with your assistance. It could,' he added mildly, 'involve you seriously in some sort of unlawful act.' He smiled at her in the silence that followed, then said, 'At the moment I'm accepting that you are a witness of sorts who can help me in my investigation of a serious crime.'

He held her unfriendly stare, willing her to tell him things. 'You were waiting for him where Sergeant Traughton found you, yes?'

'I was. You know I was.'

'He had climbed the fence?'

'Yes.'

'How long were you expecting him to be gone?'

She frowned. 'He said just a little while.'

'As it turned out, it was how long?'

'An hour and a half ... I think.' She shook her head. 'I'm confused. I was there so long, wondering where he was, what was happening. I haven't a watch and I'd been listening to the car radio for some time and I could have, sort of, dozed for a while.'

'Did you hear anything coming from inside the fence while you waited?'

'Such as?' She was showing caution. 'From Frank?'

'Anybody talking, shouting? Any noise whatsoever?'

'No. I don't think I would over the radio. And I saw nothing either. Just a fence, a lot of trees and a big rock blocking out the view from where I was.' She was suddenly agitated. 'For God's sake get to the point. I was only trying to help him.'

Rogers was patient with her. 'I want to know why Frank was in there, Miss Gadd. Just that.'

She gnawed at her mouth, leaving crimson lipstick on her teeth. 'I don't know. Only what he said without really telling me anything. He swore me to secrecy, so I can't really say.'

'I'm sure, Miss Gadd,' Rogers said smoothly, 'that having regard to your obvious connection with a brutal murder you must realize that a sworn secrecy with anybody counts for little.'

'He told me a week or so ago that he was owed a tremendous amount of money – he said it was many thousands – by a woman he'd known in the past. What it was for or who she was, he didn't say, and he also said that it was best I didn't know.'

With her nicely manicured fingers kneading at the clutch bag on the table, opening and closing it, she paused, searching Rogers's face and then Bunting's. Apparently reassured about something, she said, 'At first I thought that was nonsense. While I was with him I never saw that he did any work – he didn't need to, he said – though he always had plenty of money. Not that I never paid my share from what I earned at the agency. Then, when he said that this partner of his was now staying at the Club Farquharson and had been in touch with him, I thought there was something in it.' Speaking to both of them, she said, 'I'm dying for a ciggie and I finished what I had waiting in that bloody car. I don't suppose either of you have one you could spare?'

Rogers, suffering with her in her need for tobacco and knowing that Bunting didn't smoke, said, 'I'm sorry. Neither of us, and I'm sure there're none in the coach. Possibly afterwards,' he promised, then calling out, 'Come in!' at the double knock on the door and seeing it was his missing second-in-command. 'Just in time, David,' he said. 'You've been briefed?'

'By Inspector Blanshard; straight from the nag's mouth,' he said flippantly.

Detective Chief Inspector Lingard was a slim and friendly man, a confirmed addict of sniffing powdered tobacco into his nostrils. One of life's exquisites, he wore his blond hair a little too long and shaggy for Rogers's complete approval, and in the chillier months of the year wore replicas of eighteenth-century Regency waistcoats in emulation of his more than one-hundred-and-fifty-years-dead idol, George Brummell. He had the daunting blue eyes and the arrogantly superior nose of a man destined for high office in the police service. He was elegant in his build, his manner and in his dress. He was also moderately well-off and only the fact that Rogers hadn't yet dropped dead or had voluntarily retired, kept him from making a bid for his senior's coveted executive chair.

Rogers indicated Sarah Gadd. 'Miss Gadd's helping us in sorting out who might have killed Frank Ward,' he said. 'She's about to tell us the how and the why of his being inside the club's enclosure, and I'd like you to stay. There's no spare chair, but we shouldn't be long.' Rogers, without being downcast about it, had noticed that both Gadd and Bunting were staring at Lingard with much more interest and apparent approval than at himself.

With Lingard now leaning his spare frame elegantly against

the wall, his head not much below the ceiling, Rogers spoke to the now only lightly smouldering woman. 'You were saying that Frank had been in touch with his former partner now staying at the club. That was presumably about the money he said was owed to him?'

'Yes, but it was none of my business and I assume that Frank only told me because he needed transport to this godforsaken part of the country and I was the one with the car.'

'He named her, of course?'

'No, he didn't. It was none of my business.'

Rogers thought that she could be telling the truth, and therefore a dangerous woman to be entrusted with a secret. 'You live locally?' Being so close to him, her perfume's scent was drifting and beginning to have some effect on him. Not, he thought, the effect she might have hoped for when she put it on.

'God, no,' she said. 'Frank rents a cottage at Owlsfitten, miles away from civilization.'

'The name sounds familiar,' he said amiably, and it did, being in his own county. 'Where is it near?'

'It's near nowhere; it's on a river. The nearest place – and that isn't very near – is Amborum down along the coast.'

Rogers was familiar with Amborum-on-Sea; a bit of a yachting centre in the adjacent county south of his own. 'That's the address you have on your driving licence, isn't it?' he said.

'I was in lodgings there and I haven't had the opportunity of changing it.'

'And working there?' A chance shot.

'At an agency.'

That he would leave until later. Rogers said, 'What does Frank do when he's not trespassing on other people's land and getting himself murdered?' Just to remind her, he thought.

She had winced, barely that, and it was fairly certain she could be a hard woman only when it suited her to be. 'Nothing,' she said. 'He always told me that he had no need to work at anything much. In fact I had a job to make him take any housekeeping from me.' She looked sideways at Lingard, seemingly to intercept his looking at Rogers and possibly to flap her eyelashes at him. 'I actually lodge with him. He was never an anything else.'

'I imagined not,' Rogers murmured ambivalently. Aloud, he said, 'Part of your lodging with him was to drive him around, I suppose?'

'No it wasn't. I was doing him a favour. He didn't have a car or a licence and didn't want them.'

'His age?'

'He said thirty-eight.' She was getting restless.

'The cottage? How long have you been in it?'

She hesitated. 'Seven months. About.'

'So is Frank your lover?'

She hesitated, which meant he had been. 'No, he isn't.'

'Where does he come from? Before Owlsfitten, I mean.' Rogers was beginning to suspect that there was something decidedly odd about the dead man.

'I don't know and really I don't much care.'

'Where did you meet him?'

'At Croasdale where I used to live.'

'He lived there, too?'

'He was staying in an hotel. I forget what it was called, if I ever knew.'

Rogers guessed she was lying there. 'You said he had plenty of money. Had he a bank account?'

Christ! she seemed to whisper under her breath, then, 'If he had then I didn't know about it; I never saw a cheque book or a cheque. He was generous with what he had though. I'll say that for him. He always seemed to have plenty of fifties and twenties.'

'Where did that come from?'

'How would I know?' She had a testy edge to her voice for Rogers to heed. 'He'd get occasional small packages delivered by post and he was always in funds afterwards.'

'You saw from where they came?'

'No I bloody didn't. I'd have said, wouldn't I?'

Rogers had shown his teeth placatingly and unrewardingly, his confidence in the truth of what she was saying nearly convincing him that she was one of life's born losers; a natural victim of predatory men and he was sorry for her. 'Yes,' he said. 'Of course you would. I apologize.'

Not mollified, she was touchy with him again. 'I said I don't bloody know and all he told me about himself is what I've told you. You'd think I would, living in the same house, but I knew nothing. I just lived with him, that's all. There're no papers there I could ever find. I did look because I didn't want any wife or girlfriend he may have left blaming me for whatever just because I was there with him.' She shook her head, as if despairing.

'Did he ever mention what he did for a living?'

'No, not that I ever heard of, or saw. He probably didn't want to advertise himself.'

'Because?'

'Christ knows. He just didn't. I'm not all that silly and sometimes I thought he might be wanted by the police or by the mafia or somebody. He would lock up at night as if he was afraid of having his kneecaps shot off, and he'd spend time looking out the bedroom window to see if he was being watched.' She frowned. 'Was he being watched by you lot?'

Rogers was surprised. 'I wouldn't know. If you do live in a village in the back of beyond, that'd be none of our particular business. Unless, of course, either of you were breaking the law. Were you?'

She shook her head vigorously.

'Was Frank disguised in any way? His hairstyle changed or having been clean-shaven for example?'

'No. He was the same as he always is.'

'Did he receive any telephone calls?'

She was showing impatience. 'There wasn't a damned phone in the house or anywhere near us. How could he?'

She was silenced by a knock on the door and Sergeant Sturton came in, handing a message form to Rogers and then leaving. Rogers read it, passing it to Lingard. 'Bridget,' he said. 'She's just left for the scene and says she'll be here in twenty minutes.' To the woman, he said, 'You were telling me about the no telephone situation. Couldn't he have had a mobile phone?'

'I don't know,' she said wearily. 'I don't know. I've had it. Just leave me alone.'

She remained silent for several moments – Rogers could hear Sturton speaking on the force radio and a dog barking in the distance – seemingly being well into thinking things. Then, with a flush of red suffusing her throat and building up to a fury, with tears running black streaks down the ridges alongside her nose, she suddenly yelled, 'The prick! The bloody stupid prick! He promised me all the clothes I needed and a month in the Bahamas! Now I get bloody nothing and he owes me!'

'If he does, I'm afraid that's an uncollectable debt now,' Rogers murmured, mainly to himself because she was too wrapped up in her sudden grief – if that was what it was – to listen. Rogers himself was thinking that a bereft woman's fury was a terrible sight and thankful that it had not been directed at him. At least, he thought it hadn't.

When the fury had subsided and she was wiping away the stains of it with a tiny handkerchief and with Bunting making soothing sounds to her, Rogers said, 'Where is the agency at which you work, Miss Gadd?' He tried to make it only a matter of casual curiosity.

There was an awkward silence before she said, 'I don't want you asking questions there. I might need that job again.'

'Nothing unnecessary,' he said soothingly. 'Just for the records.'

She wasn't convinced, but said, 'They're in Amborum. Davis and Davis, Estate Agents.'

'Thank you.' He smiled at her. 'I'll now leave you with Chief Inspector Lingard and DC Bunting, Miss Gadd. Go with them to the cottage at Owlsfitten and they'll look for what they may find while you're there.'

'And then what?' she asked, still with some spirit in her. 'Can I stay there with him now being dead?'

'Probably later; it depends,' he replied ambiguously. 'But it'd be better that you come back here for the time being.'

He rose from his chair, having to get out of this broiler of a workplace, knowing there could be little more from her at the moment. Certainly not until Lingard and Bunting had searched the cottage. On his way out, having a confusion of breakfast waiters in mind, he asked Sturton to dispatch Detective Inspector Hagbourne and his DPS to him at the scene of the murder immediately on their arrival.

Outside, sorting out the buggy that Nancy Duval had allocated for his use, the sun was shining not only here, but where he could have been happily playing golf. Instead, there was the probably emotionally awkward imminence of Bridget who would probably have arrived at the scene by the time he got there and who had never been a woman to be kept waiting. Not only for his official presence at her examinations of bodies *in situ*, but also having always been impatient of any delay or lateness as a years-ago-younger lover attending to her sexual needs. Dear God, he thought unfairly as he climbed into the hot as hell buggy, did women like her never ever let go?

6

Driving the eye-dazzling white buggy past the vast crystal dome, now giving off rippling waves of reflected heat, Rogers could see, and see with some envy, that so many of the club's near-naked female clientele were spending time being cooked comatose on towels or padded loungers on the sandy make-believe beach. A few others, mostly male, were swimming or floating languidly on small inflatables in the aquamarine blue of the lagoon. Smoking his pipe and leaving a trail of aromatic smoke to his rear, Rogers felt overdressed in his suit, collar and tie; hungry too and again irritated by somebody getting himself murdered on so civilized and pleasant a day. He hoped, as he always did, that the murdered man had somehow managed to deserve it.

A smoothness of noiseless driving over pine needles and leaves through a forest silent but for the occasional raucous calling of a cock pheasant, brought him back to the small opening in the trees wherein murder had been committed. The light-blue body-concealing police tent had been erected where the dead Ward was lying and, in its shaded interior, he could see Inspector Blanshard. With him was a partly visible white-overalled crouching figure who could only be Bridget Hunter, Doctor of Medicine and Graduate in Morbid Pathology, the woman against whose persistence he had once succumbed too easily.

He was checking the presence of his troops even as he braked to a halt on the track close to the scene. Magnus, his Scenes of Crime detective sergeant, was photographing whatever detritus of criminality he could find in the locality, almost certainly having first photographed the body in specific and bloody detail and taken fingerprints from the dead hands. Four plain-clothes searchers prowled the undergrowth and the leaf-covered soil looking for significant debris and fluids, and the Coroner's Officer and his assistant – having had to walk the route carrying a stretcher and a body bag – stood by waiting on Rogers's say-so to take the dead man away. He noticed a second buggy with a driver standing by which almost certainly had been commandeered by a properly self-motivated Bridget.

Blanshard had left the tent on Rogers's approach, intercepting him and giving him a brief account of what he had organized on his behalf, assuring him that Dr Hunter had not been kept waiting for more than a few minutes.

'George!' she said, on his entering the dead leaf-smelling coolness of the tent, straightening up from crouching over the head of the dead man. 'It's been months.' She was a tall woman with short reddish-brown hair, unsettling dark-orange eyes and a mouth which in repose suggested an inner hardness; her overall appearance underlining her professionally diagnostic ability in determining the how and the why of Death's entry to a body.

'It's nice to see you again, Bridget,' he said. 'I haven't kept you waiting?'

'No more than ever,' she replied with an unusual pleasantness, squeezing her eyelids at him. 'I've been put in the picture by your nice inspector and I'm poised.'

Then, again wholly professional and detached, she crouched by the body and became intent on confirming by her visual perception and fingertip palpation of the cooling flesh of the throat that death had indeed been caused by the short, somehow wicked-looking, arrow protruding from it.

After a brief waiting silence, she said formally, 'I confirm that death has taken place.' This because no non-medical person – and Rogers was such along with a few million others – could make death a legally acceptable fact despite even a decapitation, putrefaction of the flesh or other obvious and bloody signs that it had taken place.

'Thank you, Bridget. I had a suspicion that it had,' he said drily, as he had said to her on many earlier occasions. 'I believe he was killed some time around eight this morning, and I'd be grateful to have that confirmed or otherwise when you do your examination.'

'Will do,' she agreed, straightening and picking up her instrument bag which she had apparently not opened. 'Would you take notes of what I shall almost certainly confirm later?' She stepped out from the tent with Rogers following her, having already decided that he was no note-taker, either for her or for anyone but himself.

Standing in the cool shade of the trees, the sun now overhead and casting short shadows, she said, 'I wish you hadn't told me of your estimate of the time of death, but by my calculations he's been dead for a probable five or six hours, which may or may not fit in with your own time of eight o'clock.'

She pursed her lips, seemingly scrutinizing Rogers's expression which, he thought, must be safely set in a professional gravitas. 'That small arrow thing – it looks like a dart to me – seems to have penetrated the left external carotid artery and possibly the internal one as well. As you've seen, it has entered just below the jawbone.'

'Not very friendly, was it?' Rogers wanted more. 'There seems to have been a massive haemorrhaging, so would there be time for him to have reacted to the attack?'

Bridget shrugged, frowning her doubt. 'That's difficult. Arterial damage, twice bled as it were, can bring on a rapid collapse. Two, three, four minutes? It would vary anyway. A strongly pounding heart would soon empty itself with an outflow from two punctured arteries. There's also shock to be considered and I can't be too dogmatic about that; but it can hasten collapse.'

'I'm with you,' he said, trying hard not to think of her as she was seven or so years back, his fierce and almost rapacious lover. It was difficult not to, close as her still sensuous body was to his.

She looked doubtful. 'I don't know. There is another factor to be considered. The dart could – only possibly could – have also penetrated the back or side of the larynx. That wouldn't help much either.'

'I imagine not.' Rogers thought about it and left it until later.

She said, 'You saw the blood on his hand, of course?'

'Yes. I'd assumed he grabbed at the dart after being hit.'

Bridget, though cool in her demeanour, was showing him a degree of cooperation not always present in the past when she had occasionally shown an unlikeable disagreeableness.

'I think that too, for there's no injury to it. It's not improbable that he would have touched his throat or the dart as he was haemorrhaging.'

'One thing more, Bridget,' Rogers said. 'Could it be assumed from the angle of the dart's penetration that while he may have been talking to one person, another could have shot it at him from the side?' At that, he was wondering if there had been any significance in Sarah Gadd not asking *how* Ward had been killed.

'You're thinking aloud, are you?' she asked. 'The answer's, yes, of course it could. At the same time it needn't be.' He had clearly exhausted what she could tell him theoretically. 'You know I'm not in the business of assuming,' she added sardonically.

'True,' he admitted amiably enough, though a little miffed at hearing again one of her bossy homilies; one he could have reminded her that she overrode herself more often than he could recall. 'I'd like to have the arrow thing as soon as you've finished with chummy.'

'After the p-m,' she told him, beginning to strip out of her overall and revealing an obvious fashion house's Oxford-blue business suit. 'You'll be attending, of course?' That had been a snap of her fingers demand. 'I can do it this afternoon.'

'Let me know the time and I'll try to be there,' he promised evasively, having already decided on Lingard – who also had been subjected in the past to the demands of Bridget's splendid body – standing in for him.

Her eyes were holding his in a questioning stare he found uncomfortable. 'Come, George,' she said as if divining his vacillation. 'It's been too long and we need to talk.'

He knew what she meant, though it went ill with what he had been told of her present status, that in her own area she had earned the unflattering title of *Obergruppenführer*, still with rumours of her preying on the young and unblooded hospital interns. And, he thought with some sympathy, why not if that was the measure of her need, and lucky for the interns. For himself, he could only thank God she was not now as addictive as his tobacco.

'I'm sorry,' he said. He had never been able to give a blunt refusal to a woman without feeling that he was a heartless bastard even to think it. And he felt it now. 'I really am being pushed,' he explained, and that sounded bloody wet. 'Tied down to it, you know?'

There was something of the *Obergruppenführer* in her then and she said, turning away with any softness gone, 'I know you too well, George, and you're still a dreadful coward. I'll see you at the mortuary.'

When she had been driven away from the scene in her buggy – cool and looking as if she was smiling about something or someone – she never looked back. Rogers, in his mind thinking, Oh bloody hell, could take no comfort from that.

Chewing at his pipe almost savagely, he was still trying to contrive how to get out from under when he put his mind to the release of the efficient Blanshard back to his section and the ordering of Magnus to dust the interviewing room for any fingerprints Gadd may have left unwittingly, then to attend at the mortuary and retrieve the arrow from Dr Hunter's care, finding out if he could from what weapon it had been fired.

The Coroner's Officer was ordered to bag up the body and deliver it to one of the two stainless steel necropsy tables waiting in the Abbotsburn Hospital's mortuary, retaining every stitch of the clothing for examination at the Forensic Science Laboratory.

Rogers was supervising this and deciding on interviewing Jarvis the manager and eating if he could his overdue lunch somewhere, when a mildly sweating Detective Inspector Hagbourne arrived on foot with an exceedingly thin and cadaverous male DS Hooker.

Hagbourne, as Rogers would put it, was an odd bugger. A family man saddled with too many children, he was almost permanently attached to the force's Fraud Squad. It was known that for years, when not breeding his family from an overly fecund wife, he had been reading his patient way through twenty-four volumes of a 1928 edition of the *Encyclopaedia*

Britannica. A small man, his liver-brown popping eyes gave him the appearance of being over-thyroidic, his down-turned moustache giving him an undeserved look of melancholy.

'You are professionally well-grounded on the working patterns of breakfast waiters, Thomas,' Rogers told him with a put on cheerfulness, blatantly presenting him with an application in a field of enquiry he didn't have and then filling him and the detective sergeant in with a background to the death of Ward. 'I want you to make your number with a Mrs Nancy Duval who you'll find somewhere in the clubhouse, in the dome of subtropical infidelities or worse, or even down on the beach where they moor the boats.'

He took a couple of deep drags at his pipe, enough to last him for a few sentences more. 'Speak to her, give her my regards and she will gen you up on the times and seating arrangements for the morning's breakfasts. I want urgently a list of the guests – who they are and from where they come – who were absent from breakfast, or late in arriving for it. Bend your undoubted talents to digging out a suspect or two for me in fairly short order. And that,' he ended, relighting his gone-out pipe, 'must include any of the club's own employees who have time to eat breakfast.'

He then smiled at Hagbourne who had been taking notes. 'I'm afraid that you're going to both have to walk again, but it's a nice day for it.'

After visiting the towering slab of naked rock from which Toplis had said he had heard the sounds of the killing of Ward – he thought without even considering climbing the thing that what he had said he heard might be feasible. Next he decided to return to Farquharson House and find someone who could provide him with a decent meal. He wasn't so hungry though that he could stomach the cling-wrapped fish paste and egg sandwiches on official offer from the Murder Wagon.

7

Detective Chief Inspector Lingard had arrived at Club Farquharson in his much cherished almost-a-veteran Bentley which was not insured for carrying any odd bodies such as on-duty police personnel but himself. He had therefore ordered a police patrol car and driver for his journey to Owlsfitten.

With WDC Bunting sitting in the back of the car with a brooding non-too-compliant Sarah Gadd, who held firmly on to her crocodile-skin bag and who had now apparently stopped regarding the detective as a luscious dish – Lingard felt free to sit next to the tactfully monosyllabic driver PC, occasionally feeding his nose with a Macouba snuff.

Owlsfitten, a village almost toppling into the River Calder and only just making it as an entity on an Ordnance map, was a twenty minute drive from the murder scene. Civilized enough to own to a scattering of waterside white-painted cottages, a sub-post office and grocery store, it served the appetites of the visiting sailing fraternity from the saloon and beer garden of the Two Kings public house.

Pulling up at Gadd's indication outside an isolated cottage at the end of the village, Lingard took in what there was of it while the dumpy Bunting and the head taller Gadd joined him. An attractive elderly building, it had probably stood there for a century or two; its plaster walls a cool light blue, the roof tiles of sandstone, touched only lightly by yellow and brown lichen. The lozenged windows were absurdly small and presently curtained, its door a fading green. There was a cement hard-standing for a car, backed by a small wooden shed and several hillside acres of scrub woodland.

Lingard, girding himself by charging his nose with more snuff, asked Gadd to please open the door. Gadd, taking a key from her handbag and handing it to him, said, 'You want it; you open it.'

'So be it, madam,' Lingard said, 'but you as the nominal renter of the cottage have authority to admit me on behalf of the late Mr Ward. He, in any case, no longer holds any tenure of occupation.' He looked down his nose at her. 'You are not objecting?'

'It doesn't seem right, that's all.' She was beginning to sound difficult and if she had shown an earlier partiality towards lean, blond-haired and elegant detective chief inspectors it was definitely now being repressed.

'It doesn't seem right that he should have been given the chop either,' he pointed out blandly, his back to her as he pushed the key into the door lock and turned it.

The opened door led directly into a small sitting-room and Lingard held it open for the two women to precede him. Its interior seemed to Lingard's refined nose to be full of the exhalations of a profusion of different occupants, its furniture and furnishings being adequate, but with no suggestion of feather-stuffed comfort. It was, however, Lingard admitted to himself, probably a hell of a lot more comfortable than lying on one's back on the cold stainless steel of the mortuary's necropsy table.

In the search of the room, Ward's material possessions appeared disappointingly to have been pared to the bone; his personal property being somewhat down to the scale of a transient on the flit from an arrest warrant. There were only the drawers of an occasional table to search, one producing a nameless wallet containing a thin wodge of sixteen new fifty-pound notes and a couple of trade cards. One promoted the *Davy Jones Trading Post* which dealt in sailing ware at a reasonably local Leamings Landing. The other referred to a Stanley Walley, a dealer in quality used cars at Scarborough, which was far from being local. Retaining the cards, Lingard handed the wallet and money to Bunting. Showing the cards to Gadd, she pursed her lips and shrugged, the detective giving her best for the moment and pocketing them.

There were possible places of concealment under the seats of the armchairs or other places of similar capacity for small and thin items, but searching these had been profitless. A useless trawl of a few old newspapers and a shelf of novels empty of anything but words, were telling him nothing.

Gadd, however, had been given a pack of cigarettes unearthed from under a seat cushion by Bunting. Though she unflattened one and lit it, drawing on it almost hungrily, it did nothing for the animus she was showing towards Lingard.

Leading from the sitting-room was a small kitchen which Lingard, downrating it in terms of the unlikelihood of there being anything of use in it, left for a later searching. More interested in what might be upstairs, he asked Gadd and Bunting to lead the way up the narrow stairs. There were two rooms furnished as bedrooms. The first contained no signs of being used and a quick search – while Gadd glowered – revealed nothing of interest. The second held a double bed, unmade from its last use, with a blue and green tartan bedspread and two pillows sunken in by sleeping, or not sleeping, human heads. As well as the bed there was a large and elderly veneered wardrobe, a white dressing-table with three mirrors containing a scattering of tubes and tiny bottles, and a solitary chair.

'You're satisfied?' Gadd ground out aggressively, tapping cigarette ash on the carpeting.

'Not yet,' Lingard told her cheerfully. He had noticed a growing watchfulness, an alertness about her that he hadn't seen earlier. 'The wardrobe. You shared it?'

'Of course we shared it. It's the only one in the room, isn't it? Are you stupid? I wouldn't keep my clothes under the bed, would I?'

Lingard, smiling amiably at her, was already viewing her reaction to these minor events with a professional detachment, and not inclined to be offended by his being called stupid. He opened the wardrobe door and was confronted with a short row of male and female clothing hung without any apparent separation. On the floor were two small piles of underwear and a large floppy suitcase. Pulling this out and leaving the searching of the clothing and underwear to Bunting, he snapped it open. It contained nothing but a brown paper bag containing a further wodge of ten fifty-pound notes and a yellow folder of photographs; these mainly of what appeared to be the security fencing around the Farquharson Club's forest area and a garden adjacent to the house. The money, he was sure, would not have been come by honestly.

'I assume you knew about this?' he asked Gadd who was showing a forced disinterest in what he was doing and thereby underlining the possible importance of it.

She shrugged. 'You're wrong then, aren't you. I didn't until you'd opened it.'

'You've not seen the photographs? Or the money?' With the windows closed, he was feeling stuffy in the room, the scent Gadd was wearing becoming a mite overpowering.

'No, I haven't,' she said curtly.

'I suppose not,' he agreed mildly, accepting now from her manner that she had, that she would have a good reason for not admitting it. He smiled against her intransigence, thanking God that she was no longer flapping her eyelashes at him. 'If you say the money isn't yours then that I'll accept, but you should understand that you might be called as a witness to the fact that both the photographs and the money were in the possession of your unfortunate friend.'

'I told you that I know nothing about any of it,' she said coldly, patently regarding him now as being a threat to whatever it was she might fear.

That, he knew, was as much as he might get from this intractable woman.

Bunting, while not missing out on what was happening in the room, was now doing a deft search of potential places of concealment such as between the bed covers and mattress and under any loose edges of the carpet she could find. None of this went unnoticed by Lingard and he was impressed.

Downstairs, hot and uncomfortable, certain that he now had several thousand micro-organisms infesting his underwear and skin, Lingard asked Bunting to extend her meticulousness to searching the kitchen in the presence of Miss Gadd while he had a look in the outside shed he had noticed on his arrival.

The shed was unlocked, hung with dusty spiders' webs and otherwise empty, seeming to have surrendered to unused decay. Lingard left it without any sense of having achieved anything even slightly useful about who Ward actually was or had been, what he might have done for a living in order to be in casual possession of £1300 in unused fifty-pound notes, and why he seemed to be able to live and to die without possessing the necessary documentation and licensing.

Returning by the front door and passing the apparently comatose PC in the patrol car, he moved from the eye-dazzling brightness outside back into the semi-darkness of the sitting-room. With a tightening of his chest in sudden alarm he heard a quiet whimpering coming from a moving dark bundle of something on the floor and which, his vision adjusting to the interior gloom, he saw to be a crawling Bunting looking up at him, her face blood-smeared and now trying to say something to him.

He lifted her weightiness gently, saying soothing words to calm her while his own mind was seeking the why and how the bloody woman Gadd had done this to his now suffering colleague. Lowering her on to the small settee where she lay silent, though still looking ghastly in her pain, he could see that she had a severe laceration on her forehead. It was bleeding freely and a lump was forming beneath it. Taking his dress silk handkerchief from his breast pocket and folding it over the wound, he lifted her hand to hold it in position, hoping fervently that she wouldn't be bleeding to death, though he couldn't recall ever seeing any major veins in a forehead when attending post-mortem examinations.

Holding her other hand and feeling the pulse in her wrist with his finger – it felt reasonably steady – he said, 'What happened, old girl? Tell me if you can, but I don't want you to push yourself too hard.' He felt like a bloody slave-driver.

Her eyes, reflecting her pain and confusion, looked up at him. 'My head,' she whispered. 'It hurts. She pushed ... I'm sorry, she pushed me and I fell. W-where is she?'

'I don't know. You didn't see her leave?'

She frowned beneath the streaks of blood. 'I don't know.' She closed her eyes for a few moments, then opened them brimming with tears. 'I was looking in ... I was looking in something and she hit me ... no, she pushed me against it when I had my back to her.' She looked lost for something to say, then whispered, 'Oh God, I let her escape ...'

'No, you didn't,' Lingard assured her positively. 'She was never in custody, so don't think it. Let me have a look at your head.' He held her wrist and gently lifted her hand from holding the blood-soaked silk handkerchief in place. Lifting it he looked carefully at the gash in the skin and the painful-looking bruising beneath it, then replaced its soddenness. Using his white handkerchief to wipe blood from her face, he folded it, placed it over the silk handkerchief – now blotched with red on its sage-green – then lifted her hand again to keep it there. That had been no mean sacrifice for him.

'It's not too bad,' he told her cheerfully, though he wasn't at all sure, 'but I'm sending you off to Casualty to get it sewn up.' He smiled at her. 'Egad, but you're a brave filly if ever I saw one, and I think you'll do no worse than finish up with a bit of a headache and nothing more.'

She was recovering a little and he supported her out to the patrol car, telling the surprised PC – who had neither seen nor heard anything untoward – to get her to the casualty department at Abbotsburn Hospital as quickly as possible. That and other instructions pertinent to his own prompt recovery from the scene and the immediate issue of a Wanted for Assault on a Police Officer circulation concerning the fleeing from something-or-other Sarah Gadd.

With the car and Bunting gone and himself in a necessary hurry, he re-entered the cottage, looking in the kitchen and finding a vertical smear of blood on one of the front corners of an electric cooker and thicker blood on the linoleum floor tiles. Picking up Bunting's clutchbag from where she had dropped it and confirming that the fifty-pound notes and photographs were still intact, he did a rapid search of the cottage against the remote possibility of Gadd's pulling a fast one – making an idiot of him – by concealing herself in one of the upstairs rooms.

Leaving by the open back door, he found the unfenced back area virtually cheek by jowl with the adjoining vastness of scrub forest. Ruefully conscious that he was wearing his expensively purchased summer suit and his so far unmarked shoes, both highly unsuitable for searching a forest, he did enter a couple of trees' depth into it. Even there it was dark and gloomy, but for the few bars of sunlight striking down through the foliage. It was a routine check on an unlikely possibility and he would have been much surprised to see any sign of Gadd, any glimpse of her light-blue costume or any sound of her passage, long gone, through the undergrowth.

It wasn't about to be his day, he thought, as he returned to the cottage, there charging with panache what he thought were his complaining sinuses with snuff and to continue with his search for the unquantifiable in a sort of falling on one's sword day.

8

Rogers rather liked Charles Jarvis. Visiting him in his office – he recognized in it the almost forgotten faint whiff of a smoked cigar – Jarvis had stuck out his hand and said, 'It's Charles,' while Rogers, shaking it, returned the friendly courtesy with a surprised, 'And mine's George.'

Sitting himself in the red leather-trimmed chair offered him, he took in the office which, he assumed, was an indication of Jarvis's importance to his employers. The not very crowded desk was large and of polished mahogany, inlaid with red leather, matched by a bookcase packed with real used books and file cases and what he took to be a closed drinks cabinet.

The outer wall of the office accommodated three large windows showing the eye-aching fragmented glitter of the crystal dome with the sparkling blue sea beyond it being cruised on by half-a-dozen or so white-sailed boats.

Sitting at his desk gave Jarvis a distinct aura of command, a man having matters of moment at his fingertips, his moustache now appearing larger, denser and more black. He was clearly not a man to be incautiously addressed as Charlie. He had changed into another dark suit, a fresh white shirt and a dark-blue tie. Seen in close-up he appeared to Rogers to be in his slightly dissipated well-bred fifties and still at whatever it was that had given him that look.

He said with a smile of reasonable affability, 'First of all, old chap, while I am happy – no, properly anxious – to help you clear up this ghastly matter, I do trust that you will exercise a proper discretion in your investigation of it.' He tugged at his moustache. 'I admit freely that I could be shat on from a great height were Head Office to think that I'd been discussing our clientele too freely with the police – murder or no murder. Or with the press too, of course,' he added hastily.

'In other words, I'm to identify the murderer, arrest him or her and get the hell out of here as soon as I can?' He smiled as affably as Jarvis had himself.

'Something of that order,' Jarvis said carefully. 'Given the fullest information and cooperation by myself. And by Mrs Duval, naturally.'

'I'm sure we'll be able to accommodate each other,' Rogers assured him, though only going along with him subject to how matters went.

'That's decidedly civilized of you,' Jarvis acknowledged, leaning back in his brass-studded executive chair with confidence oozing. 'I've some possibly useful information for you when you've told me that the dead man – the devil take him for being so unobliging as to be killed here – has no connection with Club Farquharson, nor has he had.'

'I can't, I'm afraid,' Rogers told him bluntly. 'He climbed in from outside as you probably know, and that could only be to further some connection with somebody in this club. His name's been given as Frank Ward and he lived reasonably close by at Owlsfitten. It could be his proper name; it need not be. He could, of course, have been a bona fide visitor here at some time and you might check your records to see if that's so. If you can, naturally.' He paused, having wondered why Jarvis had apparently overlooked this more sensitive fact, then continued, 'What is more certain is that he was murdered in the club grounds, apparently by one of your members or, less likely, by an employee.'

Jarvis looked dismayed; something produced for effect, Rogers thought. 'Not, I hope, a member,' he said. 'They're my responsibility. The staff – well, most of them – are the responsibility of Head Office.' He muttered almost inaudibly, 'I hope to God *that's* right.'

'It's my conclusion, Charles,' Rogers told him amiably enough, 'and it has the true ring of logic. You ran into Mr Toplis at breakfast, I understand. He was virtually present at the killing, a little elevated from it on the rock face it's true, but hearing what was happening below him. You know him well, I imagine?'

'More or less.' Jarvis looked easy, manifestly happy with Toplis. 'But that doesn't mean I can be overly gabby about our members. All this in confidence?'

'About Toplis?' Rogers shrugged. 'Naturally. Subject to nothing calamitous arising later on.'

Jarvis, seemingly happy with that, said, 'He's been a fairly regular member, off and on naturally, for nearly eighteen months. He uses the casino and does some climbing on Butters Rock. Sailing too, of course, but then they all do and I don't have to know of every activity our members choose to be involved with.' He looked slightly irritated. 'What the hell. I don't sleep with him and if he engages himself in other club activities that's neither my concern nor, I think, yours. For aren't we all,' he added thoughtfully, 'of the same sullied flesh?'

'Some of us less or more than others, of course,' Rogers agreed.

'He's not your average business man either,' Jarvis said. 'He talks about doing several years' service with the French Foreign Legion. That I certainly didn't tell you,' he added quickly. 'I don't want him believing that I was its provenance.' There was a touch of nervousness in his manner. 'I'm trusting you on this. Nancy tells me he's understood to be an excitable bugger and a bit short-tempered with it, so I wouldn't ... well, you get the picture.'

'I understand,' Rogers said, 'though having been a legionaire might be to his credit.' In fact he thought it might be quite otherwise, the Legion being known as a last resort for hunted men. 'His lifestyles are noted and they'll be safe with me. Unless, of course ...'

'I'm relying on your word, old son,' Jarvis said carefully. 'And while we're about it I feel I should warn you that during your investigations here you will almost certainly come across the odd – the very odd sometimes – peccadilloes, or an over-the-top naughtiness, though naturally nothing amounting to a criminal offence. It would be extremely embarrassing were there any adverse publicity over any of it and again it'd probably be my head on the block. I take it that that wouldn't be one of your interests here?'

'It mostly isn't,' Rogers assured him quite truthfully and keeping his face straight, though wondering which impropriety might be attached to what he was calling naughtiness. 'Nothing too bad, of course, and I'd speak to you beforehand if something troubled me.'

Jarvis nodded his head. 'I'm grateful of course.' Opening a drawer of his desk and taking out a flat cedarwood box, he said, 'Havanas,' showing smiling white teeth below his heavy moustache and flipping its lid open. 'May God forgive me, but the company supposes me to be a non-smoker. I'm told you favour a pipe, but will you join me?'

'I'll have my pipe,' Rogers told him, retrieving it from his jacket pocket, 'but I'll join you with pleasure.'

As they were each lighting up in their no doubt objectionable and different ways, Jarvis said, staring straight at the detective, 'Do I take it that you disapprove of the lifestyles of some of our members? No offence, old chap, but...'

Rogers tried to look something unlike priggish virtue. 'Good God, no,' he protested. 'Is that how I sound?'

'I wasn't sure. I mean, we aren't living in the backwoods about women these days are we? We seldom have them now posing as wives in order to conduct a liaison, if I may put it like that.' He smiled as if in recollection. 'Occasionally we have the executive type of woman do the booking for themselves and their, er, companions. Or, less occasionally, though definitely done, to book in with another woman with no evident sexual interest in anyone other than themselves.'

'We're losing out, Charles,' Rogers said cynically, not too certain he was right. 'It's the age of the dominant woman and we're fast becoming mere appendages to whatever lusts they may choose to have.'

Jarvis laughed. 'I like that, old chap. Is Nancy Duval looking after you? Attending to your needs?'

'Very well indeed,' Rogers assured him, his inhalation of nicotine making him feel benevolent, though not so benevolent that he didn't suspect a nuance of something or other in the question. 'We happen to be detached at the moment while she's helping Inspector Hagbourne sort out the absentees from this morning's breakfasts and I'm happy with the cooperation.'

'And I'm pleased, naturally.' He blew cigar smoke upwards to a classical ceiling of leaf mouldings and recessed panels.

'You said you've some possibly useful information for me,' Rogers reminded him. He thought he wasn't getting too much of use from a talkative but obviously canny Jarvis.

'True, old son, but if I may I'd like to get the two members who buzzed off this morning out of my mind first, and perhaps out of yours.'

'That's no big deal,' Rogers said. 'They'd a perfect right to leave, but we need to know why. I'd guess somebody's wife is on the loose, or it's a married politician with an illicit girlfriend. There but for the grace of God, or similar . . .'

'It's good you see it like that,' a relieved Jarvis said. 'May I first say that most of our members – nearly all, I'd say – are awash with big money and big opinions of their own importance; and mostly, too, able to swing big legal sticks. You savvy?'

'I've met them, Charles.'

'I imagine. So, in confidence, this man's a big noise – so I understand – in the TorontoUK Bank whoever they are.' He lowered his voice, apparently in case somebody was listening from behind the wainscoting, naming a name which the detective couldn't remember ever having heard. 'I suspect that isn't his proper name, but who am I to complain when ... well, you know what I mean. He's here at present with a lady who – how can I put it ? – doesn't seem to be the identical lady he brought here before, though who are we to assume that because she uses the same name that it is or isn't her?'

'I do see your problem, but not to worry unduly. He will have lost the lady by the time we've checked him and his car and so he should.' Rogers smiled. 'Unless, of course, he's the murderer we're looking for.'

'Don't say it, old son. It's not funny.' He was of the stamp of cigar smoker not believing it correct to tap the ash from a living cigar, the ash from his having dislodged itself on to the immaculacies of his jacket lapel and tie.

'You were about to give me some possibly useful information,' Rogers persisted, thinking he had gone a little overboard in listening to what he thought might be his good friend Jarvis's wafflings.

'Yes, I did didn't I. Well, there's a lady here you'd certainly be interested in listening to and I'm sure I'm doing you a service that you'll be glad to return if it's required.' He waited for Rogers to say something and, when he did nothing other than look calmly interested, said, 'She's told me in confidence, though allowing me to pass it on to you under a little executive pressure, that she was doing her jogging at about breakfast time this morning when she saw a man coming from the trees not too far from Butters Rock Climb, crossing her path some distance in front and entering the trees on the other side. He mightn't have actually been jogging, but, she says, he seemed to be dressed for it. Not that she's saying that he must be connected with the murder, for she's not. She's been thinking about it all morning, ever since she learned of the murder, worrying you know in case she has what she calls evidence in what she saw.'

'No detail?' Rogers needed to know more.

'I didn't want it, old son.' Jarvis shook himself. 'I don't want that kind of involvement, you understand?'

'What time was it when she spoke to you?'

'Not too long ago. Just before I had my sandwich for lunch, I suppose. One o'clock? Half past? I've been so busy, but some time about then.'

Rogers looked at his wrist-watch; it showed the time to be two-fifty. 'And she is?'

'Miss Rachel Hurt. A most charming lady and very well-off indeed. I mean, she has to be to stay here for so long as she does.' He looked thoughtfully at the butt end of the cigar he held between finger and thumb. 'She's a sensible woman and I think she'd be happy to have your assurance that she won't be treated as a witness or anything like that.'

'Ah.' Rogers was unhappy at that and showed it. 'If what she's seen is pertinent to the murder, is material evidence, then I couldn't. Apart from that, yes of course. You'll arrange a time for me to see her?'

'I've anticipated you rather,' Jarvis said, showing no reaction to what Rogers had said. 'The lady's very much against being seen talking to a policeman under the present circumstances and she's asked to meet you in the solarium at half-past three. Is that suitable?'

'Certainly, but wouldn't that be a bit obvious?'

'Not the way I've thought it out, old son. You're already wearing an appropriate pair of off-white trousers, so discard your jacket and shirt here when it's time and I'll fit you out with one of my leisure shirts.' He laughed and made a clucking noise with his tongue. 'I think a pale yellow would present you well to the lady, together with one of my Panama hats which you should carry if it doesn't fit you. When you get there, go to the far end where there's one of the clumps of palms. She'll be there – probably on one of the loungers – expecting you on the dot and will call out to you as if you're an old friend. There'll be few members there this afternoon, being that it's a fair day for sailing.' He beamed at the surprised detective.

'I expect I'll find something wrong with it at the wrong time,' Rogers said a little dourly, 'but I'm grateful for all that.'

Jarvis was back to tugging at his moustache. 'Just do your damnedest not to upset her, old son, eh?'

Rogers liked Jarvis, though that didn't mean he also trusted him. At least, not too much. He was, possibly, being too helpful to be true. 'I'm casting a wide net about this, Charles,' he said, 'but has there been any happening fairly recently concerning any of your members, or even staff, which on present reflection you think might have a connection with this murder? Even a frail one, and it's your club's murder too,' he added to underline his involvement in it.

Jarvis, allowing cigar smoke to drift from his mouth to join the blue-grey haze above them both, was clearly going through his memory's filing system. 'Yes,' he said finally, 'there is, I think, though I'm not sure that it's going to be of any use to you.'

'I'm a man who deals in fragments of information, in the debris and detritus of crime.' He smiled. 'Give, Charles. You never know.'

'It was about three or four months ago,' Jarvis said. 'I received a phone call, put through to me as general manager, from a man who said he was a solicitor in practice at Cumberslang. I think he said his name was Stevens – something like that because I've mislaid the note I made of it. He said he was acting for a client in tracing the whereabouts of his missing sister who was believed to be, or had been, staying at Club Farquharson under her married name of Kathleen – my bloody memory, old son – something that sounded like Orbit, which I wasn't going to tell him anyway. I said something about not being able to tell him offhand, but if he gave me his number I'd ring him back later. That's when he hung up on me and when I knew that whoever he was he was doing something shifty. Not necessarily criminal or fraudulent, but shifty, and he could get himself stuffed so far as I was concerned.'

'And had you, past or present, any member of that name or anything like it?' Rogers wasn't thinking much of it; a jealous or deserted husband or lover doing a furtive check; something similar from a town not more than a hundred miles away. Still . . .

Jarvis shook his head. 'No. Nancy did a check for me, going back for yonks on the members list. I'd forgotten about it until you've pushed me into being unmindful of the company's policy on the confidentiality of inside house matters.' He didn't look overly distressed about it.

'It's a bit vague for me, though it might tie in later,' Rogers said. 'But I'm grateful.'

Jarvis, screwing his cigar stub to extinction in a small and presumably odour-retaining metal can and putting it in one of the desk's drawers, said, 'No more, and what you have now you didn't get from me.' He grinned, his teeth white beneath the impressive moustache. 'Any leaking and I'll take Nancy away from being your Doctor Watson or whatever she is, and I'll also immobilize your buggy. Now wait here while I fetch your disguise.'

Rogers had been about to put his only-just-gone-out pipe in his pocket, but began to refill it instead as Jarvis left, heading for the door. He was grateful, although the scenario of his forthcoming meeting with the Hurt woman sounded very MI5 or CIA-ish and very likely to affect his supposed gravitas approach to a possible murder-case witness.

And there was one other little worry. Had Jarvis been politely warning him off Nancy Duval as a woman? If so, that really needed thinking about.

9

Rogers, not permitted to take a buggy into the solarium and having walked through a passageway into the vastness of the dome, sensed immediately the near absence of sound, the feeling of bright space held in containment. Huge panels of a lucent material in the vertical sides of the structure had been drawn aside, presumably by some gargantuan machinery, alleviating a certain greenhouse effect on an already hot day.

The lagoon, reflecting the outside blue sky and fringed by a shallow beach of raked yellow sand, was limpid and unmoving, undisturbed by the bathers and occupied inflatables he had seen earlier from outside. Around it had been planted seclusions of spaced oases of tall palms and shorter palmettos, their glowing greens of palmate and frondant leaves giving a dappled shade from the overhead sun. There were small brightly coloured birds, apparently having colonized the denser palms.

Close to the entrance Rogers had used were small red-tiled white-painted Mediterranean-style buildings. One manifestly served as a beach bar, the others as shops and salons. None appeared to be occupied and the detective, with only a minor suspension of his critical faculties, could imagine himself to be on a Spanish beach.

He could see a handful of scattered couples through the bottle-trunked palms who seemed to be observing the post-lunch ritual of a hot afternoon's siesta on the seaward side of this make-believe subtropical solarium. Those few he passed nearby appeared not to see him, the truly invisible man of a genre these *bons vivants* were choosing not to know.

Skirting the lagoon, he was pleased to be regarded as unknowable, feeling undressed and a mite ridiculous with Jarvis's additions to his clothing. He now wore a gaudily patterned acid-yellow short-sleeved leisure shirt hanging over his trousers, carrying a Panama hat too small for him in a clenched fist. There was none of it in which he would care to be buried.

The despised shirt was beginning to stick itself to his back when he heard a woman's voice calling not too loudly, but with a touch of arrogance in it, *'I say! Over here! Over here!'* He saw her then, lying on a padded lounger, only just visible in the dappled shade of a small oasis of palms; a spectacle-wearing woman in a wide-brimmed straw hat and the apparent minimum of white dress.

Close to her and having said, 'Mrs Hurt?' and receiving a cool and unsmiling nod of her head, he introduced himself and tried to assess what he was getting in the shape of a witness.

Lying half upright, she held a book in one hand and was accompanied at her side by a vanity case and a small silver-coloured vacuum flask with a crystal wine glass on an attached tray. In what he felt to be the socially polite nanosecond given him to assess her, to take in her visible status and circumstance as a presumably married woman, his policeman's mind served him well.

From what he could see under the brim of her outlandish straw hat, she appeared to be no more than a young, well-maintained forty years and therefore a woman to be seriously reckoned with. She wore her straight reddish-brown hair at shoulder length with a fringe down to her unpencil-lined eyebrows. Strongly featured and showing a golden tan, she could be considered reasonably attractive. Her eyes, behind her gold-framed spectacles, were slate-grey – a warning sign he thought of a possibly baleful glare in opposition. Her mouth was thin-lipped and curiously mobile. The sleeveless white dress she wore showed that she was sleekishly breasted with slim tanned legs. Finally, he was of the opinion that she was loaded – that always making up for any number of physical or personality deficiencies – and also certain that they were both fated to dislike one another.

'I'm grateful that you could see me, Mrs Hurt,' he said with what he thought might be excessive politeness. 'Mr Jarvis has told me that you've some information which might help us in our investigation?'

He remained standing, there being nothing other than the ground for sitting on, while thinking that whatever else he might wish she had, she definitely had a commanding presence; possibly earned by an extravagance of money.

When she remained silent as though waiting for more from him, he added, 'About the member you saw jogging somewhere near where a man was killed this morning...?'

Patently, she wasn't regarding detective superintendents as being terribly important in her scheme of things and he was beginning to believe she was going to shut up on him. That is, if he could convince himself that she had ever opened up for him.

Then she smiled, the same tight-lipped smile she might give to a policeman reporting her for having driven hell-bent through a red traffic light. 'I didn't say he was a member,' she said. 'I never thought that he was.'

'Could you tell me exactly where you saw him, and at what time?' He beamed, surely having misjudged her.

She was wearing a wrist-watch and she glanced at it. 'It was about eight o'clock.' She looked him over with what was certainly an unapproving eye and he cursed Jarvis for the hideous shirt he was wearing. 'I was doing my regular morning jogging...'

'I'm sorry,' he interrupted her. 'You were on your own?'

'I would have said had I *not* been, superintendent,' she reprimanded him. 'Allow me to tell you in my own way. As I said, I was on my morning's jogging and approaching the Butters Rock area when what I took at first to be another jogger – a man – cut across my path from my left and went into the trees on my right.'

'May I interrupt again,' he said, and doing so. 'Was he jogging or walking?'

'Walking,' she said, not pleased. 'But doing it quickly; purposefully you could say.'

Rogers, feeling awkwardly placed in standing over her – looming, he thought more apt – said, 'And then?'

'I was going to say that. Whichever – it was unusual enough for me to remember it. I don't have any positive reason for imagining that he could be connected with what happened to the poor man Mr Jarvis said was killed there, but I did feel that I should inform someone in authority of what I had seen. Certainly I believed that telling him would be enough.'

She suddenly shuddered. 'It's awful that I could have been

there within minutes. I could have actually...' She shook her head at the thought, then said, 'I assume that is what you wanted, superintendent?' She lifted her book as though to resume reading it, dismissing Rogers from her presence by implication.

Rogers smiled at her, a far from genuine smile. 'I'm sorry, Mrs Hurt, but that tells me nothing but what Mr Jarvis passed on to me. I'd be grateful if I could ask for more detail of what you saw. Murder,' he said gravely, 'is a serious matter and I am given the authority to take what are sometimes extreme steps to bring the offender to justice.'

'You surprise me, superintendent,' she said. 'Do you propose to interrogate me?'

'No. To question you on the detail of what you've already told me,' he explained patiently, believing wryly that some of his difficulties were coming from his wearing the open-neck gaudy yellow shirt and holding a too-small Panama hat in his hand. 'For example, how far were you from the man when you first saw him?'

She shrugged narrow shoulders, then stared up at him for long moments, unapprovingly it seemed. 'If I must,' she said, 'I'd guess not more than thirty yards.'

'Would you describe him to me?' His face, now a target for flies, and his back were trickling with sweat. He needed a shot of anaesthetizing nicotine. Not just a shot, he corrected himself, but a bloody bucketful.

She sighed, apparently resigned to what she thought was his unpleasantness, looking ahead through the palm trunks, her features impassive, manifestly not liking the detective at all. 'He looked,' she said, 'to be in his fifties and definitely not quite, you know? He had a shaven head like some men now have and could have been an athlete or a boxer of some sort. I can't remember his shoes, but he wore dark-blue shorts – I think – and what looked like a red golf or casual shirt. As far as I could see, he was clean-shaven. I'm certain I've not seen him here before as a member, or as a guest.' She showed her distaste. 'He looked so terribly ordinary.'

'You appear not certain that the man was clean-shaven. Could he have had a small beard?'

She looked at him witheringly, not replying.

'I take it he hadn't, then?' Rogers said, knowing that she was being bloody-minded and not going to answer him. He shook his head. 'Wrong supposition,' he told her. 'What was there unusual in his crossing your path and going into the trees?'

He was boring her and she showed it. 'Because whatever path there is there – and I know of none – would not normally be used or recognized as a jogging or walking track. It could only lead down to where they do clay-pigeon shooting, and that isn't to say it's the proper way there.'

'Why not?'

That irritated her. 'Because I say so. Because everybody knows it isn't. The steps to it are near the boat moorings and that's how you get there.'

Rogers thought that she had now decided that he was a second-class citizen of limited comprehension, and that amused him. 'Could he have returned to the house that way?'

'Certainly not. It's not impossible, but it would be completely stupid.'

'How far was he from Butters Rock when you saw him?'

She frowned. 'Not too far and obviously much nearer than I was myself.' She reached for the vacuum flask and, taking her time, unscrewed its cap and poured a little white wine into her glass while Rogers waited patiently.

When she had finished her leisurely drink, he asked, 'Did Mr Jarvis tell you where the man's body was found?'

'Yes – unfortunately.' She returned the empty glass to its tray and then yawned, stretching herself. 'Is there much more of this?' she complained.

'A little,' he told her. 'What relationship has it to where the man crossed your path?'

'Oh my God,' she said under her breath, then, 'It's close by.'

'How near to it did your jogging take you?' It was surprising him how little traffic there was within the dome. He and the woman could have been alone on a desert island, though that was an uncomfortable thought.

She was showing some irritation now, and Rogers couldn't blame her. His job had made him a persistent bugger, probably a boring one, at pushing questions at others. 'There's a turning off there before it gets to the rock,' she said. 'It leads back to the house, and that's the one I took.'

'And, of course, you didn't see anything or anybody?'

She raised her eyebrows as if questioning his competence.

'You knew a Mr Toplis found the body?' he persisted.

'Yes,' she said drily. 'He did spread it around rather.'

Against the evidence, he was beginning to believe that she wasn't so uptight as he had supposed. 'He was up on the rock actually; probably when you passed. Did you see him?'

'I rather think I would have mentioned it had I done so,' she said witheringly. 'And it mightn't be possible from under the trees anyway.'

Rogers changed tack, though not expecting to be overwhelmed by a whole-hearted response. 'Had Mr Jarvis mentioned to you that the dead man wore a beard?'

'No.' She looked surprised. 'I'm sure not.'

'Would that description suggest to you the identity of any member here?'

'Did it to Mr Jarvis?'

'No,' he admitted, knowing what was coming.

'You have your answer then. If it didn't for him, how would it for me?' Her fingers were tapping on her book; indicating, he assumed, a pointed lack of interest.

'One question more, Mrs Hurt?' he asked, feeling that he was now up against some well-established feminine obduracy, probably having been necessary against a difficult husband whoever the poor devil had been. 'Would you recognize the man if you saw him again?'

She turned the full force of her unfriendly slate-grey eyes on him. 'Superintendent,' she said down-puttingly, not choosing to give him a name, 'I may, or may not. Even if I did, I may not consider it to be my business to give you any further information about a matter which is now none of my concern.' She reached for the silver flask and then the wine glass.

Seeing him apparently unresponsive to her disinterest in his problems, she said, 'Please don't let me keep you any longer. I have nothing further to say and I wish to continue with my rest.'

'Thank you,' Rogers said, knowing when to accept a sort of

defeat. 'I'm grateful for your cooperation. I shall keep you advised of any information I may obtain about the man you've mentioned.'

She was refilling her glass as he turned away, removing himself and his abysmally unsuitable shirt and hat from her switched-off awareness of him and his investigation.

Allowing himself an inner smile of amusement at her unbendingness, he spared a mite of sympathy for the possibly existing Mr Hurt. He filled and lit his long gone-out pipe as he headed for what he felt to be an escape into what he thought of as the outside world, feeling it necessary to change back into his own no doubt uninspiring clothes before he was seen with ribaldry by any of his own staff.

Wishing to think of somebody the antithesis of Mrs Hurt, Nancy Duval came into his mind as an already existing warm and infinitely friendly aide. Or, he considered himself entitled to think, an intimate something more than that. Only natural for him to spread his affection for women around a little. As, no doubt, Angharad, cruising somewhere off the French coast, would herself endorse; for, in her own words, neither of them was to walk in the shadow of the other. And that had seemed to him always to be a happy and rewarding philosophy. It was certainly what Robert Herrick the poet had in mind – and with which he agreed – when he wrote, *Gather ye rosebuds while ye may, Old Time is still a-flying.*

10

Rogers, having returned the abominable shirt and hat to Jarvis and told him of the result of his interviewing Mrs Hurt, reported back at the Murder Wagon and to Sergeant Sturton who was almost as dismissive of him as had been Mrs Hurt. She gave him the news of the witness Gadd's assault on WDC Bunting and her flight into an adjacent wood; of Bunting's admission to Abbotsburn General Hospital and Lingard's issuing of a *Wanted for*

Assault on a Police Officer circulation before his return to Headquarters to further his enquiries, concerning which he would shortly be reporting to Rogers at the Murder Wagon.

There was also a message from Dr Hunter fixing five o'clock as the time for the post-mortem examination on Ward. Oh, my God! he muttered under his breath.

That, Sturton seemed to imply to an otherwise philosophical Rogers, handing him his asked-for clingfilm-wrapped shrimp paste sandwiches and producing a disposable carton of the dispensing machine's version of cappuccino coffee for his lunch in a dying afternoon, was how things were done while he was somewhere else and unobtainable on radio or telephone.

Fitting himself behind his desk in his cramped office, he fed himself while he shuffled through the thin sheaf of working reports left for his reading. The only one of immediate interest referred to the stopping and checking by the crew of a motorway traffic car of the TVR Chimaera II driven earlier that morning from the club's car park. The middle-aged driver – his name Jason Mathou and his address necessarily supplied – had been alone and had genially admitted that, having been told of the arrival of what he called a fornication of policemen, he had fled from any probable press publicity, dropping his lady passenger somewhere or other he couldn't exactly recall. This, he explained, had been on the grounds that her husband, a political lordling, might grossly misinterpret her overnight presence with his close friend Mathou at the Farquharson. On being pressed, he had said that he had made reservations for himself and the lady in his own name and in hers as Karen Arnold – which, of course, wasn't her true name – and this, Rogers thought, was, under the circumstances, entirely reasonable.

Knowing that their names as a member and his guest would be available anyway, Rogers said an inaudible, 'Um,' deciding that apart from a check, some time, on Mathou's antecedents, he wasn't going to fret too much about him or his inamorata, though there had to be left hanging in him the scintilla of a policeman's doubt.

Sweating in the confined heat of his office, he reflected on the apparent intransigence of Gadd – a woman supposed to be stricken with a sort of grief – who now had to be regarded with some serious suspicion, using Sturton to detach the almost skeletal DS Hooker from being Hagbourne's assistant in the breakfast enquiry and to report to the Murder Wagon. When he arrived, Rogers sent him off to Amborum-on-Sea with a description of Sarah Gadd and an instruction to check with the estate agents Davis and Davis on her employment with them, then making enquiry of her former lodgings at the address given on her driving licence. 'This immediately,' he impressed on Hooker, 'and phone in or report what you have at a gallop.'

From an intervening telephone call to the Abbotsburn General Hospital, he was assured that Policewoman Bunting was quite comfortable, though with a headache and a few stitches in her scalp, and that she needed only a few days off duty following her approaching discharge.

Having long finished his lunch and being prepared to ignore the Chief Constable's NO SMOKING notice in Sturton's cubbyhole – he half believed it referred only to her – he filled and lit a civilizing pipe of tobacco, prepared to stand and blow the smoke through the ventilating window above his head while he waited for Hagbourne who had said that his breakfast-oriented enquiries were now completed and he was on his way.

Sergeant Sturton interrupted his temporary tranquillity by transferring a telephone call from Sergeant Magnus. Magnus told Rogers that he had almost positively identified the weapon that had fired the small arrow at Ward. Probably the only one of its kind, it was a powerful compressed air pistol of German manufacture. Called a *Pfeilpistole*, it was designed to fire a ten-centimetre aluminium arrow with a claimed range of fifteen metres – round about fifty feet, Magnus volunteered – and, he thought, used for target practice and small animal hunting. A gunsmith had given Magnus this information, but was unable to either show him a weapon or an illustration of it. Magnus finished with the gun by saying that happily it was said to cost a barrowful of deutschmarks and was not readily available in the UK.

'Not to worry from where at the moment,' Rogers told him. 'It's highly unlikely the shop that supplied it would keep a record anyway. Sit on it for now.'

Further, Magnus said, as if admitting a personal failure, a

fingerprint check on the dead man Ward sent to NIB had shown that there was nothing on record concerning him, though this showed only that he had either been a wholly honest citizen or had lived a dodgy or a criminal life without being caught at it. Then he asked Rogers what time had been proposed for the post-mortem he was to attend for his photographing of the body in the process of its being anatomized and for the collection of the arrow, and that reminded Rogers that time was pushing at his back and he had better make short work of the coming Hagbourne.

He had finished with Magnus and was relighting his almost dead pipe when the sinewy and still black-haired in his late forties, detective inspector arrived, and for the umpteenth time Rogers wondered exaggeratedly why he and his terribly fecund wife seemed to want to flood the country with their flock of Hagbourne look-alikes.

'I've missed you, Thomas,' he said amiably. 'I hope you've astonishing revelations for me? I'm due at the mortuary soon so, if you have, can you make them short?' Not, he thought, that the inspector's melancholic expression promised much.

'I've had more exciting things to do totting up company accounts,' Hagbourne said, sitting himself on the dinner-plate-sized visitors seat. 'And Miss Duval has a rather naive belief in the simplicity of the breakfast schedules. Still, Hooker and I did cut out the fat of it for you and came up with some names. None likely to give you orgasms I'm afraid, but, like our dead body, something to get your teeth into.'

That had been a Hagbourne witticism and he handed Rogers his pocket-book. 'If you need the details they are in there. Briefly, of course.'

'It'll not be brief enough,' Rogers said, passing it back. 'I did say I'm due at the mortuary, so tell me.'

'You'll be baffled,' Hagbourne muttered, 'even as I was. However, as I'm told Mrs Duval laid it down for you, there are three breakfast rooms, all on the first floor and adjacent to the kitchens. One is for the members; rather palatial that one; oak panelling and period furniture: another, rather small and very business-like for the management staff. Hooker and I had a very nice lunch there with Mrs Duval.'

It must have been good, for Hagbourne's features took on a dreamy look and Rogers, slightly miffed, said, 'Spare me the details, Thomas. I'm still in a hurry.'

'Yes.' Hagbourne was unperturbed. 'The third, used by the company's perceived lower life, was all tubular metal and black plastic stuff. Not that it matters because those who could use it were either working or away from the club on leave or sick or somesuch.'

'I get that,' Rogers said sardonically, beginning to refill his pipe before it had time to cool.

'Naturally, I considered the members' messing arrangements to be the more important. They, the beautiful and the great, can take their breakfasts there between eight and nine-thirty. Or not, of course.'

Hagbourne coughed, probably a non-smoker's kneejerk response to the tobacco smoke which hadn't all drifted out through the small window. 'I'm told seven of the members breakfast in bed,' he said, somewhat disapproving of this sybaritic carrying-on, 'their breakfasts being taken to their rooms by staff. Of those who didn't take breakfast in the members' dining-room this morning, we have three who were absent as of custom from the first day – they just didn't have breakfast anyway. I have their names and addresses for checking, and I'm personally happy about them.'

He looked at a page in his pocket-book, flapping away encroaching smoke from Rogers's pipe with his free hand. 'I've a list of seven who arrived at different times after 8.15 and who you may consider to be in the running. There's Tony Grey who arrived at 8.30; Richard Yates at 8.20; Elisabet Merkel at 8.45; Martin Fisher at the same time because they came in together; Rachel Hurt at 8.40; Fiona Smith at 8.20' – his eyebrows had raised at that one – 'and Andrew Scott-Fraser at 8.45.' He turned down the corners of his mouth. 'I've an addendum to all that,' he said. 'I don't go too much of a bundle on what the waiters have said, or haven't said. I've the feeling that any or most of them could do a cover-up for a heavy tipper.'

He closed his pocket-book with a slap, saying, 'Mrs Duval is getting me their home addresses if they exist. When I get back to Headquarters I'll do a names check and so on.'

'What about the management staff's dining-room?' Rogers asked, looking at his wrist-watch.

'All those who should be there were apparently there at or about eight. I rather believe they just have to be. Anyway, I hadn't finished with the other lot so I'll recheck later. I showed my list to Mrs Duval and asked her if there was anything significant in any of the names. She said not, other than that Mrs Hurt was a close friend of Mr Jarvis the manager and had been for some time, so therefore she wouldn't need much investigating. That's all for what it's worth,' he finished.

'I imagine it might be,' Rogers said. 'It appears she saw a jogger who might prove to be concerned, though I'm damned if I can see how at the moment.' He smiled amiably at Hagbourne. 'Did the names Jason Mathou or Karen Arnold come up at any time?'

Hagbourne blinked. 'No. They damned well didn't. Is that something I missed?'

'I don't think so. They left shortly after breakfast it seems, not wanting to be identified – I suspect for adulterous reasons.' He stood, untangling his legs from the cramping recesses of his desk. 'I'm going,' he said. 'Stand aside and don't stop a man from a sort of shaking hands with the dead.'

Hagbourne stood also. 'Just one more thing,' he said with a faint glimmer of a smile. 'Mrs Duval was asking questions about you. Not directly, but from a side door.'

'Should I ask what they were?'

'They weren't about your professional capabilities.'

'Thank God for that. But should I walk carefully?'

'She did sound overly interested in your private life. Of which I know nothing of course.'

'I understand what you mean, Thomas,' Rogers said straight-faced. 'I won't be turning my back on her,' then adding, 'Trust in the integrity of my intent.' He knew that Hagbourne would be too polite and disciplined to laugh aloud at what he had meant as a light-hearted statement of assumed disinterest.

11

Moments before leaving the Murder Wagon for the mortuary, Rogers received a telephone call from Nancy Duval. 'It's been a long time no see,' she greeted him in her positively attractive well-bred voice. 'I'm terribly concerned that I'm failing in my responsibilities as your aide-de-camp.'

'I've missed you too,' he said ambiguously, hoping that Sergeant Sturton wasn't listening. 'But it's been mainly my own fault and, on top of it, I'm about to return to Abbotsburn for an hour or so. Post-mortem enquiries and all that, you know.'

'Damn,' she said tersely. 'You've eaten?'

'Something and nothing,' he exaggerated. 'It's keeping me upright, that's all.'

'I've a supper laid on for you. Some time about eight-thirty in my office. Can you make it?'

'I'd be grateful, and I'll make it,' he promised.

'You must,' she told him before closing down. 'Your aide-de-camp has duties to perform.'

Late by the ten minutes Nancy had kept him from arriving at the mortuary, Rogers offered his formal apologies to Bridget to which he received an oddly offhanded reply. He looked not too enthusiastically at the chilly and overly familiar room with its two stainless steel necropsy tables – one occupied by the naked and bloody body of Ward – its stark furnishings of white clinically aseptic working tops, the shelves of jars of diseased tissue and failed organs, a wall cabinet of the dreadful instruments used by operating pathologists and the omnipresent and unhappy smell of dead flesh. This, he thought, should be overlaid by an aromatic tobacco smoke.

Bridget, wearing green overalls, a cotton mobcap over her tawny hair, a mouth mask and pale yellow rubber gloves, was cutting into that part of the body's throat and neck from which the arrow had been removed. Sergeant Magnus, working close to her, was poised ready to photograph whatever mess of tissue and cartilage she would uncover with her scalpel. The arrow she had removed lay on the edge of the table.

As Rogers almost always did when watching death's door being opened, he spent a few seconds wondering if the dead man now knew what was on the other side; or, perhaps in disillusion, what there wasn't. Rogers knew that he himself would feel better were he to be convinced of the immutability of celestial justice, that Ward had deserved his brutal killing.

Bridget, her fingers and her scalpel still deep in the throat, was now exposing the pinkish-white cartilage of the trachea together with a short length of the collarbone. Not a glutton for observing the partial dismantlement of a human body, Rogers began to openly fidget with his pipe, a non-smoking Bridget seemingly bent on ignoring his unspoken request.

'While we were at the scene,' he said to Bridget, 'I asked you about the possible direction from which the arrow was fired. I thought it was from the side and you agreed, though saying that it need not have been. Can you be a little more explicit now?'

'I confirm that it entered the side of his throat,' she told him, 'and I would say from some little distance. I can also say that he was looking straight ahead when it happened.'

'Were the scenario to be that there were two men arguing with each other and there was a third, hidden or not hidden on the dead man's left, and he fired the arrow at chummy, would that fit the facts?'

'Yes, it would.' She was getting a little impatient, but unequivocal enough to Rogers's surprise.

He smiled at her and said, 'Thank you, Bridget,' leaving her to continue to cut her way to the truth with her scalpel.

With his back aching from leaning against a hard-edged working top and not needing to be included in the low-voiced conversation between Bridget and Magnus, he put his empty pipe between his teeth and stared hard, almost light-hearted menacingly, at Bridget. When she looked up and frowned, though not too severely, he filled the pipe, put it back between his teeth and lit it, certain that the smoke of it could only be less obnoxious than the smell of a body's interior mechanisms.

Only after Bridget had cut down the median line of the hairy chest and snipped through the rib cage to remove the heart to examine its interior, did she drop her scalpel on to the table and remove her gloves and mask.

'Simply,' she said to Rogers, being wholly Dr Hunter, Graduate in Morbid Pathology, 'my finding is that the deceased haemorrhaged to death, the heart running out of its driving fluid, if you like. I confirm this morning's diagnosis that the haemorrhaging was caused by the rupturing of the left external and internal carotid arteries.'

She paused, apparently putting her thoughts in order, while Rogers waited, wondering why the sudden coolness. 'The weapon causing the ruptures,' she said, 'also penetrated the trachea and there is the near certainty that he took only a short time to die. Two minutes, if that, from a massive outpouring of blood; partly caused I can believe by his own efforts in attempting to remove the weapon from his throat.'

'And presumably not giving him time in his dying to move from where he was shot?' Rogers suggested.

'Almost certainly,' she said crisply. 'And, having his trachea ruptured, you could say that he drowned in his own blood.'

'I'm grateful,' Rogers said, by now convinced that he had been somehow retired as Bridget's second-time-around lover and he thanked God for it. 'Can you make a stab at his age?'

'He hasn't got tree rings in him, but I'd estimate about thirty-five. Not much more.'

'We don't yet know who he actually is,' he pointed out. 'Just a man called Frank Ward and it'd help if we could have a guess at his occupation.'

'You're fishing, George,' she said, not too severely.

'In a way, yes I am. He's unknown to us other than a name, probably not his. He's unknown to anybody so far available to us, and the one person who might know is – or was – his mistress, now absent without leave and on the run.'

'I'm a pathologist,' she said with a faint show of edginess, 'not, as you seem to think, a psychic.' She took a closer look at the dead face and then at his hands, finger by finger, frowning her growing irritability and saying, 'I don't know what you expect from me, but I haven't got it. Don't you want to know what he had for his last meal?'

'I'm happy with what you've given me, and grateful.' He

bared his wrist-watch, checking the time and looking a hard-pressed man in a hurry. 'I'm sorry. I've to see the Assistant Chief about the present brouhaha,' he excused himself, though he had already sensed that he was seeing a different Bridget than the one so apparently having a need to talk with him only a few hours earlier. A Bridget, it seemed to him now, who had established a relationship with the ginger-haired Magnus. Rogers thought it would do his education the world of good, for he had always been considered to be overloaded with a potency of testosterone. Clearly for the chop, it was a certainty he would fall a victim to this beautifully bodied, sexually voracious devourer of young men.

Bridget said, a trifle mockingly and staring straight at Rogers, 'Bear up, George. It'll be all right,' leaving him, his quietus made, to guess whether she meant about the result of her examination or her dismissal of him as a once-to-be-reinstated lover.

Gratefully outside and preparing to return to Farquharson House, he felt, in a way perversely, that he had been slighted; though, indeed, an uncomfortable and unwanted load had been lifted from his shoulders.

Arriving back at the Murder Wagon, Rogers found his so far missing second-in-command seated in his hood-down cherished Bentley in the shade of an adjacent tree. Looking all but subdued and unusually irritable, Lingard was otherwise agreeably presentable in a freshly changed into off-white suit, an olive-green shirt and a patterned foulard cravat which went with the racing-green coachwork of his car. What he seemed to be saying was that anything extravagant enough for the late George Brummell was extravagant enough for himself.

Rogers joined him by climbing into the passenger seat and, aware of Lingard's always immoderate concern for his cars, was careful where he put his feet.

Lingard spoke with little of his usual panache, clearly having been put down somewhat by events. 'I'm sorry, George,' he said, 'I made a bloody ass of myself, and the lady's still hiding up somewhere. I have to accept that it could mean she's more involved than I assumed.'

'No more than I'd assumed, David.' Rogers didn't know enough about Sarah Gadd's flight to be immediately critical even in his thinking. 'Tell me about it while I get my pipe going. I've still the mortuary's stink on me.'

It didn't take much longer than it took Rogers to smoke his tobacco to ashes, and while he listened, with his critical faculties not too heavily engaged he was already deciding that Lingard was breast-beating and crying *mea culpa* much too unnecessarily.

'Absolutely too bloody awful,' he said, though smiling broadly when Lingard had finished. 'I'm sure I'd have put myself in the same position. So far as we both knew, and never mind what we suspect, she was a witness only to Ward climbing over a fence and committing, if anything, a trespass.' He looked around him for something on which to knock hot ashes from his pipe, then decided against it. 'What of the thirteen hundred pounds in notes and, in particular, the photographs of presumably eighteen ways of getting into the club's grounds? They should ring a bell or two with me.'

'Make of these what you will, George,' Lingard said, handing the photographs to him. 'There's nothing of brilliance about them, excepting somebody's application to a single subject.'

Skipping through the photographs, Rogers recognized them as an obvious novice's shots of different views of the fencing and closely standing trees adjacent to the base of the massive limestone outcrop of Butters Rock. There were also two shots of the fence blocking entry to the garden reminiscent of an Italian cemetery at the side of the house.

'Reconnaissance of an access to a known target,' Rogers suggested. 'Interesting. There was a camera in Gadd's car to go with them.'

'The best might be yet,' Lingard said, handing him the two cards he had found in the wallet.

Rogers read them both, one referring to the Davy Jones Trading Post at Leamings Landing, a chandlery dealing in inflatable life jackets and buoyancy aids, the card purporting its representative to be a Kathrin Arbitt. The other card advertised quality used cars held by a Stanley Walley operating from Scarborough.

'I see,' he said. 'The Trading Post, I imagine?'

'Yes, but look at the back of it.' Lingard was now showing a little more of his panache.

Rogers reversed the card. Written on it in pencil, in different hands, were two telephone numbers. 'Ah,' he said, scenting something useful, 'you've identified them?'

'Yes, from the dialling codes and some cooperation from the BT security bods. The first had been allotted to a house at Leamings Landing, its lessee being a Chadwick Arbitt, presumably connected with the Arbitt female printed on the card. This line was withdrawn about eighteen months ago. The other – have a guess, George – is one of the Farquharson House numbers used by the Reception Office.'

Rogers was impressed. 'Thank God we've got something out of all this. So what would Ward want with the Trading Store card? Was there any indication that he had a boat? Or was interested in sailing?'

'Nothing so far.' Lingard was feeding his nose with snuff. 'There's a connection though, there has to be. Perhaps the Arbitt woman's an old lady-love?' His expression showed that he had thought of it as a possibility. 'And perhaps she's identical with my missing – damn her – Sarah Gadd.'

'That's another thought,' Rogers said non-committally. 'You've been in touch with Leamings Landing?'

Lingard was holding the Bentley's steering wheel as though driving it in a silent and motionless journey, though Rogers noticed there was nothing white-knuckled about it now. 'Of course,' he said. 'Like a flash, through to the CID at Amborum who cover Leamings Landing. I phoned them and told the local DI that we were on a murder enquiry and what did he know of the Davy Jones Trading Post where the company owner or Kathrin Arbitt might be able to put a finger on the identity of Ward.' He pulled a face. ' He said straight away that the store had folded two or three years back before he'd arrived in the Division, but he'd find out something and call back.'

'And?' Not going so well, Rogers considered.

'So far, not. I'll give him a buzz if he doesn't soon.'

Amborum-on-Sea, being under a different police authority, needed careful handling and Rogers had been thinking about it. 'Leave the Amborum end with me, David,' he said, about to be careful that he didn't cut across his second-in-command's *amour propre*. 'I'm by way of being friendly with Bernard Trout the divisional detective superintendent and I'm sure he'll have all we want at his very bony fingertips. So, I'd like to see him myself.'

Lingard frowned, his face looking narrower than normal, an unusual expression of his objection. 'Dammit, George. I started it and I need to go to Amborum to tie it up. It's part of my brief.'

'I know it is and I don't necessarily want to do it,' Rogers said, 'but there's also the pressing matter of our dealing with the paperwork and files that are, I'm certain, already piling up on my desk. I can't deal with them while I'm up to my neck here so I'm afraid, as always, it's over to you. For a short while only – of necessity.' He smiled to soften his next instruction. 'There's also the Assistant Chief to be put into the picture with some appropriate apologies – not too fulsome of course – for having overlooked it. Fight off any half-hearted suggestion that he should come here, getting in my bloody way. Tell him that I'm up to my eyes in it and won't be here anyway for some hours, by which time he'll want to be toddling off home.'

Lingard took it – as he had to – mainly because he knew, as Rogers's second-in-command, that it was what he was there for. Rogers, climbing from the Bentley, said, 'Good on you, cobber,' in his execrable pseudo-Australian and stood there watching him drive away; Lingard not too visibly unhappy, but not too happy either.

When he entered the now cooling Murder Wagon, he found that WPS Magnolia Flowers – she was notable for her feminine sweetness and for her ample shirt-straining breasts – had taken over from Sturton. Rogers liked her, believing her to be, as yet, untarnished by man's concupiscence. She said, 'There's a call from Headquarters asking you to telephone Detective Superintendent Trout at Amborum who's been trying to contact you. I'll get him for you,' she added.

After an exchange of professional goodwill in which Trout sounded unusually depressed, he started by saying, 'It's concerning your DI's enquiry of mine about your bit of trouble with a body and the Davy Jones Store, though God only knows what the connection can be. The company, for a start, was sold over two years ago, until then being owned by a man called Chadwick Arbitt, but not I think for long.'

That hadn't put Rogers on a high and he said, 'That's it, Bernard?', his hopes of a lead also going down the pan, though with Trout calling back there had to be something more. 'You know this chap Arbitt, do you? Is there any possibility that he or his wife could take a look at our body here? He's now in the mortuary and one of them might recognize him.'

'Not remotely,' Trout told him, sounding unhappy. 'Arbitt was dead long before his business was sold. He died in his yacht when it caught fire offshore near here and God alone would know where his wife is. There's more about that on paper. At least there should have been . . .' He was silent for long moments during which Rogers could hear his heavy breathing. 'I think,' he continued, 'there's trouble brewing. Possibly for me and that'd be awkward. You'd better come straight away before the manure hits the fan.'

'It reflects on one of your lot?' Rogers suggested diplomatically.

'I'll tell you, but not on the telephone. In my office, eh? I'll be waiting for you.' Trout had sounded no happier and his words were followed by the sound of his disconnecting.

Rogers's feelings were divided. He was reasonably content that something was happening, but worried that the something might be to the frustration of his investigation. Feeling baffled, he couldn't understand why Trout should be so manifestly upset by the fact that they were confronted by an adventitiously dead man surfacing in an investigation apparently only peripheral to his death in a burning yacht and anyway in the next county.

12

Amborum-on-Sea was a neat and clean and narrow-streeted small coastal town flush with red-tiled holiday bungalows, white-painted hotels and guesthouses, all grouped on the slopes surrounding three sides of the spacious medieval harbour. In it floated lines of wooden walkways accommodating, hull to hull, sailing boats, yachts and motor cruisers. The town smelled strongly of seaweed, low-tide mud and fast-food cooking.

The Divisional Constabulary Headquarters were close to the busy harbour's edge and fortunate enough to have escaped modernization, retaining its solid saltwater-stained greystone bulk to match the harbour walls. Detective Superintendent Trout's office on the second floor was comfortably old like the building; his desk, chairs and bookcases of wood and fabric and not, as were Rogers's, of unaesthetic metals and plastics.

Trout himself was tall and rawboned with dead black hair believed wrongly to be dyed. Though gaunt in his face with sunken and seemingly suffering eyes, and despite being an occasional sufferer of melancholia, he was of a reasonably genial persona, possessing an old-fashioned decency with an inability to be more than mildly authoritarian.

With Rogers now in his office and sitting at what he called the public complainers' side of the huge desk, he sat himself as a clearly worried man. He was, as Rogers saw from an official-looking THIS IS A NO SMOKING AREA notice on his desk, suffering the same sort of tyranny as himself, though that failed to cheer him.

'You're happy that your dead man can't be Arbitt?' Trout started. 'He's been dead and buried these past two years or so.'

'I'll take your word for it,' Rogers assured him, 'though it leaves me in the dark how he comes into it anyway.'

'Not a lot more than I am.' Trout was darkly gloomy. 'Let me tell you this first. The file relating to Arbitt's death has gone missing and God only knows to where. Not only that. When I called for the back-up file from the computer mainframe I was told that it must have been deleted, for it no longer existed. You know as well as I do that files don't just go missing, nor their back-ups.'

He looked like a man who had just lost a well-stuffed wallet. 'You see what I mean, George. It's this division's files that are missing and we wouldn't have known anything about it hadn't you brought up this business of Arbitt and his wife. It leaves me up the creek just when I'm supposed to be retiring this week on my thirty-year pension. And now there's all this.' His hands were clasped on his desk and his inner agitation was being expressed by cracking his knuckles.

'Wouldn't the investigating officer have his own file copy?' Rogers could suffer for Trout and for the official enquiry he would inevitably have to endure.

'The investigating officer was Detective Inspector-bloody-Poukas who put in his resignation a few months after the inquest on Arbitt. He'd only done fourteen years, so he didn't have a pension to lose. When he was fully paid up he just went; he told someone else that he was off to Australia to get a similar job there.'

'Unhelpful, Bernard,' Rogers said sympathetically, already thinking it to be a calculated and ill-fated happening. 'You can tell me something about Arbitt and his death, I hope?' With the office's two-feet thick walls it was hot and he was sweating, the open windows not helping much.

'Quite a bit from the file Poukas originally submitted through me. Not a lot verbally, I'm afraid, because I'd gone on a three-weeks' leave before it happened. It wasn't a murder job and had I been here I'd probably not have got the department involved. Arbitt was first reported as an accidental death that needed pursuing to the Deputy Chief who pushed it over to my department for action when it wasn't actually our concern. But I wasn't here and we had it hung around our necks like a bloody albatross.'

While Rogers waited for more, Trout ran a bony finger down a page of pencilled notes he had on his blotting-pad. 'Chadwick Arbitt,' he said, 'known to his intimates as Chad I understand. He was the owner of the Davy Jones Trading Store – it was what used to be called a chandlery – and it was at Leamings Landing. That's a small fishing and sailing town eighteen miles up the coast from us and in my division. He and his wife Kathrin – she helped in the store and did some commercial travelling – owned a middling-sized yacht called something like *Poppy*. There was nothing known on paper about either of them, but his wife – she was a widow by then – later said he'd been much too fond of the bottle and had had unspecified health problems.'

He grimaced, his chest expanding with his intake of tobacco-smoke-free air, something Rogers felt he could do without. 'Some time in September,' he continued, 'he went fishing in his boat, on his own because she had to look after the store. It later appeared that he had some trouble with his paraffin cabin heater and he and the boat went up in flames and sank. This happened in Blacktoad Bay, which is not too far from Leamings Landing – if you can say ten miles isn't too far – and where he's reported to have occasionally done his fishing, or dodged having to spend too much time with his wife.'

'Was the boat seen at all? Smoke and flame, you know?' Rogers was thinking that none of this seemed relevant to the dead man Ward and he could be trotting along the wrong path. So far, it was all his friend Trout's problem.

'Apparently not. It's a bit remote there and the bay's not accessible by land, so we can't look after that bit of coastline anyway.' He shrugged that off, understandably more concerned about his missing files. 'As I said, I was on leave in France at the time and it hadn't ever been my particular pigeon.'

'There was an inquest presumably?' Rogers asked, speaking loudly against a sudden clamour from the herring gulls outside.

'Yes, but the collected evidence was all cut and dried by the time I returned, and at the hearing the Coroner found a Death by Misadventure verdict because, it seemed, nothing much could be proved or disproved with a burned and waterlogged body in a burned-out boat at the bottom of a deep water bay, and that was that.' Trout looked a little troubled, though he could have been thinking about something else.

'His wife gave evidence after she'd identified the body as that of her husband. As I said, he was badly burned and, you could say, not his usual self, but there was his wrist-watch, his house and car keys and cards in his wallet not wholly burned. Our subaqua divers who went down also brought up a gin bottle and a drinking glass which were with the body. The boat's still on the bottom; not worth the trouble of salvaging it seems and unlikely to interfere with shipping.'

'Am I thinking you're not too happy about the coroner's finding, Bernard?'

There was a look of what could be alarm on Trout's face until a sort of forced amusement took its place. 'God Almighty, George,' he said. 'Don't say that. I'm happy. I'm happy about everything but the missing bloody file and its back-up. How the hell do you delete a file from a computer to which only a very few have access, and which you'd think was past history anyway? It'll be sure to reflect on my departmental efficiency when all I want is to be a retired police officer, shot of the whole business and able to say it's all over to you.'

'I'm more than grateful.' Rogers smiled, knowing exactly to the next decimal point how Trout felt and willing to go along with him. 'Fill me in on more of Mrs Arbitt's evidence. It might do something to my thinking.'

Trout scratched a chin dark with a late-day stubble on it. 'There's nothing other than what you might expect in these missing-person-found-dead cases,' Trout said, almost dismissively. 'Mrs Arbitt told the coroner that when her husband hadn't returned by late afternoon she began to worry, first making enquiries of whatever other boat owners were at the mooring, though without anybody having seen him. Then, naturally enough I suppose, she reported her husband's unusual absence to us and also to the district's Coastguard Service which is bloody miles and miles north of where Arbitt could be expected to have been.'

Trout had been looking at the back of the no-smoking notice as he spoke, a much less than approving look in his face. He said, noticeably irritable, 'It'd taken five or six days before they found and identified what was left of the boat, for Mrs Arbitt could only guess that her husband might have sailed to Blacktoad Bay. It took a chopper from the nearby RAF airfield to find it, for the water's said to be deep and dark with a jungle of kelp along that part.'

He was silent for a few moments, Rogers thought fumbling with a long lost memory of what actually happened. 'The subaqua divers who went down and pulled out the body,' he continued, 'said that what little remained of the sails was furled and the sea anchor out, so it seems that he wasn't going anywhere when the fire broke out. His fishing equipment was missing, having apparently been destroyed in the fire that took everything over the waterline including the whole interior.' He scratched at his chin again. 'I recollect now,' he said. 'The gin bottle was found half full of the stuff; naturally, of course, but he *was* a drinker and the proper assumption was arrived at during the hearing.'

'And that was it?' Rogers asked. 'I'm almost desperately trying to find an actual understandable connection with my dead Ward. Why was he in possession of Arbitt's telephone number for a start? Might that be to call your Arbitt, or his wife within a non-business relationship? So was she the type to have an off the cuff lover or two?'

Trout looked baffled at that. 'How could I know, George, without the bloody file? Poukas would have known, I'm sure of that.'

'I still don't see too much in it for me, though my logic's niggling at my common sense and I'm unhappy about the whole thing. I seem to feel that there's something missing in what you've told me. No offence, Bernard, but it's the old instinct working overtime. I'm still thinking about the trade card and the thirteen hundred pounds found in Ward's cottage – it was rented by the way – and whether it was Arbitt or his wife who could have identified him, and said why if they could. That's a connection with Ward that needs sorting out and I feel that at least Mrs Arbitt might be able to help me.'

Trout shook his head. 'She left the area not too long after she sold the business. I did hear too that she'd collected something like three-quarters of a million pounds on her husband's life insurance from a London insurance syndicate. Whether she'd help if you found her, I don't know. That DI Poukas of mine told me after I'd got back from leave that he thought Mrs Arbitt could have killed her husband because of his drinking and his rough treatment of her. That was only one of his fanciful theories about people who'd died unusual deaths in particular and, soon enough, he told me that he'd been on the wrong track, that now that he'd dug further into it he could see that she couldn't have done it, that he'd died because of a faulty paraffin heater.' The echoes of his earlier exasperation with Poukas seemed to be still with him.

'Surely he must have had something to justify his original suspicion?' Rogers wasn't quite buying that a detective inspector would dream up the possibility of a murder on no real basis at all.

Trout snorted his dismissal of that. 'You didn't know this one. He was into self-promotion in a big way. You've had them, admit it. If he could latch on to what he could dream up as a suspect murder job in my absence, he'd damned well do so. You didn't know Poukas, George. He was the bottom and I could never get enough proveable bombast to be rid of him. Anyway, he'd told me he'd been mistaken, that after having seen Mrs Arbitt she'd impressed him with what she had said and of the obvious impracticability of her being with her husband on the boat or even being anywhere but in the store. After that had been laid to rest and the inquest had been held, he resigned as I said and took himself off to Australia. And that, George, wasn't far enough, though it did surprise me.'

'It surprises me too,' Rogers said, though he wasn't going too far with Trout on Poukas. 'Why, if it's not a silly question, should anyone remove what would be a put-to-rest file and its mainframe back-up . . .' He stopped short, showing a look of irritation. 'Of course. There almost certainly has to be information in them suggesting or showing somebody's criminal culpability in the case, though not necessarily murder. You think Poukas's?'

'I don't know what to think,' Trout answered. 'For all I know of the bloody thing it could implicate somebody else, though Poukas is the name that impresses me most. Certainly he had free access to both records.'

'You presumably read the file,' Rogers said carefully, unwilling to tread too heavily on a man's susceptibilities. 'Did nothing in it strike you as needing further enquiries?'

Trout seemed what could be called distracted. 'That's it, George. It was just an accidental death file with none of it being my department's real concern. I did skip through it, of course, as anyone would, but not with an eye to its containing anything meriting my serious attention.'

'You've not checked on Poukas's swanning off to Australia?'

Trout shook his head. 'Not yet. Probably not at all if I can get out of this bloody mess before I leave.'

'Fill me in on him. What he was like; his physical description?'

'Poukas – he's Humphrey Poukas by the way,' Trout started, 'was one of those cocky buggers who walked around believing he had what it takes to run the department himself. He was a loner, though I have to say he was a reasonably equipped detective apart from some of his fanciful theories that reflected, I suppose, his self-importance. He was unmarried, lived in lodgings and, so much as I'd heard, wasn't much of a one for the ladies or for social mixing. He's very much an average man though he doesn't look it and when he was choked off he could look like an undertaker's coffin-carrier. I can't describe him any better, but I'll get you a full description of him from our Records Department.'

'I'll recognize him,' Rogers promised him cheerfully, 'just so long as he happens to be carrying a coffin at the time.' When he saw that Trout wasn't particularly receptive of his attempt at humour, he said, 'A woman. It might not be her real name, but we have her as Sarah Gadd and she's not available to us at the moment. She was living with Ward, was with him shortly before he was murdered, and we do have to be interested in her. She's a flashy type; about thirty, thirty-five or so; tallish with a thin figure; has a sort of dark yellow hair cut short; attractive, I suppose, though with too much lipstick, eyelash stuff and a drenching of perfume. She said she was employed here in Amborum with an estate agency called Davis and Davis. I sent my Sergeant Hooker here to check and he'd have made his number with your department by now. She rings a bell?' he asked hopefully.

'Not at all.' There had been nothing in his face to show it did. 'I wouldn't know about your sergeant calling anyway. I don't seem to know anything of these buggers, yours or mine, you've been talking about.' There was now an edge of exasperation in his voice.

Rogers ignored it, only showing his disappointment. 'The Arbitts included? Don't tell me you didn't know them either.' When Trout shook his head again, he said, 'And, of course, not our dead Ward. Perhaps under a different name?'

'Not the name for sure.'

Rogers was clutching at very small straws. 'He's about thirty-five give or take; five feet ten inches on his back; average build; dark brown hair, a moustache and a small beard, yes?'

Trout was already shaking his head in an obvious rejection of anything connected with Ward when one of his desk telephones rang, earpiercingly unmelodious. Lifting the receiver and saying 'Yes?' into it, he then held it out to Rogers. 'Your Sergeant Flowers, George.'

Rogers knew trouble was looming before he took it. 'Rogers here, sergeant,' he said, wondering what the hell.

Flowers was taking it calmly, almost matter of factly, telling him that at about eight-thirty that evening – not twenty minutes ago – a woman had been found dead in the dome by one of the cleaning staff. A tremendously upset Mr Jarvis had been called to the scene and had identified the dead woman as a Mrs Rachel Hurt, a long-term guest. A sergeant and a PC were with the body which had not yet been screened from public view.

'Jesus,' he said to Trout, replacing the receiver, 'we've a woman die on us in the same place as Ward and you think you've got troubles.' Then, as he reached the door, he said, 'I'll be in touch again, when I've bottomed out.'

It was dusk outside with dark-bellied clouds coming in from the sea and beginning to rain. 'Well, it damn well would, wouldn't it,' he told himself, never having used the cliché before and even then feeling he'd borrowed somebody else's something. Turning his Citroen out of the station yard he was already filling his pipe, lighting it one-handed and beginning to seriously worry.

13

Rogers, arriving in the darkness and rain and having dumped his hard-driven Citroen outside the Murder Wagon, waved his arrival to the overabundance of Sergeant Flowers inside it. Finding the buggy provided for his use, he drove into the subtropical solarium.

With the roof lights – small, faraway hot suns – illuminating the near side of the glass dome, he was able to see the distant white buggies of those already there adjacent to a group of palms and close to where he had interviewed Rachel Hurt. Nearing them, he saw that the scene was bizarrely different from that which he had seen earlier. A few yards distant from it, clear of the palms, was a small group of obvious onlookers, the curious and the morbid, being held from encroaching by a uniformed PC.

Braking to a halt, hearing the rain beating loudly on the high glass roof and smelling the cool sea air entering from the outside darkness, he saw the scene before him as a backdrop to a staged set of three dark figures standing unspeaking in the deep green of the palms around a palely glimmering body sitting back in sleep or death. He identified the figures as an obviously phlegmatic uniformed PS Goddard, a manifestly worried Charles Jarvis and an unperturbed Nancy Duval.

Rogers, always rather formidable in the exercise of his authority, said an unsmiling 'Good evening' to them, detailing Goddard to contact Headquarters on his radio and to ask for the immediate despatch of the body-protection tent and portable floods, then to return to the Murder Wagon in one of the buggies to provide incoming transport. He put the PC – to Rogers he looked as if he had just left school – to persuading or insisting to the nearby watchers on death that the investigation into its causes needed no spectator support at the moment. Clearing the deck for action, he called it.

Standing at the side of the lounger, he took in what was visible in the deep shadow for his early information. All appeared to be much as he had seen of the live Rachel Hurt and her personal effects earlier that evening. Other than, it seemed, for the thin fabric scarf – it had a coloured floral motif – sunken tightly in the flesh of her throat. Though her head was bent forward, it did little to hide the terrible expression on the face, her eyes open in a sightless stare and her mauve tongue protruding from between the exposed teeth in the classic distortion of death by strangulation. Her spectacles rested closed on her lap, her straw hat lay on the ground well away from the lounger and her closed book was at her side.

He put his fingers against her throat, feeling unsuccessfully for the throbbing of blood through the artery, knowing she was unarguably dead anyway. Then he put his hand beneath the neck of her dress – that, he thought, might appear to be an indecency to the others – feeling the smooth flesh of her breast for warmth and finding only the growing coolness of death. She had, he thought, been dead for something like three hours, but needing Bridget Hunter to tell him sharply that he was an idiot in matters concerning the inexplicabilities of the violent dissolution of the human body.

He turned to Jarvis and Duval, smiling briefly and saying, 'Bear with me for a few moments more, will you?' then using his mobile phone to call up Flowers in the Murder Wagon. His instructions, given in a low voice for her alone, were for the immediate implementation of the Force's Major Crime Investigation Orders, these to now include finding – if he wasn't still in his office – Chief Inspector Lingard who was to drop everything not criminally fragile and to devote himself to the tracking down of Dr Hunter. He hoped that she hadn't yet started her devouring of DS Magnus who was also wanted – and to accompany her personally to the dome where a further body awaited her urgent attention.

'Charles,' Rogers said with a proper affability, having noticed that most of his meagre audience had drifted away, 'I'm sorry you've attracted to yourself another dead body. It can't have escaped your notice that Mrs Hurt was killed shortly, well relatively shortly, after confiding to me – at your initiative – that she had seen the man thought to be in the vicinity of the first killing this morning. A very nice woman,' he added, in a sort of apology for having thought her an arrogant bitch.

Jarvis, wearing a white dinner jacket with a crimson bow-tie, looked pallid in the half-light and very much shaken, his luxuriant moustache seeming to have lost its bounce. 'I wouldn't have suggested she should speak to you had I known this would happen,' he said almost accusingly. 'You must have been seen.'

'True,' Rogers agreed, his affability having fled and putting a finger to his lips in a warning against being overheard. 'And why not? Would you suggest by whom, and why?' He was conscious of Nancy Duval, to one side of Jarvis, watching him intently, making him aware that there was something going on between them, though unwanted by him at the moment.

'She approached me,' Jarvis said stiff-lipped. 'I passed on what she evidently wished me to do. I mean, how was I to know?' Something like despair showed in his face and it appeared possible that the detective was no longer one of his bosom friends. 'Jesus Christ!' he burst out. 'What am I going to say to Head Office! The bastards will have me booking in at the local Job Centre by tomorrow! One of the shirtless! Two bloody murders in one bloody day and it had to happen to me!'

'You're exaggerating, Charles.' Rogers felt sympathy for him. 'You want me to dig in with some words of well-earned praise for your being public-spirited? Tirelessly helpful to the police? I can make it hard for them to do anything drastic about you without having its injustices making big headlines in the local press. Still,' he beamed encouragingly, 'I doubt that they'll do anything cataclysmic anyway.'

'Decent of you, old chap,' a subdued Jarvis said, 'though I don't think it'll do me all that good. I mean, who else would have his establishment littered with dead bodies all in a single day?'

'You're an idiot, Charles,' the so far silent Nancy Duval told him as he chewed at his moustache in indecision. 'If you hadn't told George, I would have anyway. Tell your stupid Head Office that I did it, if you like.'

After a few seconds of thought about that, during which

Rogers could hear the rumbling of approaching thunder, he said to Jarvis, 'Fill me in on the how and when of this, will you? Was it one of your cleaners?'

'Not a cleaner actually. A Mrs Daniels – one of those employed to go out with a buggy and a bag to pick up litter, discarded wrappings and suchlike, and tidy up the lounger areas. She'll be available to you later on of course.'

'What time did she report the finding to you?'

Jarvis checked with his wrist-watch. 'Forty minutes ago? Say at eight-thirty? Since when we've been hanging about waiting for you.'

'Sorry, Charles. I was at Amborum.' He looked at Rachel Hurt's body; sinking, it seemed, deeper into the padded lounger and certainly looking displeased about being dead. 'I left her here about four o'clock which is now, roughly, five and a half hours ago. If I'm right in thinking she's been dead three hours – and God knows I needn't be – then she could have been killed between six-thirty and seven o'clock.'

When neither of them offered any comment on this possibly inaccurate hypothesis, Rogers said, 'I'd like a run down on Mrs Hurt's background later, Charles. Offhand, can you think of any connection she may have had – even in the abstract – with this morning's murdered man?'

Jarvis spoke to Duval. 'Over to you, Nancy?'

'I knew her reasonably well,' she told Rogers, 'but any connection there might be, other than sighting the jogger or whoever, escapes me. Almost certainly none at all.'

'And he certainly isn't a member here, not with a bristle haircut such as she told me. Past or present,' Jarvis added, not now looking like a man about to die.

Rogers looked at his own wrist-watch. 'I'm grateful,' he said to both of them. 'I think I've all I want from you,' then quickly, 'For the moment only, naturally. I shall want to look at Mrs Hurt's room and borrow Nancy's services in about an hour's time to open it up for me.' He smiled at her. 'A meet in your office when I can get out from under?'

On their leaving, he called the PC over, then began to re-examine Hurt's body more closely. Grimacing his distaste he lifted her dress for a brief glance at her underwear to assure himself that she hadn't been indecently assaulted or raped. The scarf around her neck – he was certain she hadn't been wearing it during his interview with her – had been tied at the back with a double knot. Faint shoe impressions in the hard sandy soil behind the lounger confirmed only that the attack had been made from the rear. It left him with the option of thinking that it had been either a stealthy and noiseless approach to her through the palm trees, or a killing by someone known well enough to be with her, she being without suspicion of his intent.

So far as he could see or assume, none of the articles she had brought with her – other than her straw hat – had been moved. Opening her vanity case, careful in handling its smooth surface, he found only a woman's cosmetics. He cursed that its opening hadn't occurred to him while Jarvis and Nancy were with him, for surely the dead woman would have needed to carry her room key with her?

Retrieving her spectacles from her lap, he frowned his mystification at finding the lenses in them were of plain glass. He could now believe that there was more to this dead woman than he had originally thought, believing that the definitely unconnected were not normally killed so soon after having been in conversation with a detective superintendent, apparently recognizable as such in spite of his ill-chosen disguise.

That Rachel Hurt had worn plain-glass spectacles gave her an intent to deceive, possibly to hide her identity. And this could mean that she had felt threatened by somebody. By the dead Ward perhaps, though certainly he hadn't risen from the dead to carry any threat he might have posed into execution. Possibly she wasn't Rachel Hurt at all, but Rachel somebody else; women – and men – liking to keep their given names even in adversity. And why had she so manifestly disliked him? And what about the woman Gadd? How did she fit into all this? Dammit to hell, his frustration led him to say under his breath. He'd leave all that for later. For now, he would tell himself not to think too ill of the dead woman, but rather to pity her.

After he had given up on unprofitable speculation he waited – mostly impatiently – for the arrival of his body tent and the flood lights, Bridget Hunter, Lingard, the Coroner's Officer and the department's assorted on-call technicians. While he did he talked desultorily to the hanging on PC, now waiting to be told what to do by somebody, and finding it hard going but being comforted by smoking his pipe in a kind of uninterfered with peace.

When he saw a buggy approaching with Lingard in it as a passenger, he knew his own detachment from the scene was imminent, even though possibly short-lived. Having missed out on Nancy Duval's invitation to eat at eight-thirty, he intended to drink enough strong coffee to keep himself standing upright before he extended his investigation to a search of Rachel Hurt's room. And, of course, there was always the prospect of the fascinating and apparently hungry Nancy Duval, a prospect about which he was now having one or two reservations.

14

Being now well after ten o'clock, time was pressing on a tiring Rogers. Parking his buggy alongside the Murder Wagon, he put his head around its door and asked the always affable Sergeant Flowers to detail one of the spare DCs to check at Reception for the names of any members who had left since four o'clock, though he thought any precipitate flight unlikely. He then told her that he would be in the main building with Mrs Duval if urgently required, in his mind praying, Please, God, don't let's have another one, not tonight anyway.

Entering the complex of the building's corridors past an unoccupied Reception Office and through the towering foyer occupied by two dinner-jacketed men – at a guess, about to smoke a couple of surreptitious cigars – he trod the blue carpeting to Nancy Duval's office. Knocking and hearing her say something difficult to understand, he walked in.

She wasn't at her desk, but standing brooding through one of the windows, apparently on the rain and the still partially lit dome. She patently wasn't very happy in doing it, turning her head to look unsmilingly at him. He saw again how patricianly attractive she was, his heart giving a sudden lurch to emphasize it. She was wearing a simple unembellished dress in black, her hair having a newly washed glossiness in it. Against her, he felt unkempt with unmown bristles thickening, the form for him this time of the night, and additionally, probably smelling of the mortuary's formalin.

'I'm sorry,' he said, showing his teeth and wondering if she could still find his beakish nose attractive. 'I feel I'm a little late.'

'Damned late,' she told him coldly, 'though it doesn't matter. I saw you coming through the dome. Are you going to tell me what it's all about?' She was eyeing him almost as if re-assessing a held opinion of him.

'At the moment I don't honestly know.' All his instinct warred against giving official information even to her who was supposed to be his aide. 'I'm still in the stage two state of unknowingness. May I now see Mrs Hurt's room?' She wasn't being the woman he thought he knew, and he felt constrained in her present mood, ready to do some growling if it continued.

'Rooms,' she said. 'She has a suite on the third floor. You have her keys?'

'No. If she had them with her they've been taken.'

'I've the master keys.' She dangled them, brass-tagged, from her fingers. 'Shall we go?'

'Where is everybody?' he asked, following her. 'The place looks deserted.'

She looked amused, which was something. 'Either in the casino at the tables, or in bed. Both have their attractions, don't you think? And are almost certainly among the reasons for their coming here.'

'I'd have thought more noise, more trotting about. An occasional laugh too,' he added.

'Not with the big money you don't.' Her eyes now showed amusement. 'Members do their own thing; discretion, some deference to the gods they hold dear and leaving them to do it are our watchwords.'

'With nobody wanting us here?' he suggested.

'Naturally not. They're sensibly avoiding anyone looking remotely like a policeman.'

'And you are actually riding herd on me?' He believed that, not being taken in too far by the helpful aide business.

Entering a lift, she smiled at him over her shoulder. 'Of course I am. It's what PAs are paid for.'

With the third floor reached, he found the passage they were in railed from the far below foyer in wrought iron and brass, its length made civilized with hanging framed prints and containers of yuccas and ferns. Mrs Hurt's suite – it had a gold-painted twenty-seven on its door – was, with its neighbours, on the outer perimeter of the building and Duval unlocked it, preceding the detective into it.

The suite consisted of a sitting-room, a bedroom, a bathroom and a lavatory. The sitting-room and bedroom were furnished in a luxurious styling of moss-green fabrics, the bedroom having in it a green-draped reproduction four-poster bed. Rogers, looking around, thought the air was permeated with the odours of the dead woman's scents and lotions.

'You've been here before?' he asked.

She shook her head. 'No. I'd have no reason to.'

'Please try not to touch anything,' he said. 'I shall be having it dusted for fingerprints.'

She looked surprised. 'You will? Why?'

'It's certain that the rooms have been entered and searched by whoever killed Mrs Hurt. I'm assuming her keys were taken from her vanity case for that purpose.'

'I hadn't known.'

'No. Sit in comfort while I look for what I have to, will you? None of it will be very interesting for you.'

There was no disorder in any of the drawers of the sitting-room's writing desk, though one contained neatly put away invoices and commercial letters addressed to Hurt. There was a noticeable absence of documents identifying who, in fact, this Rachel Hurt actually was, her status or from where she came.

When he had finished with both the sitting-room, the bedroom and the two ancillary rooms, he was certain that they had already been searched. His certainty was based on the absence of a cheque book, cheque stubs, of any document relating to a banking account, of bank or credit cards and, as significant, the absence of a handbag.

Rogers accepted that it hadn't been a five-star search, but was satisfied, subject to his not having torn up the floorboards or dismembered the four-poster bed, that nothing of importance had escaped him. Magnus would, if necessary, take the room apart when Rogers could detach him from the mortuary, Rachel Hurt's body and, he now believed, from Bridget Hunter's personal needs.

'There's no handbag,' he told Duval who had rejoined him, starting to fill his pipe. 'And I didn't see her with one, only her vanity case.'

'She has one, definitely. A lizard-skin clutch bag, quite small.' She smiled, almost apologetically, looking at the pipe in his hand. 'I'm afraid there's a quite dictatorial ban on smoking in the upper two floors of the house.' She smiled again. 'I could be shot at first light should I not have pointed it out to you.'

'I'm sorry,' Rogers apologized, again feeling himself to be a social outcast needing fumigating and returning his pipe to his pocket. 'Old appetites for nicotine die hard. I was going to say that I've finished the search, but I do have questions. In your office?'

'I'm sorry too,' she said, being noticeably more friendly. 'About your pipe I mean because I use an occasional cigarette myself. In the meantime, as I anticipated being interrogated at length, I ordered some sandwiches and coffee for us, and I'm only just along the passage.'

Following her, docilely for him, he decided that he had been mistaken in half-believing that earlier she had had a sexual interest in him and he was not about to be sorry, still having a dodgy conscience about Angharad.

Duval's rooms were smaller in size and pattern to the dead woman's, differing only in having a gold fleur-de-lis motif on a royal-blue background for the coverings and drapes. The two large windows, dripping with rain, faced the darkened sea.

Seating the detective in one of the sitting-room chairs, Duval, adopting a kind of I'm-on-my-own-ground pleasantness, used her telephone, dabbing a slender finger on two studs and ordering somebody to send up the sandwiches and coffee. Then she sat in the second chair – near enough for Rogers to smell her potent scent – and said, 'Let's get this over with. I'd like to talk about other things over a sandwich.'

'There are one or two matters I have to raise,' he admitted. 'Put aside if you will any reluctance you may have about discussing Mrs Hurt in particular. Her Majesty's Coroner will need it as much as I do now, and he can be a lot nastier than I would be if he doesn't get it.' He thought that he had said it quite amiably.

She fastened a rather amused blue-grey stare on the wary Rogers. 'You wish me to betray professional confidences?'

'Most certainly, if you have any.' He stared back at her, thinking how bloody attractive she was, how femininely enticing. 'Any that might be connected even remotely with her death, or with any other character you know with whom she associated.'

'And that's ethical?' She was baiting him and he didn't mind.

'As ethical as I imagine the prospectus of your freewheeling company to be. How long . . .'

Interrupted by a tap on the door, he paused, waiting on the entry of a white-jacketed Mediterranean-type waiter carrying a silver tray of sandwiches and a globular glass container of steaming coffee. After placing it on the table without once looking at either – Rogers thought this a practised diplomacy at its best – he left, closing the door quietly behind him.

Rogers recommenced, his voice pitched to friendliness. 'How long has Mrs Hurt been living here?'

'Eighteen months or so.' Duval smiled. 'And truly I don't have any professional confidences to betray. Help yourself to what you want. I'll join you as and when.'

'It'd help were you to tell me about her without too many prompts from me.' He wasn't liking this, eating on his own – the tiny sandwiches had a smoked salmon filling – regretting that he had come here with this too, too fascinating woman of uncertain intent, believing he was undergoing an attack of sexual priggishness.

She was pouring coffee – rich, dark and fragrant – as she spoke. 'Mrs Hurt booked with us on a temporary basis through a holiday agency. We knew only that she was then staying at a five-star Scarborough hotel – but, of course, Charles can check that for you. It's nothing unusual; it's a member's privilege not to disclose a real address should he or she choose. After she arrived, she applied for a longer stay and then another until she gradually assumed the role of a permanent resident. She's believed to be divorced or a widow, though only because there's never been a visible husband, no Mr Hurt, as a visitor. Nor, as far as I know, has she mentioned the existence of one. She's obviously well loaded if that could possibly be relevant to what you're doing about her,' then saying cynically, 'She has to be, to be able to stay here for so long.'

'Yes.' He swallowed hot, almost scalding coffee, his eyes watering. 'Mentioning that, would you know her bank?'

She frowned, though only mildly. 'No, I don't. You'll have to ask Charles that.'

'She has visitors?' Rogers was feeling a mite uncomfortable, feeling pinned down by her relentless regard of him. It was like being stared at by a tigress.

'I understand she had a normal woman's responses to attractive men, if that's what you mean. And there were lots of them coming here. One assumes, of course, that she did something about them.' She took a sandwich, holding it ready to bite into. 'You've possibly noticed this place is not an ecclesiastical retreat. Neither the men nor the women come here bogged down by too many ethics.' She smiled, then bit beautifully white teeth into her sandwich.

'She didn't think much of me,' Rogers said offhandedly. 'I thought she considered me an interfering nuisance. Obviously not her normal attitude to men?' Whatever scent Duval was wearing, it was still reaching him, troubling him with thoughts of the exotic, thoughts other than those he wanted.

'Not at all, though I'm not her confidante. I believe you saw her on one of her bad days. Poor woman,' she added sadly, then, 'Or, perhaps, she just didn't like policemen.' She pulled a face. 'Charles said anyway that he'd rather boobed in suggesting you saw her. Poor Charles,' she said in friendly mockery. 'He's having a bad day too, bless his palpitating little heart. He is, for all his worries, a senior executive manager with a seat on the board and it's only in his imagination that he'd be held accountable for a couple of deaths he could do nothing to prevent. He's just a natural worrier, but a sweetie for all that.'

She pulled a face. 'Sorry about that, but I meant it. Was Mrs Hurt killed because she was seen speaking to you?'

'It could be,' he admitted, wondering what her real relationship with Charles was. 'Would that surprise you?'

'I don't know,' she said, elegantly choosing another sandwich. 'I wouldn't care to think so.'

'Would there be names available of her more recent lovers? I assume the majority of the men she met would be that?'

'No.' She was definite, though still pleasant. 'Not even were you to subject me to your police brutality.'

'It's a thought,' he said lightly. 'Remind me about it some time. And I'd forgotten about the scarf. You saw it?'

She made no answer, grimacing her repugnance.

'I found nothing in her wardrobe drawers to suggest she wore scarves,' he told her. 'Had you ever seen her wearing one?'

'No,' she said. 'But that doesn't mean she never did. Somebody else might have. What I *can* say is that the scarf she had around her neck' – she grimaced again – 'didn't go with her dress. Or, most probably, with anybody else's.'

'Is there anything more about her that occurs to you?'

'You've been told about the boat?'

She had been looking at him oddly, her eyes large and luminous; assessing him again, he thought, though it was problematical what the outcome of it would be.

'She has one here?' he asked, the words suddenly trivial, wanting to get going.

'Yes, a Boyton cruiser; we've five of them. It's not hers though. She rents it from the company.' She frowned, though not too seriously. 'No more of Mrs Hurt tonight, please. Some other time would be better.'

Whatever her eyes were saying, she was cool in herself and Rogers thought he might be misreading her. He said, 'I think I'd wish to have it searched tomorrow if that'd be agreeable to Charles.'

'Of course.'

Dismissing the sadly gathered in Rachel Hurt from his mind, he stood, pushing himself up from the comfortable embrace of his chair. Perhaps he had misunderstood her after all, for it was late and she must want him to go. 'I'm grateful for what you've done,' he said, 'and for the sandwiches.'

'Rubbish,' she said forthrightly, standing from her chair and holding out her hand. 'I want you to stay. I might even remember things.'

With her hand warm in his and not being withdrawn, she said, 'Don't be so damned cold-blooded, Rogers. I want you now.'

He was physically tired, but not so tired that he could be disinterested in so attractive a woman – a woman so like a splendidly lithe tigress – pulling her towards him, his visual world narrowed to her eyes and mouth, his succumbing to the scent of her body in an uneasy abandonment.

15

It was ten-thirty when Rogers drove into the forecourt of Farquharson House. A brilliantly blue sky with scudding clouds in a fresh morning breeze did little for his self-incriminating post-coital mood. He had spent more of the night with Nancy Duval than he had anticipated or wanted, though it was she who had switched off at three in the morning, telling him that he really should be elsewhere so that she could catch up on her lost sleep. It had been satisfying despite her telling him at length of her fears – no, of her certainties – that with the ending of the century, the civilized world she misguidedly thought they lived in would end in a doomsday collision with a moon-sized asteroid.

She had made it clear that she believed it a certainty, intending to experience all the sensual pleasures available to her before being transmuted into a cinder. She had surprised him with a not wholly unpleasant earthiness in using him for that purpose, though the morning's aftermath, after five hours' sleep in his apartment, was downputting. He was not ungrateful, but it had only been the appeasing of a transitory lust he could have done without.

Barely rejuvenated and suffering something of a conscience involving Angharad, he said 'Good morning' to a returned and still soured Sergeant Sturton on duty in the Murder Wagon, entering his double-coffin-sized office. Politely enough, he supposed, she told him in passing that the ACC wished him to telephone when he arrived, that Inspector Hagbourne was waiting for him in the Interview Room and that she had placed a number of progress reports on his desk for his attention.

The Assistant Chief Constable was soon made content, for Lingard had effectively filled him in on the murder of Rachel Hurt and on the apparent progress of enquiries being made, satisfying his known wish for a minimum involvement at ground level. He sounded happy which, Rogers thought, was more than he himself was, and he started filling his pipe to get his sensibilities under some sort of control.

Calling Hagbourne into his apology of an office – its size requiring the inspector to stand at his side – Rogers said, 'You've interesting results for me, Thomas?' At work and leaving behind him his extramural activities he was almost cheerful, applying a lighted match to his pipe and blowing the smoke ceilingwards away from the notice of Sergeant Sturton. 'Your late breakfasters; four men and three women I recall and our murdered Mrs Hurt being one of them. There's a significance there?'

The over-thyroidic Hagbourne with his melancholic moustache and bulging eyes said first that his investigations had been limited because his Sergeant Hooker had been detached from him to enquire into the background of the missing Sarah Gadd.

'I'm sorry about that,' Rogers apologized. 'There's a report here from him and he should now be back with you.'

'Yes,' Hagbourne said non-committally, having had this done to him time and time again. 'In the meantime I've tried to sort out where these people actually live or from where they came. The majority of them booked their stay here through an exclusive-sounding agency advertising in magazines for the high and mighty. I'm still waiting for something of use about the man Richard Yates, the woman Fiona Smith and, you won't be astonished, about Rachel Hurt.'

'Her former address is said to have been at a Scarborough hotel,' Rogers told him. 'For what it's worth.'

'I know. I've already laid on enquiries with the local police to identify which one. There are dozens there, naturally. There would be, wouldn't there.' His moustache became even more downturned. 'I've had words – bloody brief words – with all six of them, not counting Mrs Hurt, and they all know to a sliver how much or how little they need admit to an interfering police officer.' He wasn't too serious about that. 'It all amounts to my having quite understandable obstructions put in the way in my efforts to find out who they actually are and where they come from. Despite that, I have to say that none of them look as though they've come bloody-handed from a murder or two.'

'Drivers' licences?' Rogers queried, knowing the answer as soon as he had asked.

Hagbourne laughed, a hollow unamused laugh. 'With all the cars off the highway? On private ground? I'll get there in the end, but it won't be soon.' He looked intently at Rogers. 'You know we haven't actually checked Mr Jarvis's arrival at the staff dining-room?'

Rogers was surprised and he frowned. 'You think we should?'

'No, but someone else might.' He meant the Assistant Chief Constable. 'You know that he and Mrs Duval were once married? Four or five years ago, I've been told.'

Rogers went cold, then feeling angry, furious that in some way he had been made a fool of, that he was now compromised, though nothing of it showed from behind the impassivity of his expression. 'Once?' he echoed, almost indifferently. 'You're sure?'

'So one of the secretarial staff told me.' Hagbourne was clearly not pointing a finger at him. 'And I'm sure because the secretary was a girlfriend of mine when I was a single PC on the beat at Abbotsburn.' His eyes were quite expressionless. 'You want me to check on Mrs Duval too?'

'Check them both,' Rogers said, feeling like a latter-day Pontius Pilate and switching subjects. 'And while you're about it, do a check on Peter Toplis, the man at the scene when it happened. He's our only evidence that there were two people concerned, so I don't want him breaking his precious neck with his climbing. At least, not just yet,' he modified his wish. 'He's told Jarvis that he's served in the French Foreign Legion so it might be as well to check that through Interpol or the local gendarmerie.'

'La Légion Etrangère,' Hagbourne murmured. 'You serve in it for a five years minimum, not uncommonly under a false name. After that you're reputed to be as hard and knotty as an oak door and permitted to wear a white kepi. It seems it's something to brag about.'

Rogers said doubtfully, 'Toplis didn't seem like that to me, but do the check just the same.' He changed course, remembering something. 'You recall I mentioned the two people who'd taken off after breakfast yesterday? Jason Mathou and Karen Arnold?'

Hagbourne nodded. 'They were checked on by Traffic and then Information Room. You've something more on them? They weren't among those late or absent from breakfast yesterday.'

'I know, it's only a thought.' Rogers gave him a short rundown on the Leamings Landing enquiry. 'People who choose to adopt a second name for whatever purposes they need, sometimes use the same initials. You agree?'

'I've met it in fraud and false pretence investigations,' Hagbourne said.

'Well, coincidentally or not, we have the initials of the disappearing Kathrin Arbitt and those of the also disappearing Karen Arnold in suspicious agreement. Dig into it rather more forcefully than has been done so far, will you? I want to be able to sleep happily tonight.'

With Hagbourne gone, he began his trawl through the batch of reports left for him. Reading through that from the cadaverous DS Hooker, he was told that Sarah Gadd had, for a period of eight months last year, been employed as a temporary clerk at Amborum-on-Sea by the estate agency she had mentioned, Davis and Davis. She had been a satisfactory worker, leaving at the conclusion of the autumn season by mutual agreement. In applying for the appointment she had offered an employment reference from a similar estate agency – the name not recalled – in Keswick, South Cumberland. For the term of her employment at Amborum, she had rented a one-room bed-sit at 43 Morby Street with a Mrs Annie Scrote who said when interviewed that Gadd was a well-behaved young woman who, to her limited knowledge, only associated with one man – name unknown – during her stay as a lodger. Something for Lingard, Rogers decided, initialling the report, though certainly not very much.

Lingard arrived as he was finishing his second cup of coffee which, he was convinced, must have been made from some evil-tasting fungi, leaving him wondering not too seriously if Sturton was bent on poisoning him.

'David,' he said, 'I'm sorry I had to lumber you with Mrs Hurt at such short notice. Were there any problems?'

'Not with the mechanics of it,' Lingard replied from his leaning position against the door post, adding flippantly, 'Only with trying to guess who'd done it.' Freshly suited in a cream jacket and narrow mustard-yellow moleskin trousers, he had obviously showered, looking aristocratically sure of himself and patently out from under the shadow of the fleeing Sarah Gadd. 'Your Mrs Hurt has been measured, photographed and delivered to the mortuary; the scene of her demise meticulously examined by myself, Sergeant Magnus and two of his searchers, without finding anything that could be construed as being useful.'

He took out his ivory snuff box and charged one of his nostrils generously. 'Bridget – being excused your absence – also attended, did her stuff with that disgustingly long thermometer thing of hers and settled on timing the lady's death to about six o'clock, give or take.'

'Not too far from my own estimate,' Rogers pointed out, then adding, 'Well, within an hour or so and I hadn't used a thermometer anyway.'

Lingard, having pinched out more snuff and charged his remaining nostril with an eighteenth-century elan, said, 'I let the Assistant Chief Constable in on what was happening rather late last night. He was in his bath when I rang him, so he gave himself immediate permission to say how grateful he was that we could manage without his presence and his finely honed intimacy with the Holy Administrative Bible, though I admit he didn't put it quite like that; but near enough.' He laughed, tapping a finger on the side of his nose and sniffing. 'You'll be overjoyed to know that the post-mortem examination, due this morning at nine o'clock, had come and gone and that I have been in attendance in your place . . .'

'Quite properly, David,' Rogers interrupted, 'and I'm quite sure you were wholly adequate.'

'Bridget, I'm afraid,' Lingard said imperturbably, 'again failed to question your absence or shed unwomanly tears, being happy with me as your substitute.' He used a yellow silk handkerchief to flap loose grains of snuff from his nose, his face suddenly serious. 'We've both slipped a trifle, George. I'm afraid we missed a thing or two in our *soi disant* examination of the lady. When Bridget was patting her fingers over the scalp she suddenly and extremely irritably said in effect, "You stupid man, why didn't you tell me about this?" And the "this" when she pulled the hair apart was a not very obvious contusion where the poor lass had been hit on the back of her head. Bridget said from her examination of it that it could have been caused by something that didn't draw blood. That sort of thing.'

'Bridget should have found it herself at the scene, not us.' Rogers was at his most definite. 'I'm not saying we didn't fail in not finding it. We didn't damn well look for it. It isn't our job to medically examine bodies. Hers is.' He had already thought out its implications. 'You're not going to tell me that she was dead before being strangled, are you?'

'No. Her Eminence was certain not. She's satisfied that her death was due to strangulation, that she seemed to have been clobbered by someone not wishing to be seen approaching from the rear . . .'

'I saw what looked like footprints behind her lounger,' Rogers interrupted him. 'They'd confirm that.'

'These were and they would,' Lingard said. 'Obviously they were male' – he smiled – 'or made by a large-footed woman of murderous disposition; but sand being sand, with absolutely no characteristic marks by which they could be identified to the shoes of the misbegotten bastard who made them.' He had allowed himself to become heated over that; understandable in that he had been present at the dissection of Mrs Hurt's body.

'And the plain-glass spectacles?' Rogers was refilling his still hot gone-out pipe, thinking how misguidedly disciplined he was in only occasionally smoking it.

'Camouflage?' Lingard suggested. 'Depending on who or what she was supposed to be?'

'Or sexual enhancement?' Rogers was guessing. 'We men can occasionally and understandably go *musth* over spectacled women.'

Putting his second-in-command in the picture about his search of the Hurt apartment and not dwelling too pointedly on the presence of Nancy Duval, he said, 'I'm concerned most of all about the theft of the documents of identity; anything on which we could expect to find her name and permanent address. To me, that means one thing, and that is they weren't in the name of Rachel Hurt at all.'

He thought on that while Lingard waited, then said, 'That mightn't go, might it? She has to pay for her stay here and that'd be by cheque or bank card. All right, or by cash. There seems to be enough of it knocking around the periphery of this place.'

'Hurt might be her proper name,' Lingard ventured. 'Why not?'

Rogers shrugged. 'I don't know. I've got it in my head that it's who she actually is that led to her murder; not what she saw, which would only be a man and him not even near the scene. Also, and bloody frustratingly, she gave her address before she came here as an hotel in Scarborough and the records here don't give it a name.'

'Quite a few people live in hotels,' Lingard pointed out. 'I do, and you should.'

'I would if I could afford it,' Rogers exaggerated, 'so let me fill you in on my interview with Superintendent Trout, because I've to see Charles Jarvis shortly.'

When he had finished – it had taken him three relightings of his pipe and a further cup of Sergeant Sturton's fungoid coffee – he said, 'You can see that there's been something odd going on at Leamings Landing and Amborum. That and our chap Ward being somehow connected, however lightly, with the dead and buried business man Arbitt and possibly more intimately with his wife, now lost to Leamings Landing with a sackful of insurance money. This raises a few unsatisfied questions in my thinking.' He paused, manifestly trying to make sense of it, then asking, 'What do you think about Detective Inspector bloody Poukas, as friend Trout refers to him?'

'I'd be thinking of getting the Mets to do some checking on him at Australia House.'

'That's being done, David, both for his address in Australia and for the details of his local police.' They were talking in a fog of tobacco smoke with Rogers hoping it wasn't getting through to the non-smoking Sturton.

'Then I'd want to know why he changed his mind about an investigation into an apparent murder, then switching it to the dead man's widow who subsequently collected the insurance money and departed to parts unknown.'

Rogers looked pleased. 'Thank God for that,' he smiled. 'I had the same old hackneyed thought about an insurance rip off. Seven hundred and fifty thousand's a fairish temptation if you own to a drunken husband and a failing business.' He looked quizzically at Lingard. 'There's a snag – naturally. Arbitt was said to be fishing on his own while his wife was twelve miles away from him and doing her stuff at home or wherever. That can be overcome, of course, but it needs a third person to be involved.'

'The former Detective Inspector bloody Poukas?' Lingard suggested. 'He sounds a right fizzer.'

Rogers shook his head, regretfully it appeared. 'It seems that while he clearly, and probably improperly, pushed himself on to it when it was only a sudden death enquiry; it was, and still is, held to have been an accidental death. Poukas would almost certainly have entered the enquiry after the death and not before. That, naturally, could have been answered yea or nay hadn't the file and its back-up copy been taken by somebody, presumably Poukas without much doubt.'

'There is a third person with us anyway,' Lingard pointed out. 'Our mysterious friend Ward or whoever. As I believe we accepted, one doesn't come into possession of thirteen hundred pounds in beautifully crisp fifty-pound notes, and God only knows how much already spent or stashed away, by being desperately honest.' He looked down his nose disapprovingly. 'Blackmail? Obtaining by menaces? By fraud? By a man of no known settled address and probably dying under someone else's name to boot? Agreed?' he asked.

'About that, David.' Rogers wasn't too certain. 'But I want more of the background from Trout who I hope to see later today.' He moved in his chair, his buttocks numbed from a prolonged unmoving contact with its hard plastic seat. 'I'll leave you with your AWOL Gadd woman.' He passed DS Hooker's report to him. 'It's adequate, but not inspirational. It might help, though apart from a previous address of sorts and a reference to a possible stud she was meeting it's not very informative. Don't worry yourself sick' – he laughed saying that – 'about the papers lying neglected on my office desk and the unread crime files in the Urgent tray. Do some catching up on Gadd. No woman can sleep with a man for months and not know who he is, where he comes from and why.'

'And Mrs Hurt?' Lingard asked, not unhappily.

'Leave her with me,' Rogers said standing, wincing at his knee joints cracking from their cramped confinement. 'If Ward is proved to have been connected with Mrs Arbitt – wherever she now is – and I think he will be, then I feel that we will have her on our hands in the shape of Mrs Hurt. That'll give me something interesting to have a stomach ulcer about,' he added derisorily, though with no possibility of allowing it to ever happen.

Following Lingard's departure, he telephoned Bernard Trout, telling him of the death of Rachel Hurt – the name occasioned no recollection of anybody with him – and arranging to see him at his office about midday.

Leaving the Murder Wagon for his interview with Charles Jarvis, he worried about what Hagbourne had told him concerning Nancy Duval's supposed marital connection with the general manager, and how he could get out from under without too much embarrassment. And not only that. There was Angharad to feel particularly guilty about too.

16

It might conceivably have been Sergeant Sturton's fungi-tasting coffee or the delayed effect of Nancy Duval's late-night hospitality, for Rogers, on his way to Charles Jarvis's office, felt unusually in a high pitch of physical excellence. The sun was still doing its stuff, the light onshore breeze fragrantly balmy, and even the Byzantine-like architecture of Farquharson House looming in front of him merited something of his approval. True, there was a niggling concern at the back of his mind that Jarvis and Duval might be combined in some odd form of collusion to compromise him, but he made it stay there.

In Jarvis's office the air was still scented from the smoking of executive-style cigars. He stood from his desk, shook hands for their first meeting of the day and invited Rogers to be seated in the red leather chair he had occupied before.

Jarvis was immaculate in a navy-blue chalk-stripe suit and white shirt, his expression not screamingly happy, but subdued and looking as though he had been chewing at his moustache again. 'My dear chap,' he said, briefly smiling, 'I'm so pleased to see you. You've good news for me, I hope?'

'Very few people expect that of me, Charles,' Rogers replied, 'but I've a few questions to ask.'

'Ah,' Jarvis said. 'Of course. We haven't had a decent chat lately, have we?' Opening a drawer in his desk and taking out two long panatellas, he asked, 'Is Nancy giving you all the help you need?'

Rogers, on immediate Red Alert, tried to read things in what Jarvis had said, accepting one of the proffered cigars, thanking him and deciding to accept his question as it had sounded.

'Yes,' he said, watching Jarvis even while lighting his cigar. 'She's been a great help and I'm grateful for your generosity, for the use of her services. You want her back?'

'Not at all. She's yours for the duration.' That Jarvis was putting on a show of mild humour was no comfort for the detective. Then he said, 'Frankly, old chap, I'd be happy to see the back of you and your CID. No offence intended, naturally. My Head Office is vastly displeased with me over this, as if I damn well invited it to happen.' He pushed his ashtray over the desk to Rogers. 'These corporate chaps can wreak a bit of murder themselves, you know.'

'I can guess,' Rogers sympathized with him. 'Only a few questions, Charles. Painless, I assure you, and I'm grateful for your patience with our trotting around the place and no doubt distracting your members.' He smiled, squinting along the barrel of his panatella. 'There won't be anything to alarm man or beast in what I have.'

'Fire ahead.' Jarvis smiled back, though a little wanly. 'Anything to get the law out of my backyard.'

'The late Frank Ward,' Rogers started. 'You know, having been at the scene, that he was killed by an arrow; a sort of crossbow bolt in fact. This was almost certainly fired from an air pistol called something in German I can't remember. The question is, are there air pistols like that used in any of the activities provided here?'

'Absolutely not. I've never heard of them and I would have told you at the time had you asked.' Ash fell from his cigar on to his blotting-pad and he paused to blow it away. 'Nor have I thought to ask you if it had been found?'

'It hasn't been, though we've searched as much of the wood adjacent to where Ward's body was found as we could. It reminds me, though, of the scarf around Mrs Hurt's throat which you must have seen. Does it ring a bell with you? She wasn't wearing it when I spoke to her earlier on.'

'Come off it, old chap; have a heart.' Jarvis looked pained. 'I've not seen her wearing one before if that's what you mean.'

'I'm sorry. I had to ask and to tell you that I've detailed a policewoman to buttonhole those lady members she can locate and ask them about it. Just so you know,' he said, laying the cigar he wasn't enjoying all that much on the ashtray to die an unfinished death. 'While we are on about poor Mrs Hurt, Charles, I'm supposing that you knew her well, she having been here for eighteen or so months?'

Jarvis said a cautious, 'Yes,' his voice not so confident.

'I'm supposing too that you would know if she had associated with any of the other members?' Though not in an attacking mode, he pointed his inquisitional nose at the manager. 'Or with any of the staff, or employees?'

After a longish thinking pause, Jarvis said, 'You've been told something have you?'

'I have,' he prevaricated, that not being too precise about what Jarvis was asking.

'I would have told you when we were there, but with Nancy as well ... you understand?' In the silence which followed, he asked, 'Can I rely on your discretion, old chap ... George?'

'If it doesn't involve you in a felony – which murder is – a misdemeanour, malfeasance or anything heinous like that,' he said genially, the ball now being in Jarvis's court.

Visibly subdued – Rogers felt sorry for him – he said, 'It was months back. I was – how can I put it? – very hungry between courses, if you savvy. It's not a gentlemanly thing to say, but Rachel, poor girl, did the running and I had felt it impolite, not done, to say no.' He shook his head gloomily. 'I don't think my management colleagues would approve of my having a sexual thingy with a club member . . .'

'I'd have thought they'd be in a fury of indifference, Charles,' Rogers murmured, quite certain that Rachel Hurt hadn't been the only one. 'There would be a certain promise of future patronage from any lady so honoured.'

For a moment or two he looked blank-faced, then, 'It's not funny, George. They wouldn't look at it like that. I don't think anyone would. What about your own people?' He didn't exactly look at him accusingly, but the detective had enough on his conscience to think he did.

'I'm not under discussion, Charles,' he said equably, hoping not. 'How long did this affair last? Until now?'

'Christ, no!' He looked terribly injured. 'It was short-term stuff, though a bit of it what you would call intense on her side. I was a fool and I knew it even then. When she became too possessive and began to haunt me, I took a holiday abroad without telling her. That finished it as I found when I returned.'

Rogers had tried to imagine the Rachel Hurt he had spoken to for such a short time to ever be as Jarvis had described, and couldn't. 'Wholly accepted, Charles,' he pacified him. 'None of my business and all that. Tell me now, to your knowledge had she had any known visitors during the time she was here?'

'Not known to me, that's for sure. Visiting relatives or friends are rare birds, and when they do come they are not in my remit.'

'Who was she supposed to be?' Now they were good friends, chatting almost socially.

'Be? You mean who she was?'

'Yes. Who did she *say* she was?'

Jarvis shrugged helplessly. 'I don't know what you mean, though when she first came here she asked to speak to me privately. She said then that she was divorced from her husband as a result of his cruelty towards her and that she had returned to using her unmarried name, which, of course, she was entitled to do. Her former husband – she said he was James Mac-Somebody or other – was an industrialist into metal tubes or something like it and was threatening violence over the divorce settlement which went largely in her favour. In short, she wanted me not to disclose her name or presence here to anyone from outside asking for her.'

He rolled the panatella he held, absently it seemed, between his finger and thumb. 'There was, she told me, a court order banning the Mac-Somebody or other from having any contact with her. It was because of this situation that I also allowed her to look over the lists of future bookings. There's nothing unethical in that, though I wouldn't like it to be known outside this office.'

'Did you have anybody enquiring after the lady in her maiden name?'

'Not at all, and by and large I forgot about it after putting a note of it in the exchange office.'

'It's interesting, Charles. How did the lady pay her charges? In cash?'

Jarvis was taken aback. 'How did you know that?'

'It's true then?'

'Yes, it is. She's never paid any differently. She didn't want that ex-husband of hers to find her through her use of a cheque or a bank card. There's nothing unusual in that, you'll understand.' His expression changed. 'I see what you're getting at now. You think her husband caught up with her here? That this chap Ward is somebody who was sent here to find her?'

'And got himself killed by somebody a few hours before she was also killed?' Rogers said drily. 'I wouldn't see it like that.' He thought things over for a few moments, then asked, 'Do you recall telling me about a solicitor telephoning you from Cumberslang? Giving his name as Stevens, you said, and asking about a client's missing sister called Kathleen Orbit. You remember?'

'I should do, old chap,' Jarvis pointed out a little testily. 'I only told you yesterday. I was cut off by the man when I said I couldn't help. He was a no-hoper anyway. We don't give out that kind of information.'

There seemed no point in disclosing to Jarvis that enquiries had been made of the Cumberslang Police and there was no Stevens practising there as a solicitor. 'It seems like years ago to me now,' Rogers said amiably. 'Would you recognize the name he gave you as, say, Kathrin Arbitt?'

'I'd say it was the same.' His forehead creased in a frown. 'You know who she is then?'

'Not yet, Charles, not yet. You'll be the first to know when I do. Had your Mrs Hurt ever mentioned a place called Leamings Landing? Or Amborum-on-Sea?'

Jarvis shook his head. 'No. Definitely not, though might I say that you're making it all so damned complicated, and somehow unsettling. So are you going to tell me that Rachel was that woman?'

'No, I'm not. Don't even think it, because I don't know.'

Creasing his eyes in a smile, he shook hands in a gesture of goodwill to a properly worried Jarvis for whom he felt a friendly sympathy, despite he himself being still hot, after a fashion, from the bed of his former wife.

Leaving the building, he confirmed to himself that it was an occasion he now regretted even more deeply, excusing himself in maintaining that there must be something particularly libidinous and pervasive in the overheated atmosphere of the place. Too, he was keeping his fingers crossed against his rashness in giving Jarvis a clean sheet in anything more than the brief intimacy with Rachel Hurt which he had so readily disclosed.

17

Rogers was almost at peace with the world when he arrived at Amborum-on-Sea. Unchoked by an overplus of traffic, its preserved Victorian town centre consorting happily with the newer not too obtrusive hotels and industrial premises, it held in it a warmth of dignified friendliness.

Shown up to Trout's office, Rogers found him accompanied at

his desk by a slim and agreeably attractive woman wearing a deep-blue business suit with a buttoned-up lighter blue shirt.

'Detective Inspector Kilpatrick,' Trout introduced her. 'Eva's on the case to represent our interest in it and to give you any help in our county you may need.' He sounded almost light-hearted; in a different mood from that in which he had been the previous day.

Rogers reached and shook her hand, hoping that his midday stubble wasn't too visible. 'Delighted, Miss Kilpatrick,' he said – which he was – sitting in the third chair on the visitors' side of the desk.

Those brief moments had given him the measure of her. She was tall, as he thought she should be, with short glossy dark-brown hair, not over-burdened with bosom – a good thing for Rogers – with a mouth, he judged, that had rarely uttered a nastiness, though his policeman's mind told him that as an indication of niceness or its absence, a mouth could be wholly misleading. Her matching brown eyes had been friendly in her regard of him, searching his face with a professional competence while she had smiled.

'I hope,' Rogers said diplomatically to Trout, thinking he looked a lot less melancholic in his linen sports jacket and olive-green trousers, 'that some of our difficulties have been resolved?'

Trout almost beamed. 'Yes, up to a point they have. I did report, of course, the unauthorized removal – well, theft actually – of the accidental death file to the Chief Constable. He had a different perception of it than I had, though he did do a bit of breast beating himself when I told him that Poukas's personal records had also been removed by somebody – obviously Poukas himself – and that a Missing Persons file associated somehow with the Arbitts had also gone astray. I'll tell you about that later, George.' He nodded genially at both Rogers and Kilpatrick, or as genially as a man with a gaunt and deeply seamed face could. 'With you and Eva following up the Poukas and Arbitt affair, the chief is happy to leave it at that; certain, he says, that our local interests will be safeguarded.'

This was normal stuff and a straight-faced Rogers told him that he accepted the responsibility and was most happy to cooperate with Detective Inspector Kilpatrick with whom he looked forward to a successful investigation.

'Good,' Trout said, having understandably washed his hands of any further responsibility, together with it seemed of his yesterday's melancholia. 'Now I suggest we get out of this stuffy office and initiate a small conference at a little bar I'm disgustingly familiar with on the quayside. The hospitality's on me, naturally.'

The Ram on the Strand inn, a few steps' walking distance from the Divisional Police Headquarters, had scarlet geranium-filled windows actually overhanging the green water of the harbour. Through them, Rogers could see an agreeable assembly of motor cruisers, small sailing boats and herring gulls, and what he was told by Kilpatrick was a replica of the eighteenth-century *Mayflower* moored to the quay wall.

The interior of the bar was oak-beamed with white plaster walls and filled with the smell of tobacco smoke and the civilized murmur of hungry and thirsty humanity. Seated at an obviously reserved table adjacent to the window, Trout, with all the generosity of a happy man, ordered wine and stacks of sandwiches.

Getting down to business, he said to Rogers, his voice pitched low against being overheard, 'Since we met yesterday, I've been in touch with my Detective Inspector Longrigg who's on a course at Bramshill Police College, and who, unknown to me, worked as a detective sergeant with Mr bloody Poukas for a day or two on the Arbitt business. I telephoned him at the college and had words with him on the side . . .'

A girl carrying a tray checked him, pouring out glasses of white wine, leaving the opened bottle and another on the table. She was followed by another with two platters of smoked salmon and ham sandwiches, while an impatient finger-tapping Rogers, hungry though he was, wanted more from a hoped-for garrulous superintendent.

Trout, saying 'Cheers' and sipping at his wine, started again, his voice dropping to a deep bass confidentiality. 'In brief,' he said, 'Longrigg told me that Poukas, as his DI, took him on his investigation into Chadwick Arbitt's death on his yacht. Even then Longrigg, not being privy to what was going on in Poukas's mind, was wondering what the hell. He was told very little of

Poukas's thinking, suspicions you could say, even when his DI was way out over Arbitt's death in believing that it was no accident and that Mrs Arbitt was possibly involved. There was some sort of evidence that Mrs Arbitt was working in the store that afternoon while Arbitt was fishing at Blacktoad Bay. Poukas had mentioned this to Longrigg, and it was at this stage that Longrigg became convinced that his DI was holding an unjustifiable suspicion of a criminal act having been committed, when to him it was becoming clear that on the evidence available it could be nothing more than an accidental death. That, you'd agree, would be of no interest or concern to a CID man.'

Trout engulfed most of the ham sandwich he had chosen, chewing at it for the best part of ten silent seconds. 'What particularly struck Longrigg,' he continued, 'was Poukas's sudden U-turn. From, one moment, digging into something more than an accidental death, then to pooh-poohing any suggestion of its being anything but and dropping Sergeant Longrigg from the enquiry. And not only that, but choking him off for ever questioning a decision made by his senior officer. And you'll understand that nothing of Longrigg's two days' involvement in the case ever went into the missing file. It couldn't really, could it?'

He was silent for a moment, looking at a gull preening its plumage on the geraniums outside, then said, 'In view of what I've since heard, I now feel that that damned Poukas was right in the first place and that there could have been a real suspicion of dirty work in Arbitt's death.'

'With a pay-out on a life insurance of seven hundred and fifty thousand pounds and a vanishing wife, I'm convinced of it,' Rogers agreed. 'And with a strong suspicion that Poukas was somehow involved in it, even if after the event.'

'I'm with you there,' Trout said. 'As is my chief constable. It's why you have Eva here to help out.'

'Every bad circumstance has in it a complementary good side,' Rogers said looking at Kilpatrick and hoping he had got it right, not laying on the flattery too thick.

'There's something more though.' Trout looked at Rogers and Kilpatrick as if he had just joined them in marriage, refilling his glass and pushing the bottle over to them. 'The abominable

Poukas had also mentioned to Longrigg when he was in good odour that he was interested in a missing man called something Seaforth-Major – he's the man the subject of the Missing Persons file by the way – who Longrigg understood had been associating, probably improperly, with Mrs Arbitt. This before her husband's death, he thought.'

Trout seemed to have eaten his way through seven sandwiches in between his speaking, Kilpatrick and Rogers following less voraciously, both trying to concentrate in his wake. 'I'll come to Seaforth-Major later,' he continued, 'but I'll deal with the Arbitts first. It's been made clear to me now that Chadwick Arbitt was a hard-drinking man, though he wasn't a weakling by any means. He wasn't much good at business, and his trading store was heading downhill fast. What with that and his wife being very much in the driving seat at the store, there wasn't much going for either of them. Before his death – the coroner had very positively ruled out suicide – their home at Leamings Landing and their boat had been remortgaged with the business definitely tottering.'

'Is the business still in being?' Rogers asked.

'No, it isn't. There's nothing for us there. The building was taken over as a restaurant when Arbitt's business folded and went down the drain.' He eyed the remaining untouched bottle speculatively, but did nothing about it. 'About the Seaforth-Major man who'd gone missing and who'd been having it off with Mrs Arbitt here in Amborum, Longrigg said that Poukas had given him the evil eye when he'd mentioned it to him, believing he was being helpful.'

'That's the information I really care for,' Rogers said. 'We might be getting round to finding our third person. Can we get more on this?'

'I think so.' For a moment Trout had looked annoyed. 'I say that because Poukas was dealing with him as a missing person, apparently on a second complaint, which anyway is none of the business of the CID. Unless of course there is cause to fear some harm has befallen the party concerned,' he quickly added to it. 'Now the bloody Missing Persons file itself is missing, though fortunately that's nothing to do with my department. I don't know, and neither does Longrigg, how long before Arbitt's death he was associating with Mrs A, if he ever was.'

'Do we know how Seaforth-Major came to be on a Missing Persons report?' Rogers saw that Eva Kilpatrick was now taking notes of their conversation in a form of shorthand.

'I don't because, as I said, it was never any of my department's concern. Longrigg said it had been reported to us by a Mrs Constance Seaforth-Major from Little Salton, which is in the north of the county. In fact, it's about twenty miles up the motorway, and there's no record of her address. Furthermore, we don't know his age, his description, why he went missing or bugger-all else. Just a name and just an odd remark from that goddamned Poukas that Seaforth-Major had somehow met Mrs Arbitt and was having it off with her.'

'Would the woman be his wife?' Rogers asked.

'Longrigg doesn't know any more than that she reported him missing, and that'd be second-hand information anyway. It would be on the missing file which isn't much help with anything. We don't even know whether he was found to have returned home or not.'

'Mrs Seaforth-Major,' Rogers said diffidently. 'She sounds very traceable just so long as Little Salton isn't a couple of hundred acres of unnumbered city streets with nobody on the telephone.'

'It has a population of plus or minus a thousand reasonably civilized inhabitants and some of them are on the telephone,' Kilpatrick intervened, her mouth curved in a smile. 'I know it well.'

'I'm grateful,' Rogers said, then turning back to Trout. 'Could I ask Inspector Kilpatrick to find her address for me? Perhaps it'll be in the local directory.'

'Eva,' Trout said to her. 'You can do?'

'I've already made a note to do it,' she replied crisply, looking directly at Rogers who was wondering if somehow he had offended her.

'Thank you,' he said. 'Through her we might find out what this Poukas fella wanted so badly to hide.' He drank the last drop or two of the only glass of wine he had had – breathalyser scared, he told himself – thought about lighting up his pipe, but deciding not because he appeared to be associating with a couple of rabid non-smokers. But he suffered.

'Bernard,' he said. 'I don't know that what I have to say is going to please you or not, but I believe I know where your Mrs Arbitt is now.' He paused, eyeing them both, then deciding that whatever he was to say wasn't going to trigger off an earth tremor. 'I think she's in the mortuary of the Abbotsburn Hospital; that she is, or was, a Mrs Rachel Hurt, a long-stay visitor at the Farquharson House Club, where she was murdered last night.'

Trout said a surprised 'Bloody hell!' then 'Are you sure?' while Kilpatrick initially frowning her perplexity, then made notes in her pocket-book.

After Rogers had given his reasons – they weren't sounding so watertight as he had first thought – he then said, 'You'll see that it can't just be a coincidence that an hour or two after I had been poking around her, interviewing her as a witness, she was murdered. It needs to be proved, I know that, and even when it is it may not tell us exactly why. Nor, manifestly, by whom.' He spoke to Kilpatrick. 'You know about our first dead body? The man Frank Ward?'

When she answered, 'Yes, I do,' he spoke to both of them. 'Because Ward was involved before his death in possessing fairly large amounts of money in unused fifty-pound notes and telling the Gadd woman he was living with that a woman staying at the club – for what that's worth – owed him much more, there could be a significant connection there. Whatever it is, or was, the subsequent murder of Rachel Hurt has to be connected with the death of Ward.'

He smiled; not the smile of a shark, but certainly that of a hungry hunter. 'So, who is the man who called himself Ward? And there's one thing I know about him for certain. He died in greed: he died, I believe, in demanding money – necessarily illicit money – by menaces from a third person. And that third person either killed him or caused him to be killed. And this third person could have been connected criminally with the woman he must have killed: Rachel Hurt who must, to make any sense of my theory, be your missing Kathrin Arbitt.'

'You know?' Trout queried, not overly surprised, but with eyebrows raised.

'Not about Mrs Hurt, I don't. That's a logical surmise. As is my surmise that your ex-inspector Poukas never went to Australia and never intended to.'

'I'd believe anything of Poukas,' Trout grunted.

'If you've the time now, Bernard, I'd like you to pay a visit to our mortuary and have a look at Ward. He might, only just might, be Poukas.' It was a shot in the semi-darkness of a not really knowing for Rogers, and it couldn't wholly be a waste of time. 'You'll do?' he asked.

'It'll do me the world of good,' Trout agreed, 'only don't expect to call me as a witness. The south of France is waiting for me as soon as I'm a free man.'

'I'll have a High Court warrant of extradition sworn out for you,' Rogers joked with him, 'and I'll come down and arrest you myself. Can you suggest anyone in your bailiwick who could do a possible identification on my Mrs Hurt?'

'Not offhand, George,' he said, rising from the table, 'but I'll have a look at her too, though I can't recall ever meeting her.'

While Trout was paying the bill, Rogers and Kilpatrick walked outside into the warm sunshine – dazzling after the twilight inside the inn – to the edge of the quayside. For Rogers, satisfactorily fed and watered and now filling his neglected pipe, the unstained blue sky seeming nearer the sea than usual, the wooden black-painted replica *Mayflower* and her flotilla of smaller sailing boats and dinghies pulling against their anchor cables on an ebbing tide was, together with the company of this attractive woman with him, an unexpected pleasantness in a rather murky investigation. For all that, he was determined, please God, not to become sexually attracted to her, though he felt there to be an acceptable rapport between them, possibly a shared professional empathy.

'I'm pleased to have you to work with me,' he said, rather fumbling with his words. 'Is it possible that I can use you straight away?'

'I'm free.' She smiled. 'I haven't anything much I can't delegate.'

'I'm wondering if you could organize a visit for me to Blacktoad Bay this afternoon. I'd like to survey the scene where Arbitt died.'

'There's no approach to it by land,' she pointed out. 'I could get the use of one of our motorized inflatables, if you wish.'

Rogers thought that they were both being too bloody formal, but could see no way around it yet. 'That'll do fine, Miss Kilpatrick,' he said. 'Do we have a driver?'

'We could, but need not. I've done a course on handling the brute.' Her mouth curved in a restrained smile. 'You're insured against being drowned?'

'The thought has never occurred to me.' He smiled back at her. 'But I can swim a yard or two.' Then he said, 'There's one other enquiry you might possibly unload on to somebody else. I need to know what Mrs Arbitt's full name was before she married. It's possible?' Her eyes attracted him. They were large and a deep soft brown that could do things to men's imaginations and they were being held steadily on his.

'Yes, it is. I was going to ask you about it.' She hesitated, then said, 'We don't serve in the same force, so could you find it possible to be informal enough to call me by my given name? It would make the job a lot less stuffy.'

He saw Trout emerging from the inn, looking for them. 'I'd be most happy to,' he said, really meaning it and thinking that she was going to be a force to be reckoned with now that the investigation had come alive in his hands.

'Thank you, George,' she said without a trace of a smile. 'I knew you would.'

Rogers thought much about what she was doing and intending to do for him in an abstract sort of way as he hit the road for Abbotsburn and the hospital mortuary, his passenger Bernard Trout being about to metaphorically shake hands with a couple of dead bodies.

18

After the blue sky and golden warmth of Amborum's harbour, the Abbotsburn Hospital's subterranean mortuary Receiving Room – windowless, harshly lit and smelling of formalin – struck an added depressing note to Rogers's existing perception of death, though he comforted himself with the thought that so far it had always been somebody else who had died.

Eighteen dark-green metal cabinets lined one wall, all humming quietly in the refrigerating of the dead. From the display of white name cards on the pull-out drawers, any who cared to look could see that the body count in them was twelve. A closed door at the end of the cabinets led into the mortuary proper, the ghastly workroom wherein Bridget displayed temporarily her bloody skills in the dissection of the human body.

An overly cheerful girl attendant in bright scarlet lipstick and dun-brown overalls had shown Rogers and Trout in, remaining with them it seemed to resist any impulse either might have to steal a body.

Asked to produce for inspection the body of Frank Ward, she pulled open the sideless drawer number ten, dropping a pair of folded-back metal struts to take its weight.

'Thank you,' Rogers said tactfully, not being disposed to have her ride too close an escort on any official conversation he and Trout might have, and looking pointedly at the door. 'We can manage now without worrying you.' He smiled at her. 'I'll give you a shout when we need your help.'

With her having gone, Rogers folded back the white sheet, uncovering the upper half of the body, momentarily experiencing his old never realized fear that at some time unclosed dead eyes were going to stare up at him to reflect the horror of their owner's death.

Ward was peacefully, if bloodily dead with his eyes closed. Bridget's scalpel had made a rawly sliced and bloody-boned mess of the side of his face and that part of his throat penetrated by the arrow which had killed him.

'He's all yours, Bernard,' Rogers said, standing to one side. 'There's a whole lot of expectations riding on this particular horse.'

Trout's face showed nothing but its misleading built-in melancholia as he looked down at the mutilated face; long enough for Rogers to put his half-smoked pipe between his teeth and to put a lighted match to it.

When Trout turned his head to Rogers, he said, 'Damn it,

George, I should be able to. I'd known him for over a year, though that's two years ago. My recall isn't what it was and what with this cove sporting a beard and moustache – which Poukas never did – it's going to be difficult.'

'We can't shave him, I'm afraid.' Rogers was disappointed. 'You're sure?'

'No, I'm damn well not,' Trout growled. 'That's the trouble. Give me a minute to recollect how I saw the bugger last.' He turned his back on the body, and on Rogers too; cupping his chin in his hand and screwing his eyes closed in deep concentration.

Rogers had smoked his tobacco down to its dottle when Trout turned back to him and said, 'I've got him now, I'm certain.'

Again approaching the open drawer he crouched, his eyes level with the dreadful face of the dead man, viewing it in profile, unblinkingly and without expression. When he stood, grimacing at the pain in his ageing knees and looking again at the dead man full-faced, he whispered loudly enough, 'Yes, yes. He's that conniving sod Poukas all right.' Louder, he said, 'I've done it, George, and I'm sure. I'd swear it on a shop full of bibles, ancient and modern.'

'I'm proud of you, Bernard,' Rogers said happily. 'Have you any reflections or emendations on him now that he's upstairs trying to argue his case for being a goody?'

'Once a devious bastard, always a devious bastard,' Trout retorted, 'and I've no respect for him now that he's dead. I'm not in the business of forgiving, that's for God to do if he wants to; not me.'

'Think about his deviousness then,' Rogers urged. 'While I'm satisfied that the late Mrs Hurt is identical with the gone away and wealthy Kathrin Arbitt, and that she was being blackmailed by your Detective Inspector Poukas, I do need some further evidence of it. Any comment?'

'I've said it before; I'll believe anything of him and don't say that he's my Poukas.' He was slightly nettled. 'I washed my hands of him two years ago.'

The girl, not so cheerful now, had come in from wherever she had been waiting. Rogers, feeling himself to be on a winning streak, gave her an affable smile. 'I was just about to call you in,' he said, not wholly truthfully. 'Could we now see Mrs Hurt?'

When drawer number eleven had been pulled out, he made no request for her not to be there, for he had no confidence that Trout had ever seen Mrs Arbitt and that even if he had, an identification would lead to no significant discussion.

Exposed, Rachel Hurt's features showed an even greater exaggeration of the pathological signs of death by strangulation; never pleasant by any means, but not bloodily horrific either.

Trout, having stared at her briefly, shook his head. 'Never,' he said. 'So far as I remember I have never met or seen the lady.'

'She must be known to somebody at Leamings Landing,' Rogers pointed out. 'Can you detail one of your staff to do an enquiry there to see if there is?' He reached and re-covered the dead woman's face, then thanked the waiting attendant and left with Trout.

'I'd like someone other than Inspector Kilpatrick to do it,' Rogers continued. 'I shall certainly need her for the next couple of days.'

'It'll be done.' It was patently no skin off the nose of a man who was leaving the service on pension within the next forty-eight hours.

Reaching open air – the daylight and sun on Rogers's face felt beautiful after the tomb-like atmosphere of the mortuary – and approaching his parked car, he said to Trout, 'Have you any serious push with your county banks? It seems likely that Poukas has had whatever money he's gouged out of Mrs Hurt stashed away in one. Probably under the name of Ward. And there's Mrs Hurt, too. It'd help.'

'I've no push at all,' Trout said positively, 'and certainly will have none after tomorrow when I hand in my warrant card. You know the drill as well as I do. No talk about a client's account without a court order, no matter how unscrupulous or criminal the client might be.'

'I can but try,' Rogers said, unlocking and opening his car's door to let the hot air out and Trout in. 'Perhaps a gentle twisting of Inspector Kilpatrick's arm once you're out of the way.' He was joking, as Trout well knew.

'Be careful with her, George,' he said as he climbed into the passenger seat. 'She's shown too much interest in your background – suspect as that must be – to be good for your health. And, as I believe, being virgo intacta, not for the likes of you.'

19

Detective Inspector Kilpatrick, her intriguing slimness now dressed in a blue shirt with narrow white trousers and trainers, was undoubtedly the Amborum Division's most attractive senior officer; a not unwilling Rogers, away from his own bailiwick, found himself unusually content to be managed. But gently, and only just.

With the afternoon's sun beating on their shoulders, Kilpatrick led Rogers along the wall of the quay, still within view of the police headquarters, to an iron gate with a POLICE ONLY notice on it. Unrailed concrete steps led down to two dark-blue 12-footer inflatable dinghies, both with POLICE stencilled on them in white, floating in the harbour's turn of the tide water.

Preceding him down the steps to the one dinghy equipped with an outboard engine and a pair of oars, Kilpatrick, pulling out two lifejackets from under a board seat, said, 'Force orders, I'm afraid. As well as having me to crew the boat, you're required to wear a jacket while you are on board. Don't worry about it. It'll inflate automatically as you hit the water.'

'I'll try not to,' Rogers said almost sardonically, taking the jacket from her and forbearing to mention that he had been distance swimming from his boyhood.

Out of the harbour and turning to port, Kilpatrick followed the mostly steep and rugged coastline at what Rogers thought to be a leisurely speed. Sitting uncomfortably and low down on one side of the dinghy, he was breathing in the smells of stranded seaweed, hot rubber and the occasional wafting of their outboard engine's exhaust fumes. It decided him to smoke his pipe after satisfying himself that the smoke he chose to regard as aromatic was going nowhere near Eva, as he now thought of her.

With the noise of the engine and the slapping of seawater against the dinghy's sides making conversation difficult, Rogers was able to concentrate on not being humiliatingly seasick as a result of this rubber contraption's ability to side-swing, to roll and pitch queasily, in a sea of baby-sized waves.

There was a long twenty minutes of this before Kilpatrick, manifestly accustomed to an inflatable's sick-making movements, switched off the engine. Retrieving the two short oars from beneath her seat, she said, 'We shall drift if I don't hold her steady with these. Let me introduce you to Blacktoad Bay while I do it, this being approximately the position where Arbitt's boat sank. I've been told you can no longer see the hulk of it for the kelp that's since grown over it.'

'I'm pleased to be here,' Rogers told her, looking over the side of the dinghy and seeing deep below them an indistinct sand-filled blur of flowing brown kelp. It wasn't an exhilarating sight and he said, 'I see what you mean,' looking up and turning his attention across the eye-dazzling blue-green water to take in the bay itself.

The high reddish-brown cliff face, with its arms reaching out each side of them, had been eaten into by the waves of rough seas, their violence bringing down boulders on to the already rock-strewn and inaccessible beach. The cliff's crests, steeply sloped and scrub-covered, made access impossible for any but experienced rock-climbers and the suicidal. Even with the afternoon's sun on them, they looked alien and inhospitably grim.

'No access to the beach, Eva?' he asked, turning to her. Already he was beginning to heat up beneath the air-stifling lifejacket, while she wore hers coolly and attractively.

'Only by boat and that would be wholly stupid,' she said. 'There are rock-falls almost daily with the face of the cliff falling into the sea.'

'I won't ask you to take me there,' Rogers promised. 'Tell me what you know about Arbitt's boat.'

'I've not seen it,' she said, holding back on the oars, 'but it's a single-masted Quatro 23 with a mainsail and jib, and capable of being sailed single-handed should whoever it was know port from starboard. She would have an open and very draughty cockpit with a two-berth cabin just big enough to sleep and eat in . . .'

'And to die in,' Rogers interposed.

'... and a couple of other things also,' she agreed. 'There's not much room on it for an adequate dinghy or life-raft of any type, but it would be fitted with lifebuoys.'

'I have it now,' Rogers said, looking at her with some approval. 'You research remarkably well.'

'Thank you,' she said, not the type to get sloppy over a man's compliment, or his admiration. 'Talking of which, I've since had a telephone access to the coroner's report of his finding on Arbitt's death. You've a need to know?'

'I certainly have,' he agreed, 'being still ignorant of much about him. Enlighten the darkness of my unknowing.' He needed a further fix of nicotine and began filling his pipe, promising himself that it would be his last until later in the evening.

Still paddling gently with the oars, keeping the dinghy on station, Kilpatrick said with her unsettling way of holding Rogers's gaze with an almost hypnotic regard, 'I had it read to me over the phone, and I don't believe it's too helpful for us. The coroner referred particularly to the post-mortem examination without too much questioning of it, finding that Arbitt's death was due to the inhalation of smoke and water due to the boat he was fishing from catching fire and sinking.'

She looked away for a moment, recollecting her stored memory it seemed. 'He accepted that the cause of the fire lay with a fault occurring in either the paraffin heater in the cabin, or in the injudicious use of the propane gas cylinder used for cooking. Mrs Arbitt gave evidence that her husband was fishing on his own on a quite chilly day and that he would invariably cook and eat some of the fish he had caught.' She stopped until Rogers, trying to light his pipe in the onshore breeze, had finally produced smoke.

'I'm sorry, Eva,' he said contritely, though not enough to stop doing it. 'I was taking it all in.'

'I didn't doubt it for a moment.' She was quite amiable about it which, he thought, was right and proper.

'I was about to ask if there was any evidence that he had prepared or eaten a meal.'

'No. If he had, I'm sure the pathologist would have noted it and given it in evidence. What it did show was that there had been a heavy ingestion of gin, even after the several days immersion under water, and the coroner accepted that this could have left him helpless or stupefied in the face of a sudden fire.' She added doubtfully, 'And the half-empty gin bottle could support that, I suppose.'

Rogers shook his head. 'Not with me, it wouldn't. It could be argued that it was half empty, or half full rather, when Arbitt set out to fish.' He smiled. 'Perhaps I'm being bloody-minded about it. You think?'

'It's a point,' she said, 'though it was the coroner's, not mine.' She wrinkled her forehead. 'Can you deliberately get a man, possibly a trusting husband or friend, drunk like that?'

Rogers scratched thoughtfully at his emerging chin stubble. 'A bit doubtful. I was waiting to ask you whether the pathologist processing him gave evidence of finding any injury to the head.' He was wishing the dinghy would stop its unsettling wallowing.

She was definite. 'There's nothing in the coroner's report to suggest it.'

Rogers shrugged. 'Even were there, he need not have found it. Especially not when Arbitt had been sunk a few fathoms down for several days. Nor need there be much to find if whoever it was used a sock full of wet sand, or a rubber cosh. As I think someone did with our Rachel Hurt who will, I hope, turn out to be your Kathrin Arbitt.'

'I rather think that she's yours now, George.' She smiled. 'Mr Trout would certainly believe so.'

'Whichever,' Rogers told her cheerfully over the relighting of his pipe. 'I've very little doubt that Arbitt was murdered here and that Mrs Arbitt was either an active party to it, or knew or suspected what had happened to him.' He frowned. 'That has to be; otherwise the apparently abominable deceased Poukas, who was investigating a believed accidental death that wasn't his concern, wouldn't have had anything with which to blackmail her for large amounts of her insurance money.'

He was looking down into the water as if for enlightenment in a crystal ball. 'It seems to me,' he continued, 'that having suspected early on that there had been dirty work in Arbitt's apparent death by drowning that he did a sudden change of direction – probably suspecting correctly that Mrs Arbitt *was* involved – and became certain that there was money in it for him.'

'So far an agreeable hypothesis,' Kilpatrick murmured. 'BA Sociology stuff, in fact.'

'I'd be surprised,' Rogers smiled back at her. 'With a total lack of evidence for it, I believe that Mrs Arbitt, having collected the insurance money, did a runner and changed her name to Hurt to lose contact with the no doubt money grabbing Poukas. Thereafter, he'd be on the hunt to find and bleed her; none too difficult a task for an ex-detective inspector who had already taken care to destroy the crime files and any reference to his implication in the missing Seaforth-Major character.'

He was absently tapping his teeth with the stem of his gone-out pipe. 'Doesn't all this indicate to you that there has to be a third person involved in killing Arbitt on the boat?'

Kilpatrick was already there with him. 'If there were two of them on the boat out at sea and one killed the other, it would pose a problem for the murderer in getting back to dry land unless he used the boat to do so. Which he obviously didn't.' She stared at him questioningly. 'You aren't thinking that Poukas was the third man, are you?'

'He's not remotely a front runner, Eva. Arbitt had to be dead and long immersed before Poukas could have become interested. Why he decided to investigate what had been reported as a missing person and then an accidental death will probably never be known.' He held her stare. 'Did you know him, Eva? Serve with him?'

'I applied for a transfer to here from Manchester after Poukas had resigned; so no connection between the two,' she said with cool amusement. 'I was never his associate, his friend or anything else at which you might hazard a guess. I'm reasonably fresh from a senior course at the Police College and preparing myself for, I hope, an assistant or deputy chief constableship.'

A discomfited Rogers smiled with her. 'You've shot me down in flames,' he said. 'Not that I was being curious in that sense, God forbid. I want to get to know Poukas, that's all; to know what made him what he was.' Feeling parboiled, he pulled open his lifejacket to allow air to circulate beneath it. 'Could we drop Poukas,' he said, 'and see what we can make of the probably still missing Seaforth-Major?'

'Make of him as what, George?'

'As the third man. Poukas was interested in him, therefore so must I. Why not?' He answered that himself. 'With Poukas having no title or reason to make enquiries about a reported missing man, then there's a curious something about what was going on in his mind.'

'Could he have been an accessory to Poukas's criminal determination?' she asked. 'Or been a victim of some sort?'

'I don't know. You've given me my own alternatives, so let it be for the moment. At least until we see his wife, if such she is.' He hesitated, wondering if he was not piling it on too much. 'I don't suppose you know of a Sarah Gadd? She was employed in Amborum by Davis and Davis the estate agents, and until yesterday – when we lost her – she was living with Poukas at a village called Owlsfitten. She was, I believe, into some of his activities near the scene of his murder.'

Kilpatrick shook her head. 'I know you've already had enquiries made of the agents and her late landlady, but she rings no bell other than that.'

'Tell me,' he said, 'being here in my boat, as Arbitt was, how would you get to me with murder in your mind? By another boat? To be seen or heard approaching? To board the boat if I didn't want you to?' He showed his teeth in a tight smile, making his suggestion of gaining access rather unlikely. 'Alternatively, by swimming? By stowing aboard at the point of departure?'

'You're in a prosecuting counsel mode now, aren't you?' she challenged him amiably enough. 'Swimming to here or stowing aboard are as unlikely and as impossible as you intended them to be. By another boat? That is possible – of course it is, though it would mean either that his intending murderer was known to him, or at least be a person having a feasible, possibly an official reason for demanding it.' She shook her head. 'I don't go anything on that either.'

'What if our murderous friend did use a boat? Where's the nearest boat-hire facility to here?'

'There's a small fishing village called Cliff Bagot about half a mile around the cliff outcrop that does things for holiday people. You want?'

'I'd be grateful. I know it's two years back, but it's a chance.'

'I'll put a DS on to it,' she promised. 'If anyone did, he'll turn him up.'

'It'd help, even in a negative sense should we get nothing from it.' He paused, clearly trying to sort things out in his mind. 'I think – rather unimaginatively at the moment – that Arbitt had company with him at the time of his death. A lover, male or female? Our third man or, possibly, a third woman? At a guess, why not his wife who would certainly profit from his death by an accident or by some faulty bodily mechanism acceptable to an insurance company. As indeed she has done by what I suspect to be criminal chicanery, if I may call it that.'

'The logic's good,' she approved, 'and you're keeping your options open. I'm happy with them.'

'Don't have a rush of blood to the head about them, Eva,' he cautioned her. 'I can be found riding the wrong horse now and then.' With women as well, he told himself.

He busied himself in scraping out ash from his gone-out pipe and then refilling it, putting his need to smoke it in neutral for the moment. 'If the boat can be located in that kelp,' he said, 'would you do a dive with me to look it over?'

'Yes, I would,' she replied without thinking about it. 'Subaqua, necessarily?'

'If I can borrow the equipment.'

'You're on,' she told him. 'You can and I will, but what had you in mind?'

'The boat was obviously examined with only the assumed fatal accident in mind. That might not attract the same intensity of purpose that a suspected murder would. We might, for example, find the remains of a meal, possibly even two meals or none at all. I don't know, it's all guesswork based on probabilities anyway.' He shrugged his uncertainty. 'It's a thought and you could convince me otherwise.'

'The need for locating the hulk would come first,' she reminded him, 'and I believe our underwater unit could do that.'

'Good,' he said. 'I'm immensely grateful. 'There're just one or two things before we go. How far are we from Amborum?'

'Eight miles, though it might seem more in this inflatable.'

'It does,' Rogers assured her. 'I'm told by Bernard Trout that Leamings Landing is eighteen land miles from Amborum, which means that Arbitt was sailing the equivalent of ten miles to do some fishing. What fish would you find here that'd be worth sailing that far for?'

She pulled a face. 'I don't know, though I'd imagine the pleasure of sailing a boat itself would be part of whatever he got out of it.'

'Or perhaps an escape from his wife and a failing business?' When he didn't get an answer to that, he said, 'That's the lot then, Eva. Do you want me to give you a compass course back to base and home?'

'God forbid.' She smiled back at him as she stowed the oars and started the outboard engine. 'But I'll find out about the fish.'

Being motored back to Amborum – he couldn't bring himself to think of it as sailing – both were silent and reflective against the staccato racketing of the engine and the noise of the dinghy's flopping over the waves.

Rogers was vastly approving of Kilpatrick, being presently at peace with his more masculine instincts. He could look at her sexually dangerous attractions with an almost complete detachment, for he was of the breed of policemen who found it disciplinarily improper to look upon a woman police officer as anything but that.

A pity, he thought, as he refilled his pipe and struck futile matches at it. While it may have happened on the heels of Nancy Duval while he was still emotionally depleted, it was still the unacceptable made taboo in his own mind.

20

The evening sun had lost some of its heat when Rogers returned to the still glittering crystal hemisphere of earthly delights and the garishly white Farquharson House, to the contained sweat-making heat of the Murder Wagon and its custodian, the amiable and abundantly bosomed Sergeant Flowers.

Referring him to the reports of Action Taken awaiting him on his desk and producing her own non-constabulary cup of cappuccino coffee, heavy on the chocolate, she told him that Charles Jarvis had been asking for him, wishing to be contacted urgently at his office.

Telephoning and arranging with a rather terse-sounding Jarvis that he would be with him in fifteen minutes, Rogers set fire to a recharged pipe of tobacco and finished off his coffee, wondering what had been downloaded on the usual old-boy chumminess of the general manager.

Sitting in the visitors' chair in Jarvis's office, Rogers thought the air heavy with unsaid things. There had been no cordiality in Jarvis's greeting, but a perceptible lukewarmness. It was apparent from the set of his features that he knew about, or suspected, Nancy's transgression.

Jarvis, accoutred in a well-tailored white twill suit and showing his teeth in not quite a smile and avoiding meeting the detective's eyes, said, 'I'm sorry to have to see you at such short notice, George, but it's a Head Office diktat again. It seems I've overstepped something or other in loaning you the services of Nancy. I've been carpeted and told she's to be returned to normal duties.' His eyes belied even the pallid friendliness he was showing.

'I'm sorry,' Rogers said. 'Nancy's been most helpful.' What he wanted to say was that it had been in ignorance, in complete and bloody ignorance and that he was desperately sorry. But how could you tell a man that his wife, or ex-wife, had initiated the liaison which had clearly been intended to lead to a one-night stand. There was dismay in him, a feeling of being small and somehow belittled, for here he was, having cruelly hurt a man he liked and admired.

'I'm sorry too.' Jarvis might have meant that, but if he did it didn't show. 'You know how it is with these Head Office wallahs.'

'There are many things an investigating officer doesn't happen on,' Rogers said in a veiled defence of himself, though that was visibly making no impact. 'It's an opportune moment as it happens, for my enquiries are now centred in another county and I don't believe we shall be treading on your toes for much longer.' He rose from his chair. 'I do understand, Charles,' he said, sympathetically and possibly cryptically, 'though I certainly didn't before.'

Leaving his buggy where he had parked it, his injured *amour propre* deciding him against any further use of it, he returned on foot to the Murder Wagon, his bad mood neutralized by a further cup of Flowers's cappuccino coffee, even stronger on the chocolate, and began dealing with the paperwork overspill from his in-tray.

A report, dictated by Lingard and timed in the late afternoon, informed Rogers that he had unearthed information that Sarah Gadd had been seen returning to the cottage at Owlsfitten which she had shared with Ward, presumably knowing where a spare key had been kept. She had been observed by a neighbour to enter the cottage and stay for a few minutes only – Lingard suggested that she had retrieved money overlooked in the interrupted police search of the cottage – then being seen waiting at a coach stop in the village on the side of the road serviced by the Dumbarton-bound coaches. He, Lingard, was then going to follow the route taken by whatever coach she had boarded to effect her arrest.

The other reports were largely routine and negative bumph which he could, with a clear conscience, pass to Flowers for collating. It was as he was noting these that a call came through Flowers from Detective Inspector Kilpatrick; a something that, though he hadn't eaten yet, made his evening much brighter.

'Events,' she said in her cool voice, 'are piling up on us. First the up side, and this has to be done in a hurry. A nephew of Chadwick Arbitt has been traced and interviewed and says he is willing, subject to your paying him his expenses, to attend at the Abbotsburn Hospital to identify his aunt by marriage, Kathrin Arbitt, should your Mrs Hurt be the same person.'

As he scribbled notes he could tell she was happy about this, and so she should be. She continued, 'His name is Leonard Longstreet and he lives with his parents here at Amborum. He's employed locally as an auctioneer's clerk and there's a snag, though that's not it. He's off to Italy tomorrow morning with his lady-love so I've had to arrange for him to be taken direct to the hospital this evening and to wait there on your arrival, tentatively given as half-past eight.'

He checked the time on his wrist-watch as ten minutes to eight. 'I can make it,' he said optimistically, 'if I don't take too much notice of bends in the road. I imagine he'll wait if I'm a minute or two late?'

'With one of our drivers taking him there he'll not have much choice.' She was amused. 'One other matter, the down side one in a way. We've traced a Mrs Constance Seaforth-Major, with a hyphen, to an address in Little Salton, remotely in our bailiwick, though she has not yet answered our telephone calls to confirm we are on to the right woman. I'm off duty now, so if anything comes in about her you'll know tomorrow morning.'

'I'm grateful, Eva,' he said, already standing cramped from his chair, replacing the receiver and about to take off for the Abbotsburn mortuary. Much, he qualified to himself, like a fagged-out foxhound on a not very fresh scent; this particular one smelling of dead body.

21

It was comfortably past eight-thirty when Rogers turned his car into the Abbotsburn Hospital's almost empty car park, the sinking sun's growing redness already being reflected from the hospital's windows.

An irritable-looking Leonard Longstreet, climbing out from an unfamiliar police patrol car, was young and tall and gangly with a lumpy forehead, a prominent Adam's apple, a thin moustache and hair caught back in a thumb-sized ponytail. He wore new-looking jeans, a cream-coloured jacket and a gold ring in the lobe of one ear.

Rogers, holding out his hand and being genial, said, 'I'm sorry I'm late, Mr Longstreet,' withdrawing his hand and geniality when Longstreet appeared to ignore both. 'If you'd come with me, we'll get this business over with quickly.'

'This is a nuisance for me and I'm attending under protest,' Longstreet said. 'I assume I shall be paid for my time and inconvenience. I should be getting ready for my flight out early tomorrow morning.'

'Put an expenses chit in,' Rogers told him, leading him around to the side of the huge red-brick building with its two centuries of worrying about the sick and disabled. 'I'm afraid dishing out expense money isn't my department's problem.'

'Are you going to tell me who killed her?' he demanded.

'We don't know. Not yet. When we do I'm sure you'll be told.' Rogers thought handling him might become a small problem.

Escorting the none-too-pleased Longstreet down the tunnel entrance to the subterranean mortuary, Rogers said, 'You are, I'm told, the late Mrs Kathrin Arbitt's nephew, is that so?'

'She was my aunt by marriage, if that's what you mean,' he gave out grudgingly. 'I wouldn't say that was family, if you understand what I mean.'

'I do,' Rogers beamed at him, trying to bring some sunshine into his life. 'Would you know what her name was before she married your uncle?'

The smile hadn't done much for him. 'I've never had anything to do with her, or him, if it comes to that, but I believe it was Kathleen Hurt. Or something like it,' he added indifferently.

'Not Rachel Hurt?'

'If it was I never heard of it. He called her Kathy. My uncle I mean.'

'You were close to them?'

'No, I wasn't. They lived miles away at Leamings Landing, so I only saw them occasionally, mostly just to say hello, that sort of thing. We weren't too family like.'

Rogers could understand that. They had reached a badly lit entrance to the Receiving Room with the detective pushing open the doors to a harsher light and death's own smell of formalin.

There was no attendant there to stop them from snatching a body or two should they wish and it was what he expected, having been on professionally familiar terms with many of the previous occupants of the body drawers.

'Your aunt is in drawer number eleven,' he told Longstreet. 'You've no objection to viewing her dead body? She is rather, ah, unpleasant about the face.' He added expressionlessly, 'I wouldn't want you upset about it.'

Longstreet shrugged his indifference. 'I'm being paid for it,' he said. That was, apparently, the be-all and end-all of his personal philosophy.

Approaching the drawer, Rogers pulled it open with Longstreet standing behind him and giving off a noticeable increase in the rapidity of his breathing. Drawing back the sheet from Rachel Hurt's distorted face, he said, moving to one side, 'She's all yours, Mr Longstreet. Please take your time.'

He took it, moving from one side of the drawer to the other, blank-faced and giving nothing away. Rogers, waiting patiently and preferring to look at the far end door, filled his pipe and put a match to it, believing the smoke to be an efficient fumigant against the no doubt dangerous putrefaction-associated bacteria floating around him in their millions, all waiting to pounce.

'Yes,' Longstreet said at last, standing back from the corpse, 'this is my uncle's wife. I do recognize her.'

'Your aunt known when alive as Kathrin Arbitt?'

When Longstreet nodded his agreement, Rogers asked, 'Did you ever know of her using the name Rachel Hurt?'

'No, never. Just Mrs Arbitt.'

'Tell me what sort of a woman she was.' Rogers pushed the drawer shut with a metallic clang that made Longstreet jerk as though startled.

'It won't go further than you?' he asked.

'Of course not,' Rogers assured him. 'At least, what use we might make of it won't be attributed to you. I know much about her already, so don't hesitate about telling me all you know.' He spoke as if with a doubt in his mind. 'Before that and while we're here, would you mind having a look at a man who was killed yesterday and who had lived and worked in Amborum some time last year or earlier? He could conceivably have known your uncle and aunt and you might recognize him.'

'My aunt by marriage,' Longstreet corrected him again, 'and I'll tell you if I do.'

Rogers moved to the drawer where Poukas's body was kept and pulled it open, turning his head away from a growing smell of corruption. Longstreet had followed him docilely enough and stood with him, apparently having no nose for bad smells.

Pulling back the sheet from Poukas's face, he said, 'Look at him carefully, try to imagine him without a moustache or beard. Take your time and tell me if you've seen him in the company of either your uncle or your aunt by marriage. Or, possibly, in anyone else's.'

Longstreet was already frowning and shaking his head, though not detaching his gaze from Poukas's ruined face. 'No,' he said. 'Not at all,' then grimacing and looking at the undamaged side of the face in profile.

Rogers had thought him paralysed until he straightened his back and muttered, possibly to himself, 'I've seen him with someone, I'm sure, but God knows who or who he is. I'm needing time to think.' Then louder to Rogers, he said, 'I'll let you know if I can. I must be sure . . .'

It had been a close-run thing and Rogers was by no means put out. 'Let's go,' he said, banging the drawer closed, 'and tell me now about your aunt by marriage on the way.'

'I didn't like her, that's for sure,' he said, as he followed Rogers through the tunnel and out into the open air. 'Most of what I know I got from my mother who was Uncle Chadwick's older sister and hated his second wife.'

'That should be a good reason for your not holding anything back,' Rogers pointed out, 'so tell me why both you and your mother felt unable to like her.'

Rogers, grateful to be done for the day with dead bodies, steered Longstreet to a low wall, sitting him on it in the florid warmth of the dying sun. 'Let me have it, Mr Longstreet,' he said, 'and then we can get you driven home before it's suddenly night.'

'I, or I should say we, didn't like her at all,' Longstreet started. 'This, I think, because she'd been married before and divorced – well, uncle had been as well, though that was different – and mother thought she had married him for what money he got from the business. That was failing even then, I'd heard. Uncle drank, they both did. She was pushing him, that's for sure.' The lumps on his forehead were glossy with a light sweat.

'You *know*?'

He shrugged bony shoulders. 'I heard it, same thing. She was also a cold fish so far as my mother could make out. All talk and no do, so she said. As it turned out it was obvious that, one way or another, she had spent most of his money before he'd died.' He was twisting his fingers together, watching Rogers with careful eyes.

'How long had they been married before he died?'

'About five years.' He frowned, then said, 'I did think at one time that she had a boyfriend. Somebody'd said they'd seen her and some man in a pub in Amborum. I don't know whether uncle knew, but he'd have been a fool if he didn't. She was money mad my mother thought, and when she got the insurance money from uncle's death she took off and we never heard of her again.'

'Your mother was sorry, I suppose, about her brother's death?'

'So-so,' Longstreet said. 'They weren't that close. Not on visiting terms anyway.'

'You'll be able to tell her something now, won't you?' Rogers thought there had been little grief at his passing. 'Your uncle. Describe him to me, will you? His age, what he looked like; his temperament, that sort of thing. Then I'll keep you no longer.'

Longstreet had been showing signs of wanting to leave; shifting his position on the hard brick wall and looking ostentatiously at his watch. 'He was about forty – perhaps a bit less; I don't know exactly. He was sort of a biggish build with brown hair. He didn't have a beard or anything like that. When he wasn't with her he was quite easy-going, even though touchy at times.' He looked towards the car park as an indication of his need to go. 'Isn't that enough?' he complained. 'I can't remember anything else.'

'Did you like your uncle?' Rogers was ignoring his impatience.

Longstreet shrugged. 'I could take him or leave him. He did cut himself off from his family when he married her.'

'And her?'

'I've told you. She was nothing to us. We weren't even invited to his funeral and we didn't go.' He showed his teeth, not in a smile, standing up from the wall. 'That's your lot for today if you don't mind. If there's anything else I'll be back in ten days' time.'

'You've been helpful,' Rogers said, 'and I might be in touch. Put a chit for your expenses in to Inspector Kilpatrick and I'll see that you're paid for your time and attendance.'

It was something to see Longstreet actually attempt a brief smile as he left, a gangly and rather disgruntled young man, manifestly not in dire need of the usually grudgingly paid expenses he would get very much later than he might expect.

With the Murder Wagon now certainly closed down for the night – except that is for the reporting of an utterly unthinkable third murder – Rogers returned to his office at Headquarters. Ignoring the files and papers accumulating on his desk, he read a telephoned message sent by Lingard complaining that he had been unable to contact Rogers personally and was now advising him that he was returning to Headquarters with Sarah Gadd who he had traced to an hotel in Cambarton and arrested on a charge of assaulting and wounding WDC Bunting.

Rogers, as much at ease with the world – apart from the affair with Nancy Duval – as he ever would be, decided that he needed a meal of sorts at the Solomon & Sheba Inn and then to bed after a supposed accidental removal of his telephone plug. If anybody wanted him about anything less than bloody murder he intended not to be available until tomorrow morning. He hoped fairly firmly that Eva Kilpatrick would stay out of any dream he might have.

22

Rogers, not having dreamed of Eva Kilpatrick, but of being trapped in dark-green tangling seaweed and drowning in Blacktoad Bay – a premonition, he thought on waking – had shaved and showered with the thought of Charles Jarvis and Nancy Duval still troubling his conscience.

It was one of the early morning occasions when, staring at his reflection in the bathroom mirror and mowing the stubble from his face, he did a bit of self-analysis about how he must appear physically to other people. On this occasion, he considered that he wasn't too disgustingly unattractive to women; his thrusting nose not too inquisitorial, his dark-brown eyes not reflecting a too strong cynicism of his fellow *Homo sapiens*. He thought he could comfort himself that he didn't look too much like a man who made a habit of feasting on other men's wives, or even other men's ex-wives.

Outside, when he had reversed his car from its garage, he found it slate-grey and shiny with heavy rain. Arriving at his office at Headquarters, he was once again convinced that it was not his favoured habitat. Its staring white walls were broken only by two windows, a few crime graphs and a NO SMOKING notice signed by his steely minded chief constable. His executive chair in a glossy black PVC waited for him at a desk cluttered – that being Rogers's word for it – with an *Archbold Criminal Pleading*, an elderly Glaister's *Medical Jurisprudence and Toxicology*, a Moritz's *Pathology of Trauma*, and three overburdened trays of uncleared reports and crime files. Investigating murders was not by far his only responsibility. On a windowsill near his desk was a civilizing pot of freshly cut yellow carnations, supplied by his shared secretary who translated his reports and correspondence into computer-speak and, unrevealed, fancied him.

Fitting himself into his chair and waiting on the arrival of Lingard, he ignored the trays of files waiting on his attention, dealing instead with a note from Detective Inspector Hagbourne asking to be unloaded of the results of his enquiries.

'Fill me in, Thomas, and make it brief,' he said with reasonable amiability for that time of the morning, when Hagbourne arrived clutching papers and sitting opposite him. 'I hope that whatever it is, it's something useful.'

'The late breakfasters, sir,' Hagbourne started. 'All those I'd given you seem to be stainless in the criminal sense. The lady with the same initials as Mrs Arbitt is entitled to them.' He turned down the corners of his mouth. 'I've no real results at all with any of the others, a lot of them having already left; all being relatively clean and proper. At least, on paper they are.' He looked hurt in having to say that; to him, it was a failure.

'No matter,' Rogers said. 'I believe we've progressed since then; gone out of the county for our more likely material. You've a reply on Toplis, you say?'

'We've something of a hard man in our midst.' Hagbourne pulled out a sheet of paper, passing it to Rogers. 'Peter Nigel Toplis. He's been checked and reported on by the Deuxième Bureau as having enlisted in La Légion Etrangère at Aubagn sixteen years ago. He's seen active service with the Second Foreign Parachute Regiment in French Guyana and Lebanon, *en route* having collected himself the Médaille Militaire. Not much of the Sahara Desert about him though. And nothing recorded against him on the PNC.'

Rogers thought about what was obviously the career of a hard and resourceful soldier; and of macho-man Toplis who hadn't quite revealed that background to him. 'Sixteen years or so ago,' he murmured almost to himself. 'Time softens and ravages us all, I suppose. Still, better do a home address check on him. On the double if you would. And, I think, how many visits he's made to the club. And when,' he added quickly.

Hagbourne blinked and made a note, waiting for the inevitable next.

Rogers made his voice impersonal. 'What about Charles Jarvis and Mrs Duval?' The flesh of his face tightened momentarily at his own mention of their names, though dammit, he had no reason for the guilt implied by Charles.

'People of the status of Jarvis don't often enter our records, as we've always known,' Hagbourne said. 'So he's one of them. In the time given I can't even find where he comes from. Or what he's ever done before coming here.'

'It was an outside shot,' Rogers admitted. 'I didn't suspect him of being involved in anything. The same for Mrs Duval?' He wanted her out of any reckoning he might eventually have.

'Absolutely, though I've taken her no further than a routine check with the PNC.'

Receiving no comment from Rogers, Hagbourne said, 'About

Mrs Hurt and Scarborough. She was living at the Hotel Imperial for eight months prior to booking in at the Farquharson. In that name she's remembered as a big spender and a generous tipper of the hotel's staff. She left at short notice, telling the manager in confidence that her divorced husband, then in Ireland, had found out where she was living and she had been advised by her solicitor to move. She never said where she was going and the manager told me that there had been no later enquiries there from anybody likely to be her ex-husband. Or in fact,' he added cynically, 'anyone else.'

When Rogers remained silent, seeming unusually satisfied with the meagreness of one result, Hagbourne, retaining his melancholic presence, said, 'I've had two DCs chasing up on guests who don't seem to mind being questioned about the scarf used to strangle Mrs Hurt. So far, all we've found out is that none who actually knew her can recall her wearing a dress scarf, several pointing out that in any case it wasn't really the weather for wearing one around the neck unless to mop up undue sweating.' Finished, he reordered his papers and waited.

'Not your fault, Thomas,' Rogers told him. 'The investigation's probably on standstill at the scene anyway. Unless you've anything more I'll release you to your figures and percentages.' He smiled. 'For me, I'm visiting the washroom for a quick fix of nicotine before I have a convulsion.'

Afterwards, still waiting on Lingard's arrival – it was now nearing ten o'clock – and reluctant to dive into the mass of paperwork not yet gone away, he sat drinking bitter canteen coffee. He was wondering whether he dare risk flouting the Chief Constable's oppressive No Smoking order, his need not having been satisfied by his brief visit to the washroom, when his unlisted telephone rang. Guessing correctly that his caller would be the cool and elegant Kilpatrick, he was grateful that her voice didn't raise his emotional temperature. He was, he considered, now much inclined to a monkish mood of abstention from any outside attraction of a female presence.

'I have,' she told him, 'managed to contact Mrs Seaforth-Major – her name is Constance – who has confirmed that it was she who had reported her stepson missing, though I thought she seemed more concerned about some lost furniture than him. His forename is Edward and she calls him Teddy, and she's not heard of or from him since she reported him missing from her home two years ago. Subject to your agreement, I've arranged a meet for both of us this afternoon. Is that convenient for you?' She was, properly, being business-like.

'It is,' he agreed, he thought a little too enthusiastically.

'There's more,' she said. 'Apropos the late Chadwick Arbitt's boat – it was called *Poppaea II* had you not been told – I find that this had been allotted an eight weeks' mooring pass in Kathrin Arbitt's name by the harbour-master's office here in Amborum. This was five weeks prior to her husband's death, if you can fathom the sense in it.' She sounded as if she herself had not and was irritated by it. 'Unfortunately, the harbour-master's away for the next three days and not available for more details.'

'It's significant enough to have me worrying whether I'm on the right track or not.' He was also trying to make sense of it, not being helped by hearing her quiet breathing from the other end. 'It certainly makes nonsense of Arbitt's going fishing in a boat that's now known to have been moored sixteen miles from where he lived.'

'The bafflement is mutual,' she said brightly, 'though I'd say rather useful for us, particularly as I've been informed that one would be idiotic or overly optimistic to go fishing in Blacktoad Bay anyway; its being well-known to be almost barren in the sense of finding any fish there.' She laughed. 'We'll discuss later on a prepared agenda, shall we?'

She had paused and he heard the quiet rustle of paper from her end. 'So,' she continued, 'Mrs Arbitt herself. I've had our Registrar of Births, Deaths and Marriages seen and he has a record of a Registry Office marriage between Chadwick Austin Arbitt and Kathrin Rachel Hurt two years before his death.'

'Ah,' Rogers breathed out, deeply satisfied. 'Poukas would have been a fool not to have cottoned on to that. And no doubt he did.'

'I'm sure,' she agreed. 'The Registrar said he could recall that the local CID at that time had already made an enquiry about the possibility of a wedding though nothing came of it and nobody said why.'

Rogers could tell that she had been smiling over the telephone as she changed tack and said, 'Bernard's gone and he asked me to say goodbye to you and good hunting. I should tell you also that I'm now his locum if that's the proper word; Temporary Detective Superintendent until any replacement that my Chief Constable has decided on arrives and takes over.'

'It couldn't happen to a better detective inspector and I'm delighted for you.' He felt that to be a little overdone, but ploughed on. 'I hope the replacement – no ill-will intended – breaks a leg or something before we finish this enquiry.'

'While I'm riding high in the polls,' she said, 'I have to tell you that the Chief gave me a thumbs-down on the scuba diving. It's a fact of life that the force insurance covers only the official underwater unit. You're disappointed?'

'Staggeringly,' he lied, though having had, after his dream, aquaphobic doubts about ever being in deep water with seaweed abounding. 'They'll dive for us?'

'It's already arranged. It only needs you to say what they'll be searching for.'

'I'll say now. Any physical evidence suggesting that Arbitt was with another person, male or female, on the boat immediately before its sinking.'

Kilpatrick was efficient, he would say that for her, but he knew that he had to be careful not to be swamped by her need to work her way to a chief constableship. Such women – and men – were dangerous. He said, 'I'm grateful, Eva. I'll pick you up at your office. I presume you'll be sitting in Bernard's chair? And about one-ish?'

Closing down he reached for his pipe, about to head for the open air and to smoke it in peace before Lingard arrived when his internal telephone rang. It was the Assistant Chief Constable, presumably realizing that when there were a couple of corpses on the force's plate it might be politic to know something in detail of what his Detective Superintendent was doing about it. Rogers, not at the moment of the same inclination, lost much of his feeling of well-being in thinking belatedly that it might also be that a whisper of the affair Duval might have reached his ears, though this proved not to be the case.

But, he felt, it could have been a shot across his bows, and he took a wobbly sort of inner vow of a future sexual abstinence. Something, he felt, he had done not infrequently before.

23

Rogers, late in attending Sarah Gadd's interrogation and taking a spare chair in the closely screened Interview Room, found that Lingard, elegantly suited in a light-weight dog's-tooth tweed, was well into it. Gadd, sitting opposite the chief inspector and accompanied by a heavyweight uniformed WPC, wore a pink dress – certainly finishing, Rogers thought, at mid-thigh – and was in full female warpaint, heavy on the scent, her scarlet lipstick a thick paste on her mouth. Sitting with a swirl of cigarette smoke above her head she was, manifestly, no helpless ninny incapable of caring for herself in her present calamitous circumstance.

'I was detained by the ACC,' Rogers explained his lateness to Lingard after his brief smile to Gadd had been ignored and his being treated as a non-person.

'Miss Gadd has been cautioned, has declined to have a solicitor present and that the interview' – he nodded at the tape recorder on the table – 'was to be taped.' He redirected his present benignity at the woman. 'Miss Gadd was about to tell me of her association with the late Frank Ward – a reassessment of her earlier account of it. Please carry on,' he said to her. 'You remember? Mr Ward as a seeker after financial justice and so on?'

She spoke. 'I see now that I was fooled into helping Frank with something I should never have considered.' She was tense and seemingly fraught with forebodings. 'I know that he used me; left me to explain what the hell I was doing, sitting like a bloody idiot waiting for him while he was being killed . . . left to explain how I came to be mixed up with him and his bloody affairs. What did you expect, for Christ's sake!'

She was sucking in and blowing out smoke from the cigarette

she held between her red-tipped fingers, baleful in her regard of Lingard and ignoring the disapproving frown on the policewoman's face. 'I did lie at first, but what the hell was I to do? Found there, not knowing what was happening with you bastards crawling all over me. I was frightened about him being killed and me having to explain about helping him.'

'The money, Miss Gadd,' the imperturbable Lingard reminded her. 'The money you told me about last night.'

'I didn't say anything but what Frank told me. He said he was owed the money and lots more, because the woman he had to see lost her husband and came into it.' She shook her head, almost fiercely. 'I told you that and it's true. He said he had an interest in the money she had because he'd invested in their business, that she had left and hidden herself after her husband died and she came into the money. Thousands, he told me.' She had spat the words out like an angry cat. 'And we were going to the Bahamas for a holiday. Then to settle in Australia where he'd been promised an executive job with Qantas Airways.'

The outburst had been the mangling of the stump of cigarette she held while she raged her disappointment, and she took another from the packet in front of her with shaking fingers, holding it in her mouth for the policewoman, her temporary custodian, to light.

Lingard, changing tack, asked, 'What do you know about the woman you mention, apparently a guest at the Farquharson Club?'

'Only what Frank told me. He said she was living there permanently under a false name. In hiding from him, he always said.' She brooded on that for a moment or two, then said, 'She was the one who killed him, wasn't she' – not a question, but a statement.

'Why do you think that?' Lingard was watching her eyes, not wholly screened by the black eyelash mascara.

'Wasn't she?' she said aggressively as if it mattered. 'She was the one he was seeing. She was the one who owed him his money.'

'Of course.' He smiled. 'I'd forgotten. Didn't he ever mention her name? Something like Hurt? Rachel Hurt?'

'No.' That had come instantly and there had been nothing in her eyes to contradict her denial.

'What about Arbitt? Mrs Kathrin Arbitt from Amborum?'

'Damn you, no! I've told you.'

'Might you think that either Mrs Hurt or Mrs Arbitt could tell us that he had?'

'I don't give a damn what they say,' she snapped. 'I told you he didn't.'

Lingard, though now reasonably satisfied, was still watching her reactions to his questions. 'I'm fairly happy about that,' he said mollifyingly, 'but could you have heard mention of the name Poukas? Humphrey Poukas?' seeing immediately her blank incomprehension.

'If I had it wouldn't mean anything,' she said. 'For God's sake!'

'Did Frank ever say anything about the death of the woman's husband?' He pinched snuff into his nose with a Beau Brummellish flourish.

She shook her head impatiently. 'I told you, he never mentioned those sort of things. I wasn't his bloody confessor, was I?'

'You don't need to be when you're living with a man and, in a way, having a connection with his death.'

'You bastard,' she said contemptuously, 'you know I wasn't and don't keep on about it. Frank didn't tell me and I didn't know. He had his good points, but he wasn't a talker. He gave me money for the housekeeping, for running my car and for any clothes I had to have – full stop.' She sucked in cigarette smoke and coughed. 'He wasn't a man for telling me anything either and I wasn't encouraged to ask. Nor, if it comes to that, could I call him a liar about what he'd told me and chance leaving the cottage with nowhere else to go. He gave me money when it was needed, and it was his problem where it came from.'

'That's not a particularly credible story, is it?' Lingard said. 'I'd suggest that your Frank was blackmailing Mrs Hurt – for that's who the woman you keep mentioning was – over something criminal in which she and her husband had been involved.'

'That's rubbish,' she told him angrily. 'How dare you! How dare you try to involve me in that!'

'A suggestion, that's all,' Lingard murmured, just audibly,

'though it's obvious that your Frank was getting pay-offs from her once he had discovered where she was. You were with him, I know, waiting in your car while he climbed over the fence to collect whatever money she had for him to collect. Not, we do know, for the first time.' In the silence that followed his no more than a guess of an accusation, he saw the sudden strain showing in her expression. 'How many times, Miss Gadd?' he asked gently, almost sympathetically. 'I think I know, but I'd like you to tell me.'

'Yes,' she agreed, her staring black-lashed eyes almost hypnotically on his. 'Three ... four times. I didn't know what for though. I could only guess.'

'So what did you guess?' Lingard asked. He felt like a priest taking confession.

When she shook her head blindly, he said, 'You saw whoever it was he was visiting?'

'Of course I didn't.' She was getting back her spirit, apparently feeling that she was on safe ground. 'They were in the trees inside and I couldn't even hear them, seeing that I was in the car with the radio on.'

'How long on previous occasions had he been gone?' Lingard was still gentling her, not letting her off the hook of his disturbingly blue eyes and the mental willing of her to answer him.

'Ten minutes ... sometimes more. It wasn't ever very long. Not until the last time when I became worried. I should have gone then,' she said bitterly.

'Perhaps you should,' Lingard agreed. 'I'm finishing now, so think things over before I see you again. Then tell me a little more about Frank and what he was doing before he met you.'

'Don't bother,' she said, holding a fresh cigarette in shaking fingers as her guardian WPC prepared to put a match to it.

Lingard looked across to Rogers, raising his eyebrows questioningly, accepting the slight shake of Rogers's head that he had no wish to ask any questions himself.

Standing and stuffing tobacco into the bowl of his stone-cold pipe, Rogers said, 'See me in the Mess, David, when you've cleared your decks. And make it fast, please.'

Heading for the comfort of a strong coffee, perhaps some

smoked salmon sandwiches, he was happy that he still had a promising Mrs Seaforth-Major to come, for he had heard very little that seemed useful from an understandably shattered Sarah Gadd.

24

The Senior Officers Mess was not one to inspire a gourmet appetite and Rogers, for survival only, ate in its tastelessness of plastic chairs and tables, venetian blinds, unadorned walls and a patterned red carpet that hurt the eyes. The food was fair, but the coffee, drunk incautiously, was a scalding dark-brown bitterness.

Rogers and Lingard were in conference in a corner of the spacious room, away from their peers. Rogers, now with emptied plates on the table and conscious that he was due to collect Kilpatrick in a little over an hour's time, was anxious to have the conference shortened and had asked Lingard to fill him in only with what he hadn't heard from Gadd herself.

'Finding her was simple,' Lingard drawled over-modestly, 'and she was no bother in being arrested. When we got back to base I had her charged with assaulting young Bessie Bunting and occasioning her actual bodily harm. She said in answer to it that she was sorry but she hadn't meant to; only to push her out of the way so that she could do a runner. I'm happy with the truth of that, too.'

'She wasn't officially under arrest, anyway,' Rogers agreed.

'No, she was not.' Lingard was clearly not pushing for anything punitive. 'She did say before you came in that she'd returned to the cottage after I'd gone. She'd been watching me from the trees, she said, recovering a spare key from where it had been hidden in the shed, and collecting some of her clothing and a couple of hundred in emergency money she'd kept somewhere in the kitchen.' Lingard did a quick grin. 'I suspect that to have been the property of the late Poukas, but good luck to her.'

Lingard, having finished his slightly charred lamb chops and sensibly refusing both the pudding and coffee, fed snuff into his sinuses, the Chief Constable having overlooked indicting powdered tobacco as a noxious substance. 'I'm inclined to believe the lady,' he said, 'though only insofar as Poukas told her little or nothing of the real reason for his abstracting large amounts of money from Mrs Hurt.'

'Gadd's no real problem then?' Rogers didn't believe she could be.

Lingard shrugged. 'She's no stainless virgo intacta, that's for sure, but I think she was genuinely fooled by Poukas in doing what she did.'

'Bail her then,' Rogers said good-humouredly. 'Let any fall-out be on your own head. I think she was only a Pottifer's Calf anyway.'

'Don't you mean a Jacob's Goat?' Lingard had looked baffled.

'No, I don't, though I'll admit to probably meaning an Isaac's Ass.'

After they had both laughed at their biblical absurdities, Rogers said, 'Time's pushing, David, so let me spell out for you a not too impossible hypothesis about the death of Chadwick Arbitt; something that happened two or more years ago and about which, until now, there had been no suspicion of murder.' He shook his head wonderingly. 'Odd that ... considering. Still, this has now to be coupled with the death yesterday of chummy's wife, who took on the name Rachel Hurt, and Poukas, using the pseudonym Frank Ward, being the discredited ex-DI from Amborum.'

He finished off his coffee, grimacing and accepting an offered pinch of Lingard's snuff, though a poor substitute for his outlawed pipe. 'I'm probably repeating myself, but there are a few details you mightn't have caught up with, having been galloping around the country like a blue-assed fly,' he said, untroubled by his mixing of metaphors. 'Chadwick Arbitt ran, probably with some assistance from his wife, a chandlery called the Davy Jones Trading Store at Leamings Landing, this thankfully being in the next county. The business was already in trouble when Arbitt died in his burning boat – which sank with him still in it – while fishing in Blacktoad Bay. That, you probably wouldn't know, is about ten miles south of Leamings Landing.'

He was silent while he shifted his position in his uncomfortable chair, then continued, 'I'm told that his body was recovered from the boat a few days later and identified by his wife who presumably has now gone to have further words about things with him. An inquest was held at Amborum with the coroner finding that his death was due to misadventure. Some months later, Mrs Arbitt was paid three-quarters of a million pounds on a life insurance policy. This, I am going to assume, was the imperative for her getting rid of the failing business and disappearing into then unknown territory.'

'Strewth,' Lingard murmured. 'I wish I'd known. Wealthy widows in fine fettle have always fascinated me.'

'Same as,' Rogers smiled, 'though not with suspect ones like Mrs Arbitt. Once she was bedded down at the Farquharson Club as a presumably life member and using her unmarried name of Rachel Hurt, she indirectly underlined the privacy and protection she needed by alleging an unidentifiable divorced husband supposedly looking for her with evil intent. We can guess now that she was hiding from Poukas, knowing him as a DI at Amborum and who was, to put it at its best, privy to something blackmailable she had done.'

His eyebrows were down, scowling his deep thinking. 'I'm beginning to believe,' he said, 'that there are gaps in it and some matters a bit too obvious; such as that her husband was murdered in order that she should qualify for a life insurance payout. Not necessarily killed by Mrs Arbitt herself though; and that's not because she was a woman, for we know that the ladies have committed even worse crimes than the killing off of a husband or two.'

'But relatively rare birds for all that,' the gallant Lingard interjected. 'And rather pushed by circumstance?'

'I meant that she can't be a five-star suspect because of the practical improbabilities of her doing it. And that underlines my point. If she had been with her husband on that fishing business, killing him and setting fire to the boat, then she had somehow to unload herself from it – there wasn't an inflatable or anything similar on board at the time – and return to Leamings Landing. That's unlikely in the extreme, I think.'

'You believe there'd be somebody with him other than his wife?' Lingard asked. 'The somebody who killed him?'

'There had to be. And supporting that, there's an oddness about Arbitt's boat being moored at Amborum prior to his death. Eva Kilpatrick was on to me this morning with something she said could point to some decidedly tricky goings on. She found on enquiry that five weeks before Arbitt's death, his wife had booked and paid for an eight-weeks' mooring for their boat, *Poppaea II*, in Amborum's harbour. That surely indicates that the Arbitts were using, or intending to use, the boat while it was harboured there. The even odder bit. It happens that Arborum is eighteen miles north from Leamings Landing, so to go fishing from there to Blacktoad Bay, where I'm told the fishing is poor, is odd indeed. Particularly so when the bay is eight miles nearer to Leamings Landing itself.' Pausing for a moment, he added, 'There must be an underlying purpose in that, David; something nasty, dishonest or unlawful, if I could only think of it.'

'A possible scenario,' Lingard said, not too confidently, 'is that the boat could put out from Amborum to Leamings Landing specifically to take Arbitt on board for whatever purpose, then to sail part of the way back to the bay where he dropped dead or was murdered, whichever that was.' He thought about that for moments only, then said, 'Dammit, George, I've fallen at the first fence. That way lies lunacy. It can't make sense.'

'Paradoxically, it may do in a moment.' Rogers was groping for the logic of it. 'First of all, I forgot to mention that I'm almost certain that the bay was chosen for Arbitt's murder because it's all but concealed between uninhabited cliffs. What makes less sense – at least it does to me – is that Mrs Arbitt booked the harbourage at Amborum when she and he had one at Leamings Landing. A mooring for a day or so to dispose of the apparently unwanted Arbitt would have been understandable – but eight weeks! There's no specific mention of Arbitt in this booking of the harbourage, though certainly she couldn't do it, or take advantage of its facilities, without his knowledge and agreement. Damn it! It was his boat and he was using it. So was he, in a way, preparing for his own death? Sacrificing himself for an insurance pay-out? If only in the metaphorical sense, then having whatever it was going horribly wrong?'

He was chewing what appeared to be his bafflement on his bottom lip. 'Mind, it isn't necessarily an answer, but where does this missing chap Seaforth-Major fit in? I know nothing more about him than he went missing after Arbitt's death, having been somehow adjacent to Mrs Arbitt. It was Poukas who brought Seaforth-Major into the frame by dealing unofficially with a Missing Persons enquiry. Why? Why, for God's sake?' he almost shouted. 'There wasn't a bloody reward out for the man, and friend Trout insisted that Poukas had had no authority to do such an enquiry. On top of which, Poukas undoubtedly stole or destroyed the Arbitt and Seaforth-Major files. So who's covering up for whom? Might it be that when I've seen Mrs Seaforth-Major, that light will be manifest, eh?'

'After which, much will probably be made clear – I'm sure,' Lingard said with the confidence that only a man not in charge of the investigation could have.

He had left his open snuff box between them on the table and Rogers, needing a fix of nicotine, took a pinch of it. 'I'm guessing now,' he continued, sniffing it in, 'because it's possible that there's a third man to be considered. Other than Poukas, who was involved at the wrong time for what I'm considering and almost certainly not concerned in Arbitt's death until the fall-out from it afterwards. Anyway, he's now been cut off in his prime and not likely to be a source of information.' He scowled quite formidably, then growled, 'It has to be a man and one having access to the Farquharson Club premises; not only because he needed to strangle his probable partner in crime, Mrs Arbitt, but also to steal what must have been incriminating documents from her apartment.'

'You do have to get round to it that Mrs Arbitt was privy to at least her husband's death, be it by murder or whatever,' Lingard said. 'And she's now gone from us; deaf to any awkward questions we might have felt inclined to put to her.'

'There's a logic to it,' Rogers pointed out. 'She certainly didn't disappear and change her name for having got her hands on three-quarters of a million pounds, paid out on a dead husband who was accidentally killed and his boat sunk. I *know* she was involved, but that doesn't help much unless I can get her husband dug up.'

'Dug up?' Lingard echoed. 'Don't you think he's there?'

'Somebody – perhaps the coroner – was happy he was, and certainly his wife identified the body.' Rogers was at his most cynical.

'Or said she had, you're meaning.'

'That's it, David. At the moment we've only got her word for it. If this develops after I've seen Mrs Seaforth-Major, I'll have to think of somebody getting an exhumation order.'

'Don't ask me to have anything to do with it,' Lingard said firmly. 'I don't approve of bodies which have been down with the worms for years. In any case, all this happened in Eva Kilpatrick's territory and she'll be in the driving seat.'

'As I know only too well.' Rogers was looking a little happier. 'It'll depend on this afternoon's interview I think. If we have to get an exhumation order, it'll be Eva's chief constable's problem, if I can get him with us.' He pushed back his chair and stood. 'If the salmon croquettes don't kill me, then the coffee certainly will,' he complained. 'As you seem to be running out of things to do, perhaps you'd care to sit down in my office and do your stuff with the files you haven't so far looked at. I have to leave now, Eva will be waiting and I'd rather be on your bad side than on hers.'

'You've got it bad, haven't you?' Lingard smiled at him.

'I've never given her a thought,' Rogers lied with an appropriately expressionless face as he turned and strode briskly from the room.

He had given her a thought or two, but was determined that that would be all there was to it. He had never wished anyway to be tied emotionally to a future woman chief constable; the thought was terrifying. Unless, of course, she smoked, and didn't mind others doing the same.

25

The Priory at Little Salton was an imposing-looking early Victorian brownstone house, architecturally out of place in the Mercedes, double-garaged, tennis court, pantiled-roof side of the town. Using the heavy black knocker on its lofty panelled door, Rogers and Kilpatrick were admitted by an anonymous-looking young woman in a blue tunic who said that they were expected by Mrs Seaforth-Major who was in the drawing-room and would they please not keep her too long.

The room into which they were led – it smelled strongly of a woman's perfume – was large with tall windows and a late Victorian decor. To Rogers's undomesticated eye it looked to be seriously underfurnished. Constance Seaforth-Major was seated on an oatmeal linen-covered sofa with a black ebony walking stick by her side.

Rogers, introducing himself and Kilpatrick, took the pale hand she had offered with a wan smile while asking them to please sit down and be comfortable, and would they care for a coffee, not really listening to their acceptances.

She was a slender small-breasted woman; her age probably about fifty. She looked ill with her pellucidly white skin and one in whom ageing had blemished her high-cheek-boned attractiveness. She wore her lightly greyed tawny-brown hair in a bob, her dark-brown eyes alert and questioning; her mouth showing suffering and not wholly concealing an invalid's understandable irritation with her condition. She was wearing a knee-length mustard-yellow cocktail dress made for a woman half her age and from a different era, and wearing it well. The detective thought that in a different milieu she could well be a woman to be pursued, though not conceivably by himself.

'I'm sorry to have inconvenienced you by our visit,' he said. 'It's concerning your son Edward, as Miss Kilpatrick explained to you.'

'Yes.' She seemed now to be wary, watching his mouth.

'Though Teddy's my stepson, not my son. I married his father, who died seven years ago, and he was his son by a former marriage. Miss Kilpatrick told me that you were enquiring after him.' She paused, widening her eyes at Rogers. 'Are you going to tell me he's dead?' There was a tenseness in the way she said it; its seeming to Rogers to be something she had anticipated.

'Not at all,' Rogers protested, though wondering what the hell he *was* going to tell her. 'We only know he is missing because you reported it at Amborum two years ago. We are interested in his then association with a woman – a quite proper one, naturally – who was to be seen in connection with the death this week of the policeman who was dealing with your enquiry about him.'

'Oh, dear, I remember him, the poor man.' She sounded only offhandedly sorry. 'I spoke to him on two occasions, but he wasn't successful in finding him, was he?' She smiled tight-lipped. 'And I don't think you have either. I would prefer, Mr Rogers, that you told me precisely why you are interested in him. I am not a stupid person to be fobbed off by evasions.'

Rogers exchanged glances with Kilpatrick, then said, 'You are right, of course. I was having a regard to your being his mother as such. There is a possibility that he is connected, possibly innocently, with the commission of a serious offence, and we're anxious to trace his whereabouts.' He was hoping that she wasn't too soft on her stepson.

'I can't help you with that, but I can – I should – tell you about the furniture and my beautiful Bechstein piano, and why I think he has disappeared; why I don't know where he is.' She sounded angrily hurt, tears welling in her eyes. 'I do . . . I really do feel so very much put upon . . .'

'I'm so sorry I'm upsetting you,' Rogers apologized, taken aback at what he had done.

Kilpatrick intervened. 'We would be immensely grateful,' she said, certainly more used to dealing with another woman's emotional outburst than Rogers. 'There really is a seriousness about the business that brings us here.'

'Yes, of course there is and I'll really try not to be silly.' She stared down at her hands, restless on her lap. 'I promise,' she muttered, then speaking to both of them, said, 'In the spring of two years ago when Teddy was back living with me, I was taken ill with a quite unexpected and humiliating complaint and was told that I should be in hospital – a private one, of course – for about two months. Having been told that, and because there was no one else to to help me, no other family but Teddy, I was idiot enough to be persuaded into giving him Power of Attorney. Then...'

Emotion had caused her to bite at her lip, the words to trail off. 'I'm sorry,' she whispered in the waiting silence. 'That was silly of me. I was saying about the Power of Attorney I gave Teddy. I had no possible reason to suppose he would do what he did – not my husband's son whom I had treated as my own in so many ways. He had visited me as much as said he could, the hospital being sixty miles away from here, which wasn't very often for he said he had to be away from home for days at a time doing his courier work.'

She was silent for a time, during which Rogers could hear somebody, probably the woman who had let them in, doing things with china in a remote room.

'When I had been told that I could return home earlier than expected,' she continued, 'the hospital people telephoned and told Teddy, but though he had been warned he wasn't there when I arrived.' Her lips had tightened at that recollection, her growing anger showing. 'It was when I arrived in the hospital's ambulance car and let myself in that I realized what he had done to me. He had taken away – stolen, as it happened – most of my drawing-room's good furniture, my Bechstein piano – that was the cruellest blow – and a few oil paintings. Also, which hurt me even more, my own family's Georgian dining table and chairs, which are irreplaceable. What he had left behind was, I thought, due to my unexpected return.' She was clearly reliving the anger and frustration she had experienced and was being hurt again.

'What could I do!' she seemed to be asking the two silent detectives. 'He was my husband's son. Even though he had been grown up, well into his twenties when his father died ... it wasn't that I was surprised he was so dishonest, but that he lied so much, that he had stolen from me furniture that I had shared with his father.' She was looking down at her twisting fingers again, her eyes hooded. 'I couldn't report it to the police, and the insurance company told me they wouldn't, couldn't, consider a claim until I did so . . . so do you understand?'

'I understand,' Rogers assured her, though in relation to her stepson she had left much to be understood. 'But you did report him missing?'

'That was later,' she told him as if he should have understood, 'when I found my latest bank statements in his room, where they should not have been. I couldn't believe it when I saw that he had withdrawn four thousand pounds from my deposit account and overdrawn my current account by nearly six hundred pounds. I realized then that he really had left me and wouldn't be coming back. The Power of Attorney had only been meant for my domestic and hospital expenses while I was away. He understood that, it had been made quite clear by my solicitor.'

'The Power of Attorney was at Teddy's suggestion?' Rogers asked.

'Yes, it was. At the time I thought there had been some ghastly mistake; that having been in hospital something had happened to Teddy and that I was misinterpreting what had necessarily to be done.' She had sounded vacillating in those few words. 'When that silliness had gone, I knew I would have to see him. After a week when I hadn't heard from him, I took a taxi and reported his disappearance at Amborum police station. That's all. I didn't wish to say anything about the furniture or the money. Teddy would have had it one day anyway; the house and furniture that is. But my Bechstein . . . that was cruel.'

'You saw a detective inspector there?'

'No. A young woman not in uniform. The inspector called on me here a week or so afterwards.'

'He gave you his name?'

'I've forgotten it, I'm afraid. It sounded foreign, but he wasn't and he did show me his card.' She was troubled, looking frail. 'Is that important?'

'I think not. Could you tell us what he wanted?'

'Yes. He wanted to know about Teddy's association with a man and his wife at Amborum whose names I've now forgotten. I had never heard of them and told him so. He also asked what he did for a living and I found that I couldn't tell him about that for he had never mentioned even to me who he was employed by or why he was so irregularly away from work, and so often having to borrow money from me. Personal things like that about which I said I didn't know, and which made me sound a little foolish. Under the circumstances I felt that I should say nothing about the furniture and the money.' She hesitated, then said, 'I hope you don't mind my saying it, but the policeman wasn't a very nice man and I didn't like him.'

'Did he ask about Teddy's knowing or contacting anybody at Amborum? Or Leamings Landing?'

'He asked me if Teddy had associated with those people I mentioned, but I hadn't known and I said so.'

'You said you saw something in his room that suggested he had gone to Amborum?' He raised his eyebrows at her, needing something more than he had been given. There was something about her that made him feel he wasn't being told the truth, or not the whole truth at least.

She hesitated, looking at Kilpatrick and, in effect, answering her. 'It was a newspaper clipping, a Personal Column advertisement in the *Amborum & Saltash Chronicle*, and not in good taste. It was a sort of Wants column called "Couples" or something and Teddy had marked it as if he was going to answer one of them.' She was annoyed. 'I think that it was despicable of him. It was about a woman who said she was from Amborum and wanted to meet a man interested in sailing. And plainly,' she said downputtingly, 'wanting someone with enough money to support her lifestyle and her boat. There were other things which I found quite disgusting. I suppose I can understand him answering it, if he did, because he does have an interest in sailing boats. He has rented them and crewed them, though never owned one. And Amborum, being not all that far away, would be convenient for him.'

'Do you feel that's where your money went?' Rogers asked as gently as he could.

Receiving no reply, though her lips had thinned, he said, 'Would you let me see the clipping, please? And anything associated with it if you'd oblige us.'

She rose and, using her stick, walked not too unsteadily from the room. At least, a standing Rogers thought as his gaze took in his surroundings, the apparently despicable Teddy hadn't taken the vast expanse of expensive-looking carpet as well as the furniture.

When Mrs Seaforth-Major had returned to the sofa and Rogers felt able to sit again, she handed him the closely folded page of a newspaper.

'There was nothing with it?' he asked.

'No, I'm afraid not. That had been in the waste paper basket where I found it.'

Rogers said, 'Excuse me,' and read it. The Personal Column which was called 'Couplings' had an insertion ringed in red pencil and seemed, he thought, to have been written in high excitement:

> Amborum. Attractive slim lady yachtie with own boat; divorced in her 30s, maturely passionate nature and fond of good living, seeks 35/40 gentleman sailing companion for adult fun and games afloat. Must have no ties and be solvent. No landlubbers, please. Reply with photo to Box No. 1217.

Rogers said, 'Ah!' and passed the page to Kilpatrick. To Mrs Seaforth-Major, he said, 'It's the thing today. A bit over-heated, but it's suppose to take the place of the old Lonely Hearts column making for an easy access to whatever these people don't get from their normal social life.' He added sardonically, 'It also provides an opening for criminal deception and villainy.'

She looked sour. 'I think I know what you mean.'

'Might I see Teddy's room, please?' he asked.

She hesitated, then said, 'Please, not now. I've had all his papers and books put in the attic.'

'Have you a photograph of him?'

She flapped a hand in apparent frustration. 'I'm afraid I haven't. I was angry once at something he did so I tore them up. He had been hateful and there were only two anyway, and they were taken years ago.'

'What had he been hateful about?' Rogers asked gently. 'Tell me.'

She bit on her bottom lip, not being very happy. 'There were women, common loud women. He wanted to bring them here . . .' She shook her head. 'No, I don't wish to think about it.'

'Could you describe him for me?'

'Not very well. I'm not very good at that sort of thing, I'm afraid.'

'Try,' he urged. 'Compare him with me if you can.'

'He was about your build,' she said after eyeing his length and breadth, 'though perhaps bigger. His hair is brown and he wears it sometimes down over his collar. Not too much, of course. I think his eyes are a grey colour and he has very good teeth. He isn't exactly handsome, but he is quite persuasive when he wants anything.'

'In speaking to women do you mean?'

'Naturally.' She was suddenly sharp with him. 'Have you finished?'

'Not yet. What was he like as an individual? Emotionally, temperamentally? That sort of thing?'

'He was friendly when he wished to be, very, very bad-tempered when he didn't. He could, from what I'd heard, be violent and hit people. I was – at times – frightened of him. I still am, I suppose.' She suddenly clamped her lips together, shaking her head.

'I think I understand,' Rogers said, now suspecting that he wasn't about to be among the pantheon of those she admired.

Kilpatrick came in then. 'Did you like your stepson at all?' she asked.

Mrs Seaforth-Major looked sharply at her, hesitated, and said, 'Not really. Certainly not since, though I never thought he would do to me what he did.' She frowned. 'I distrusted him in so many ways.'

'Would you tell me in what ways?' Kilpatrick pressed her.

She shook her head, her mouth forming a silent, 'No.'

'Are you frightened of him?' Rogers asked gently.

'I could be,' she said as if reluctant to say it.

Rogers thought he could understand why she hadn't done so many things and he said, 'I'm sure that Miss Kilpatrick will take any steps necessary to ensure that you aren't disturbed or interfered with should he return, though I'm reasonably certain that he will not.'

'He's really not dead then?' There was clearly no anguish in her question, though possibly fear showing in her eyes.

'I don't know. I honestly don't, but I promise you'll be told the outcome of our enquiry.' He smiled to give her confidence, though already there was a possibly unworthy thought in his mind about her. 'Now that we've to go, could I ask who the young woman is who let us in?'

She looked surprised. 'I'm sorry, I thought you would know. She's my private nurse until my illness requires me to return to the hospital. Or not.' She didn't sound too optimistic. 'It's so very much end of the road stuff now you know.'

She had, it appeared, forgotten about the coffee and Rogers was glad. Something much stronger seemed more relevant to the feeling he now had that Edward Seaforth-Major could possibly – though only possibly – have already made his accounting in the next world for his stealing the furniture and money from the rather off-putting woman who had been his stepmother.

26

Rogers was not unduly uplifted by what he had learned from Mrs Seaforth-Major; though he was as intrigued by her possible relationship with her stepson as by his with the Arbitts.

It was still only halfway through the afternoon and no more than a few minutes after leaving Little Salton for the cliff-top road back to Amborum that he said to Kilpatrick, 'I'd like your opinion, Eva, on what might well be a dodgy hypothesis and what you might make of Mrs Seaforth-Major's little effort. For myself, I'd accept the theft of her furniture and what must have been the grievous loss of her Bechstein. What I find less acceptable are her reasons for not putting her Teddy's head on a block. An unfortunate woman, I suppose,' he added as an afterthought, 'with very little to look forward to.'

'I thought her rather clever in some respects,' a possibly sceptical Kilpatrick said from her seat at Rogers's appreciative side. 'I had a probably different view of her and her stepson from you. She was almost certainly concealing a closer relationship with her stepson than she was prepared to admit to us.'

'Feminine intuition?' Rogers asked, respecting it.

'Not, I think,' she said. 'Perhaps a better judge of the vagaries of my own sex.'

'I did have the same impression, if that is what you had,' Rogers agreed, 'but only perhaps. I saw her as a quite attractive woman for her age, having lost a much older husband who had left her in a sort of *in loco parentis* situation with a sexually mature and probably attractive stepson. Possibly you meant that in saying there could have been a closer relationship?' He added, 'Shoot me down in flames if you think I've a dirty mind.'

'I thought it went with the job.' She smiled. 'I believe it could be the reason for her reluctance to make a complaint at the time about a really nasty theft. It'd never be an unlawful incest, certainly, though she might have thought it to be.'

Rogers was pleased – gratified really – to have some confirmation of his thought-to-be-unworthy suspicion. 'She needs only consider the scandal that would bounce around in her social circle should the son of her dead husband blow the whistle on their improper – if it is – relationship.'

Kirkpatrick looked blank for a moment. 'You think it was a factor in his going off?'

'I doubt it, unless he had a later conscience about it, and that's not likely knowing us men.' He smiled. 'For whatever reason, the theft of the furniture must have financed it, and her being in hospital facilitating it.' The road being unusually clear of oncoming traffic, he turned his head to speak directly at Kilpatrick instead of to his windscreen. 'At the moment,' he continued, 'I feel sorry for her. The situation must have been difficult and I can imagine her pride and what she probably thought to be a terrible sin. That and her illness.'

Kilpatrick shook her head. 'She would have had him back at any time he wished, furniture or no furniture.'

Having thought about Constance Seaforth-Major while keeping his eyes on a road far less attractive than the woman at his side, he said, apparently offhandedly, 'The possibility's certainly there that she would, but can we come to an agreement that you're with me in not bringing her possible sexual activities into this investigation? I not only believe they are irrelevant, it may also be unnecessary, for she obviously believes she's dying. And so do I – well, at some time, I imagine,' he amended, which was a safe bet always.

'You interest me,' Kilpatrick said, peering at his profile as if to read in his expression whatever he had meant. 'You think there's more in this about Seaforth-Major than there is on the surface?'

'Yes.' He didn't sound overconfident. 'We could be, only could be, in a wrong body situation. It might be interesting to do a check on him at NIB, and I'll have it done.'

Slowing the car down, he pulled into a lay-by which, he thought, could have been a damn sight more interesting had it not been raining again and had been at night-time with both of them having a less professional purpose in mind. Having parked in the shade of an overhanging tree, he pushed open his door and unharnessed himself, with Kilpatrick doing the same.

Preparing to commit violence against the incoming horse-flies – old adversaries of his – he said, 'It's all a guess, Eva, and I wouldn't put any serious money on it. While we have the well-attested bodies of Poukas and Kathrin Arbitt on the hook, I'm not so sure that we have her husband's. You're surprised?'

'Not awfully,' she said, amused. 'An advertisement offering a sexual romp being answered by a rather questionable character who then disappears prior to the violent deaths of two other characters concerned with it, does rather suggest the disappearance might be fraught. You have other reasons?'

'Foggy ones, like, for example, Mrs Arbitt's apparently sole say so that the probably well-corrupted body she was shown was that of her husband, by whose death she stood to be paid sickening amounts of insurance money. Do we need another motive?'

He smiled at her, having to admit that she was a damned good listener and so interestingly attractive in her dark-green linen skirt and jacket. 'Seaforth-Major,' he said, 'dishonest as he must be, though apparently singularly trusting, could have been the sacrificial lamb offered up on the altar of the Arbitts' greed.' He grimaced. 'A bit flowery that, but I'm certain that one of the Arbitts – I'm betting heavily on Mrs Arbitt – put the advertisement in the "Couplings" column of your local rag; a reason you might think for harbouring the boat at Amborum in the first place. You'll have that checked for me, will you?'

'Immediately we've finished here,' she told him. 'Convince me about the undead Arbitt.'

'Firstly – and it's mostly supposition – he was in serious financial trouble with his chandlery store and needing money, probably by the bucketful. His wife would know that and, having spoken to her as a potential witness when she lied to me, I found her most uncooperative and arrogant. I've no doubt that she would be in on it as an accomplice if not being the actual instigator. I mean, murder seems to be a relatively trifling crime these times, doesn't it? So, she and her husband set up the entrapment of any man answering her advertisement found likely, I imagine, to be a suitable corpse.'

'That sounds to me quite cold-blooded,' Kilpatrick said. 'Terribly so.'

'So it is and it fits. Though I doubt they would have worried themselves sick about it.' Rogers was at his most sardonic. 'I assume they rented the harbourage at Amborum to use the boat as an accommodation address – Mrs Arbitt was, you told me, definitely involved there – necessary for receiving any answers to the advertisement in the *Chronicle*. Taking the wording of the "Couplings" entry, it did represent a calculated and ruthless intent to murder some unfortunate who wanted his share of adult fun and games afloat. That sort of thing would certainly have its attractions,' he mused. 'And, before I let it pass me by, there is a something very pertinent about how the substitution of an intended body was to be done?'

Kilpatrick smiled wryly at that, saying, 'So we're back to thinking where might Mrs Seaforth-Major's "Teddy" be, if anywhere?' It was a statement, not a question.

'At the moment I am. Not too frantically, but it's an angle, the only one. I admit that the *modus operandi* of the reeling in and the killing of Seaforth-Major doesn't quite register, other than that he was possibly chosen because he was similar in age and appearance to the male Arbitt who, as a corpse, would be a valuable commodity, but as a standing up, living and breathing body, worth nothing. And the corpse, of course, would be identified by Mrs Arbitt as that of her late much-loved husband, and God only knows how she got away with it as she did.' He smiled cheerfully, if not all that convincingly, meeting again the cool and somewhat unsettling stare of Kilpatrick's brown eyes. 'Of course,' he said, 'that's not the whole of it.'

'No,' she told him pleasantly – he thought warmly, 'it does seem a little incomplete. There's the late ex-Detective Inspector Poukas being on ice in your mortuary, and yours to worry about.'

'Yes, though not too much. It's fairly obvious he'd ferreted out something about Arbitt's supposed death and was putting the bite on Mrs Arbitt. You can imagine how she felt when this nosy interfering detective inspector started digging into what was going on in the Arbitt ménage. She'd be terrified of any mere hint about her husband's non-death and more so about what would have been the murder of Seaforth-Major. And if we do assume an undead Arbitt, then he couldn't show his face anywhere near Amborum or Leamings Landing to do much about Poukas's interference, though the Farquharson Club would give him an opportunity later on. And that's when, I feel, that Mrs Arbitt, frightened of any disclosure, possibly moved her money away from wherever it had been and fled, changing her name to Rachel Hurt.'

'And you are suggesting by implication that Arbitt eventually killed both Poukas and his own wife?'

'Why not? It's been done a million times before. You know how they died. And in my bailiwick, too. I'm a great believer in the thought that there's never ever enough money for more than one.' He pulled down the corners of his mouth. 'There's a further suggestion, naturally, but not the time.'

He leaned forward to switch on the ignition, then drew back. 'I'm thinking now in terms of your coroner or your chief constable getting an order for the exhumation of whoever's buried under the name of Chadwick Arbitt. I need it, Eva, before I can go any further. And really in a hurry.'

'I'll try,' she said, not so concerned as he was. 'You want me to jump on the coroner's face presumably?'

'Or your chief constable's.' He was almost apologetic. 'I know I'm pushing you, but could you first have someone see the Longstreet family; their son identified the body of Mrs Arbitt who's his aunt by marriage, but he's now somewhere in Spain. Mrs Longstreet is Arbitt's sister, so could she or her husband be asked if they would identify, or try to, a disinterred body? It's a lot to ask them, but with their son on holiday...'

'I'll see them myself,' Kilpatrick promised, 'though I don't hold out much hope of getting your exhumation order for days, even if we can get one. You haven't much evidence for it, have you?'

'You mean that I don't have much of a case for it, and you're right. I can but try.' He switched on the ignition. 'And would you detail one of your staff to dig out the editor of the *Chronicle* and have him hand over the name of the fair yachtie wanting a sea-going and solvent lover. Without that,' he exaggerated, 'I've nothing.'

Getting into gear and edging the car back into the road, he thought rather wryly that he could probably suffer quite well with being the casual lover of Kilpatrick as a chief constable. Given half a chance, of course, and not being too final about parting from his beloved Angharad.

27

Rogers, at his desk and writing up his notes on Constance Seaforth-Major and her thieving stepson, had only just escaped from the Assistant Chief Constable who had, unusually, demanded an in-depth report on what had been going on, not quite under his nose, but near enough.

Understandably irritated, the part of Rogers's mind not engaged with Mrs Seaforth-Major was now casting itself back on the unloading of his incautious theory of the two Arbitts' conspiracy to murder on to Kilpatrick. Not having known the male Arbitt, it was difficult to picture him as a man closely concerned with the execution of a murder, yet having to accept the logic of what the two had done in order to defraud an insurance company. It was the gruesome garrotting of Arbitt's own wife that stuck in Rogers's throat. Killing a blackmailing Poukas, driven by necessity, was understandable; but not his wife, his partner in the crime. It worried him because he couldn't fit his thinking, his theory of the original murder, into an acceptable pattern.

He was experienced enough in human self-deception to know that theory was often a word used for making a speculative guess at something and, unless bottle-brained, rarely expecting it to be right.

There now seemed a lack of feasibility in what he had unloaded on to Kilpatrick. It unsettled his confidence so much that he decided to defer his asking for an Exhumation Order – a legally awkward instrument to obtain at any time – and to telephone the Amborum Divisional Headquarters to speak to Kilpatrick. She was, predictably, out and assumed to be unobtainable, though she would be asked to call him when she had returned; a familiar situation when somebody was wanted urgently.

He supposed with a kind of sick humour that whatever disaster might happen, it would be preferable to falling under a bus; but only just. The late afternoon's sun shining through his windows seemed then of little comfort.

Finishing his notes while waiting for Kilpatrick to call, he took the few routine reports from his departed investigative team from his in-tray and began dourly to read them. One from the overly potent Hagbourne prompted Rogers to tell himself in the stirring of his optimism that he must try and get Hagbourne a peerage, a knighthood or something for what he had put down in black and white for his senior's pleasure.

It was a very short report, submitted in response to Rogers's own request, stating that the man Peter Toplis's recorded postal address had been given as the Hotel Imperial at Scarborough, the hotel at which Mrs Arbitt, using her Rachel Hurt alias, had stayed prior to her moving to the Farquharson Leisure Club.

That was it for Rogers though, his elation spent, when he thought about it logically. Toplis, having stayed at the same hotel as Rachel Hurt – as she was – need not signify anything more than a coincidence. But, it was a connection of sorts, when each also admitted to a Farquharson Club membership. Accepting that Toplis might be the killer of Poukas at least, it might also be accepted that he had acted the horrified bystander and, as such, the only man with a seemingly foolproof reason for being late for breakfast. It couldn't, and didn't, escape his notice that Toplis might be either the supposedly dead Arbitt, the missing Seaforth-Major or just himself.

If I only knew for certain, he growled to himself, trying to fit Seaforth-Major into an Amborum grave and wondering should he not leave the exhumation business active in Kilpatrick's hands.

Leafing quickly through the remaining few papers, he was informed by a fax from NIB that Edward John Seaforth-Major of the address given had a record of convictions for Theft (fined £50); Assault Occasioning Actual Bodily Harm (two months' imprisonment); Demanding Money by Menaces (three years' imprisonment) and Obtaining Money by a False Pretence (six months' imprisonment). There were no unserved warrants or unexecuted summonses. It fitted, Rogers thought.

Uncradling his telephone receiver, he put a call through to Farquharson House, asking for Charles Jarvis. 'Charles,' he said, hoping that he might somehow be back in good odour with him, 'I've an important development in our investigation. I can't name names, but would you call me back hotfoot with a checklist of all members at present in residence?'

'Bloody hell, old chap,' Jarvis got out after what sounded like a dismaying pause. 'I thought we'd lost you. Is this necessary?'

'So necessary and fraught that your giving it to me over the phone may avoid my having to call on you personally for it. So much more police visibility, Charles, for you are likely to have our murderer – well, the presumed murderer – still with you.'

'But you'll have to come here if he is. He is a he, I imagine? Can't you give me his name?' Jarvis had little of his usual suavity.

'No. Call me back with the list, there's a good chap. We can do all this on the quiet, without fuss, if you'll cooperate.'

'I'll call you back.' That hadn't been agreed too happily.

'Within minutes, and I'd be grateful.' Rogers replaced the receiver, now hoping that Kilpatrick would call and let him know the best or the worst, should he be able to recognize the difference between either.

He needed time now, and it was moving faster than he wanted it. Time to get Toplis identified, if he actually was Toplis, and he, Rogers, wasn't found to be wholly brainless about it.

Sitting there for long silent minutes and sucking at his empty pipe – he didn't believe that it could be construed as a disciplinary offence – he was delivered from too much unfavourable introspection by the ringing of his telephone. It was Jarvis – probably doing a light sweating – with his list of the Club's members which he read out to him. Toplis's name was unexpectedly among them, for Rogers had assumed in a fatalistic way that he would have decamped.

'Is there a chance of any of them leaving later today, Charles?' he asked.

'No,' Jarvis told him glumly. 'They'd have been gone after breakfast. So what's happening?' he demanded.

'As he's still with you, nothing. So not a word outside your office if you want him removed from the premises without loud words and an unpleasant scene.' He replaced the receiver without elation, an emotion he was fairly certain he wasn't to experience.

When the telephone rang again, he knew who it would be and was grateful. 'Rogers here,' he said, going a mite soft inside on hearing Kilpatrick's voice.

'George,' she said, 'I've been told you wanted urgent words. Is there trouble?'

'There could be. Have you done anything about the exhumation thing?'

'No. There's no need.' She waited a moment. 'Have you ever had a house fall on you?' She was, he thought, somehow unemotional.

'If I have it's escaped my notice.' Ominous now, but he waited.

'You're about to, though it's not all bad. Mrs Longstreet, née Arbitt, saw her dead brother in his coffin at the undertakers the day before he was buried in the municipal cemetery. No doubts. No chance of an error. No nothing but a straightforward and uncomplicated woman wanting to say goodbye to her brother estranged from his family. Chadwick Arbitt is dead and buried, George, with all our ponderings gone agley.'

There was relief in Rogers; the falling house hadn't been very big. 'I owe you, Eve. She didn't think you mad about the identification business?'

'No reason, George. She'd heard from her son about the death of Mrs Arbitt and it all came out. She had had her brother's death nagging at her since he was hauled out of Blacktoad Bay. He had been, she let me know, dominated by his second wife and would do almost anything merely to please her. Needless to say, she didn't like her, which is why she chose not to attend the funeral. A brother's blood being thicker than the bad blood of a family's hostility, she chose to have a last goodbye look at him the day before without any interference.'

He could almost hear that she was smiling when she continued, 'I had accepted by then that you mightn't still wish me to jump on our poor coroner's face or alienate myself from my own chief constable over such a trifle as an Exhumation Order.'

'My many thanks, Eva,' he told her. 'I'd already sprinkled my head with ashes. Still, dimmish as I seem to have been, I had anticipated something like that. I'm now almost convinced I have Seaforth-Major here in my own backyard in the guise of a character called Toplis. Only *almost* convinced, for he's the man who'd said he had heard Poukas being killed. And if you work that out, so he would have in a quite different sense.'

Telling her about Toplis in more detail, he then said, 'I want to arrange some sort of a confrontation, an identification, this evening, which I'd like you to attend if you would.' He smiled, knowing she would sense it. 'Can I persuade you to see Mrs Seaforth-Major again and find out if she's in the mood to be brought here to identify her missing stepson who is believed – only believed – to be here; having been concerned in a most serious crime. Not to push it too hard, Eva, but we do need her identification of him. Possibly you could imply that we aren't all that interested in other people's sexual habits. Somehow,' he added, knowing how damned difficult that could be.

'I'll do just that,' Kilpatrick promised ironically. 'Have faith. Vengeance is a remarkably potent weapon.'

'Irrespective,' he said, 'when you are speaking to her, ask her if her Teddy was ever associating with a Peter Toplis. Or just knew of him. It's a shot in the dark, no more.'

'It will be done instanter,' she promised, 'but before, I've the result of the *Chronicle* enquiry. The ad was entered in the name of Kathrin Arbitt – surprise! surprise! – her address being given as care of the Amborum harbour-master. There were three replies, all sent off to her by post. You're happy with that?'

'Delighted,' he said, hitting something of a high. 'Call me after you've seen Mrs Seaforth-Major, will you?'

'Will do.' She paused, then said, 'George?' with an odd warm softness in her voice.

'There's more?' he asked, wondering what was coming.

After another pause, during which he thought he had lost her, she said almost crisply, 'Sorry about that. It was something ... nothing actually. It'll keep.'

Replacing his receiver, he did a five-second think about unfathomable women in the mass before returning to the presently more pressing problem of Seaforth-Major.

28

While Rogers was calling Farquharson House at fifteen-minute intervals for an elusive Jarvis, the offices in his Headquarter's building were echoing a growing one-by-one emptiness until he felt isolated from humankind. At six-thirty, with the sun midway to sinking into the coming darkness, he had Jarvis at the other end of his line.

'Charles,' he said, 'what time is your evening meal? I've a need to know.'

'For God's sake!' Jarvis didn't sound too happy. 'You're not eating with us, are you? They'll have seen you here before and know there's something nasty on the go.' He made a mildish groaning sound. 'You'll definitely have me skewered by Head Office.'

'Come off it, Charles. We don't want to have your place labelled as a sort of sanctuary for the murderously inclined do we?' Rogers was trying to comfort him. 'It'll all be painless, and there'll be a lady with us. Would you have, more or less, a full house?'

'All but two ladies have indicated their intention of requiring a dinner. It's the custom on our Guest Night, for then we know exactly how to cater for the most prominent meal of the day.' Jarvis didn't sound any happier. 'So what is it that you're hoping to do?'

'To intercept the target – I still can't name him for you – between his room and the restaurant, then use your office or Mrs Duval's for his interrogation. I'll give you his name at the start of the exercise so that you can advise where we can intercept.'

There was silence, but not so much that Rogers needed to worry. 'I'm relying on you, though God only knows why,' Jarvis said at last.

'And so you may, up to the point of human fallibility. There'll be no uniform bodies on show and we'll dress in keeping with your evening's activities. We shan't be obtrusive.' Rogers was trying to placate him. 'And we will almost certainly be out of your hair after tonight.'

'It all sounds so bloody ghastly.' Jarvis didn't sound as if wholly appeased. 'Still, if I have to . . .'

'You don't *have* to do anything I've asked,' Rogers pointed out. 'But there is an alternative if I'm forced to it – you know, the full panoply of the law and all that – and you wouldn't like it one bit.'

When the unfortunate Jarvis made silence his answer, Rogers asked, 'What time does the meal start, Charles? Not that I shall be at it or near it, though I must be at a point of interception, chosen by you, where I am most likely to meet with my target.'

When he had finished with an apparently much more amicable Jarvis, he was told by a switchboard operator that a Detective Inspector Kilpatrick – a female – from Amborum had been calling for him.

'Eva,' he said when connected, 'I'm sorry. I've been tying up with Charles Jarvis for later this evening.' Speaking to her even on professional matters, gave him a *frisson* of an earthly need, his conscience making it rather despicable so soon after Nancy Duval.

'A hit,' she told him, 'but Mrs Seaforth-Major first. Though she'd been rather shaken by our earlier visit, she's not at all antagonistic and she needed no persuading to help put the finger on her Teddy, if it be he on whom we have our eye. After I had assured her that nothing of a domestic nature would be exposed as public information, she agreed to attend at Farquharson House to identify Teddy from a safe distance, with no possibility of a communication between them. I am to be her escort and to provide suitable transport. Justice is otherwise being done about the stolen money and furniture, and I have promised to try and locate the Bechstein piano. She's a hard woman when roused, George, and he won't now be getting the house or its contents or any spare cash after she has seen her solicitor...' She stopped abruptly, then asked, 'Are you still there, George? I thought I heard your door being closed.'

'The last man but me leaving the premises,' he said, 'and I was wishing you were here with me.'

'That's interesting,' she said obliquely. 'I don't much like the telephone either. I was going to say that Mrs Seaforth-Major did rather reinforce our belief that she and her stepson were, or had been, lovers. It was rather pathetic actually, for she's probably aware that there's nothing much after him, only more hospital and probably death. She's well rid of him.'

'He doesn't deserve her, the bastard.' Rogers meant it, a contemptuous dislike of the man rising in him. 'I'm pleased you've persuaded her. You've added to the debt I already owe you. What was the hit you hinted at? Not a painful one I hope?'

'The hit's for your friend Toplis.' She was clearly teasing him. 'Mrs Seaforth-Major was quite forthcoming in saying that yes, she knew of a Mr Peter Toplis. He was a second or third cousin of Teddy's – one of the family anyway – and had not been heard of for over three years. Teddy had known him quite well in the past – admiring him tremendously, it appears – when he was living somewhere in France, but had since lost touch. She knew from what he had told her that Mr Toplis had once served with the French Foreign Legion. She couldn't say whether or no her stepson had seen him lately, though she thought not. She had never met this Toplis man, even should he actually exist.'

Rogers had heard this with some disquiet, for it required some mindmaking-up from him. 'She's rather confused the issue, Eva,' he said, 'though I'm still rather stuck with Seaforth-Major for the chop. If I've ever seen a man who wasn't the physical product of five years with the Foreign Legion, it was the Toplis I have in my own backyard. However, good for you, and I'm indebted. Is there anything more?'

'Nothing that won't keep.'

'Meet me here at seven-thirty with the lady, would you?' he asked. 'My finger's on the trigger; and I hope the gun's not loaded with a blank.'

Being once more alone in the acreage of silence from which people with homes to go back to had fled, he thought he might fine-tune his thinking with the smoking of his pipe. The last pipe, he convinced himself, for he had bought a packet of slim panatella cigars – to which Jarvis had introduced him – to pacify his palate during his desertion of it. Filling the pipe with the last charge of the aromatic tobacco he used, he was already brooding not wholly about the job in hand, but also about the unfairly attractive and beguiling Eva Kilpatrick, a future lady chief constable if ever there was one.

29

The second-floor corridor of Farquharson House, heavily carpeted and lined each side with head-high Spanish Dagger palms, gave access through a further flight of stairs to the third-floor suites of rooms. From the corridor's tall windows could be seen the setting sun, its fiery crimson reflected from the glass panes of the looming, almost omnipresent, crystal dome.

Rogers, standing with Kilpatrick at one of the opened windows, and with a late hour deference to her possible sensitivity to his pipe, was smoking a now appreciated panatella cigar, blowing its smoke to join the warm outside air. They were partly screened from an approaching view by the window's heavy blue drapes and a neighbouring palm.

Rogers, who wore a white dinner jacket and matching bow-tie – *de rigueur* on the club's guest night – and Kilpatrick, in an all-cream evening dress and most agreeably splendid, were both looking out over the dome to the spectacular reddening sea and talking. A plain-clothes WPS and Mrs Seaforth-Major – sitting palely in a chair – were waiting near the far end of the corridor, both inconspicuous behind a palm. The corridor, used by the members leaving their rooms, had a plain-clothes PC, at both ends, each bulky in a dark suit and both apparently absorbed in viewing the paintings on the walls.

Rogers had been discussing the investigation with Kilpatrick, making up for time lost and saying, 'It isn't so often that we can be concerned with the deaths of three people dying so brutally and having no particular sympathy for any of them.' He tapped cigar ash on to the soil of the potted plant; a spiky dangerous thing, he thought. 'I quote, I think,' he said. '"All are gathered unto the dust by the greed that killeth them." And one to come I hope. Not, of course, necessarily dead.'

'And not too sure of who he is?' Kilpatrick commented. She was wearing a most engaging perfume, a perfume that Rogers found dizzying and much too close to him on what was a serious investigation.

'I don't think it would astonish me too much should we find ourselves dealing with the real Peter Toplis.' He shook his head. 'No, that's idiotic. My instinct, my professional opinion, tells me that's too far-fetched.'

'The big money's on Seaforth-Major then? As mine is.' Kilpatrick had an unsettling way of holding his gaze intensely as though trying to fathom what lay behind it.

'There's something I meant . . . damn!' He broke off, recognizing the figure of Toplis turning the corner leading into the corridor. Alone and wearing a blue dinner jacket with dark trousers, he had seen and recognized Rogers almost at the same time and, though there had been a momentary jerk in his walk, he came on as if oblivious of the detective's presence. From the edge of his vision, Rogers had seen the signal of agreed identification from the WPS with Mrs Seaforth-Major.

Rogers stepped forward into his path, Toplis's expression showing a sort of frowning recognition as he was forced to stop. 'Do you mind?' he said, not unpleasantly. 'I'm about to eat and this isn't the time for whatever it is you want.'

'It's an explanation about your identity I need; your use of the name Toplis,' Rogers told him unsmilingly.

There was nothing in Toplis's face to give encouragement to the detective as he stiffened and said, 'I don't believe I can help you. If you believe I can, and I don't, see me later. So damn well...'

Over Rogers's shoulder he had seen Constance Seaforth-Major, now exposed in her chair, as she stared at him from the end of the corridor. Momentarily only disconcerted, then recovering, he said, 'I'm in error it seems, but keep that bloody woman away from me.'

'Mr Jarvis's office is a suitable place for an explanation,' Rogers said, keeping a careful eye on him as they were joined by Kilpatrick. 'I'm sure we'll come to some understanding about what you've been doing.'

Toplis's attitude changed surprisingly to a strained cordiality, though his pale-grey eyes remained cold. 'You're a little severe on a man, superintendent,' he said. 'I've a lady friend here and it's not unknown for a man to try and impress one. Forgive me if I've misled either of you.' He made a small bow, almost mockingly, to Kilpatrick. 'I shall be pleased to join you if it will help.'

He walked between the two detectives along the corridor and down the flight of stairs to Jarvis's office, more like a stiffly correct host than a man walking into trouble. Rogers was feeling uneasy about the curiously unlikeable man who had such an air of confidence about him.

Inside the office, flushed red from the sun through the three tall windows, Rogers asked Toplis to take a chair in front of the large mahogany desk; Kilpatrick with her notebook and pen to sit next to Rogers who intended to use Jarvis's leather-trimmed executive chair. The two duty PCs had followed Rogers who had already detailed one of them to remain outside the office door as a sort of guardian of the gate.

With the contained air in the office companionably scented with the ghost of Jarvis's secretly smoked cigars, Rogers sat and without speaking took in again what he could gauge of the Toplis – or Seaforth-Major – persona, already on record as having been three times imprisoned for criminal offences. He saw a man of strong fleshly appetites, possibly possessing a gluttony in both food and sex, with much that was shifty in him. Possibly bombastic too, were he allowed to get away with it. Now he seemed to have believed he had taken the measure of Rogers and looked geared to self-assurance.

'You are not under arrest,' Rogers told him, 'though I'm afraid you won't be allowed to leave until you can give me a more satisfactory reason than you've done so far for taking over another man's name; even taking for your own use his service in the French Foreign Legion.' He locked his steady regard on the man. 'Do you confirm that you know we are also investigating the deaths of John Ward – you've first-hand knowledge of that, of course – and of Mrs Rachel Hurt whom you would know?'

Toplis had creased his forehead in puzzlement at what was being said. 'All that's common knowledge here,' he said, 'but what the devil is it to do with me other than that I am a witness to what I heard happening to that man Ward and no more? And little thanks I'm getting for that now.'

Rogers smiled, not a very comfortable smile for Toplis, for he now had the small item of information he needed. 'I'm reasonably satisfied that you haven't committed a serious offence in calling yourself Toplis – using the name of a probably dead man – though your identification by your stepmother does confirm your being the former Edward Seaforth-Major of the Priory, Little Salton.'

'I know all that,' Toplis said testily, 'and I shall go on using the name I've chosen as my own. You know, or you should know, that it's quite legal under certain conditions and you've no right to detain me. I want to go now.'

'No,' Rogers said, flatly refusing. 'Not yet. There's a formality to these interviews which I'm required to observe. Before I question you further, I'm to tell you that you don't have to say anything unless you wish to do so, but it may harm your defence in any hearing or trial which may ensue if you do not mention when questioned something which you may later rely on in court for your defence. Further, anything that you do say may now be given in evidence.'

Toplis had shaken his head and Rogers, coldly amiable towards him, thought irritably for the umpteenth time how the legal caution was a certain way of stopping dead in its tracks any wish that a suspect, even an uptight and arrogant one like Toplis, might have to say something he really wanted to.

'Could we start way back,' Rogers said, 'when you left your home in such a manner that your stepmother reported you as a missing person to the Amborum police?'

Toplis almost sneered at him. 'I shall tell you exactly what I choose to. Are you going to bring her in to damn me, as she would?'

'I wasn't, but should I?'

'No you shouldn't, but will you get on with it. I've a lady waiting for me in the restaurant.'

'You may forget that, I'm afraid,' Rogers told him. 'I asked you about your stepmother reporting you missing.'

'I just left, that's all; not intending to go back either. Do you want to know why?' He was arrogant now, obviously disdainful of Rogers's ability to get any information from him other than what he chose to give. When the detective merely stared disquietingly at him, he said, 'The silly old bitch wanted me to sleep with her. To take father's place. She wouldn't take no for an answer. It was frankly disgusting, so while she was in hospital I took off, not intending to go back.'

'Together with a load of furniture and her piano, despite what you infer to be the improper sexual advances,' Rogers reminded him, regarding him with unconcealed contempt.

'No comment. Ask her who she's left it to. And who said I could have it anyway.' He looked at Kilpatrick, then back at Rogers. 'The lady's taking notes. Is she your shorthand typist?' he asked insolently.

'Miss Kilpatrick is a detective superintendent from Amborum and is associated with me in this investigation,' Rogers said coldly. 'Your stepmother found a news cutting from the Amborum *Chronicle* in your room after you'd left. Did you find the lady agreeable in handing out the adult fun and games she promised?'

'She could have been, though I didn't follow it up,' he denied resentfully. 'In any case, I wasn't the only one.'

Rogers's eyebrows lifted. 'No, you weren't. But how would you know that?'

Toplis was obviously casting about for an answer and not finding one. 'I just knew,' he admitted lamely.

As if he hadn't answered at all, Rogers said, 'I know you answered the "Couplings" advertisement, and from that it appears you met Mrs Kathrin Arbitt, an alleged divorcee, and stayed with her on her boat *Poppaea II*, moored at Amborum.' He added, as if pained, 'Please don't lie to me, Mr Toplis. It does you little credit.'

'And I don't need you to tell me that; or to discuss my private life with policemen,' he almost snarled.

The sun had moved away from colouring the room its dying red and Rogers switched on the desk's equipoise lamp. Satisfied with the way the interrogation was going, he said, 'None of us do, but sometimes we have to. Particularly we do if it's already known and proveable. By Amborum's harbour-master for example, who must know.'

'I don't have to tell you. You said so yourself.'

'That was, in a way, against any wish you might have for incriminating yourself.' Rogers was forcing him to justify, if he could, his innocence. He now found himself able to see this man as Peter Toplis; yet also in a parallel sense as Constance Seaforth-Major's thievish Teddy.

'Shall we start again,' he said, 'in accepting that it's not yet a criminal offence for a man and a woman to engage in casual sex?'

'Two weeks,' Toplis said reluctantly, 'and might we skip the details?'

'Why such a short time?'

'We decided we didn't have the same ideas about what were fun and games.' Toplis glanced at the silent Kilpatrick. 'We were incompatible if I can put it that way.'

'And that ended the relationship?' When there was no response to that, he said, 'Before you left, you did some sailing with her?'

There was a short thinking pause before he said, 'Once or twice. Only locally and not overnight.'

'Locally, such as Blacktoad Bay?'

There were a few seconds of unspeaking silence until a

suddenly tight-faced Toplis wagged his head and jerked out, 'I've never heard of the place. Why?'

'Leave it,' Rogers said. 'How well did you get to know Mrs Arbitt? She was divorced, she said, and few women can resist saying what a miserable miscarriage of justice the cast-off husband was.'

Toplis was clearly becoming unsettled and, with it, he had a hard edge of anger. 'For Christ's sake, man,' he almost shouted, 'why the hell do you keep on about the bloody woman! I don't give a damn for her or her husband.'

Rogers was happy, thinking he now had what he wanted. 'There's no husband now, I'm told. He was drowned or burned to death while sailing the *Poppaea II* we were talking about; after you'd said you had left his wife. Odd,' he said thoughtfully, 'when she so specifically said she had divorced him. And then there was the business of the life insurance. Three-quarters of a million pounds, wasn't it?' He tried to look baffled with it all. 'You'd not heard about it?'

'I might have. It was a long time ago and I'd left the place.'

'I can understand that, I really can.' Rogers cocked his head sideways; staring, always staring with a hardness his words belied. 'Did you go back to your stepmother at Little Salton?'

There was an apparent inner perturbation in Toplis and he must by now have been hating the sight of the interfering and probing detective. 'No, I didn't,' he rasped angrily. 'Where I went is none of your business.'

Rogers raised the hand of peace to him. 'I apologize,' he said. 'I really shouldn't get too personal about the way you live your life. Let me ask you again about the man Ward you heard being killed below Butters Rock, a man who's believed to have been associating with the lady member, Mrs Hurt, who was strangled to death the same day. You were told his name was Ward, I believe? I mean, you didn't know him beforehand or anything like that?' Rogers tried to look guileless.

'I didn't know,' Toplis said reluctantly.

Rogers was reading the man; an unintelligent man, he considered, of surface bombast and living with an inner funk. 'While you were at Amborum with your Kathrin Arbitt, had you any reason – not necessarily blameworthy – to have any dealings, however briefly or casually, with a Detective Inspector Poukas?'

'What do you mean? What are you getting at?' Toplis managed to get out, visibly shaken.

Rogers look perplexed. 'You surprise me, Mr Toplis; you honestly do. Inspector Poukas was investigating your being missing from home – you remember your stepmother reporting you being missing? – and had in fact compiled a file about you.' He smiled companionably at him. 'Doesn't that ring a bell with you?'

'Not in the slightest and I don't know what you're getting at.'

'I'm trying to get at the truth, Mr Toplis,' Rogers said mildly. 'Inspector Poukas was also known to be investigating the activities of both Mr and Mrs Arbitt, possibly even while you were having those adult fun and games with Mrs Arbitt, presumably without her husband knowing. Or did he?' He shrugged, letting it go. 'There's a police report about it somewhere,' he equivocated, looking hard at a perceptibly worried Toplis. 'The dead man, the murdered man I should say, was in fact this Inspector Poukas you could have met or even heard of.' He frowned his apparent perplexity, really pointing his inquisitorial nose at him now. 'That's a strange coincidence that you should be so near him when he was killed, eh? Aren't you surprised?'

'It's – it's bloody nonsense,' Toplis managed to get out, his face a dull red as if still flushed by the departed sun. He half-rose in his chair. 'I've never heard of the man and I'm bloody well going.'

'Sit down,' Rogers said sharply, waiting while Toplis sank slowly back in his chair. 'It was only a question, not an accusation. The body you saw was that of the same Poukas we are talking about, apparently doing an undercover job for himself after he'd retired from the force. Odd that, Mr Toplis, don't you think? Of all the people it could have been, it had to be you – somebody he'd been making enquiries about a couple of years earlier – that had heard him being murdered.'

Toplis, not answering, was staring with a deep hostility at the detective, his clenched fists with their restless fingers, held lying on the desk.

'I suppose it'll all come out in the wash,' Rogers said to nobody in particular; then to Toplis, almost cheerfully, 'Do you know what I think?'

Toplis mouthed words soundlessly, clearly something ugly.

'You're probably right,' Rogers agreed, 'with whatever it was you said. I think Ward – or Poukas, your inspector as he was – came to this club to blackmail a woman – it seems to have been the late Mrs Hurt – over the death of Mr Arbitt and the unlawful – well, criminal – insurance pay-out.' He let that rest with Toplis for the moment, then said deliberately, 'You'd have known Mrs Hurt as a fellow club member, of course? You'd have seen her about the place over the past months you've been here; been told that she'd been murdered here. Yes?'

'Everybody knows. Not just me.' The words seemed to be sticking in his throat.

Rogers put on an expression of deep perplexity, staring even more intently at the shaken Toplis. 'Mrs Hurt has been officially identified as the Kathrin Arbitt with whom you've admitted having been closely associated, not only in a two weeks' fun and games romp, but also as a guest at the Hotel Imperial at Scarborough and, without doubt, here at Farquharson House.' He hardened his voice accusingly. 'Despite that, not once have you said at my specific mention of her, *Yes, I know Mrs Hurt; of course I do. I knew her as Kathrin Arbitt.* You knew her at Amborum, knew her in the biblical sense too, and therefore you would have really known her intimately – for God Almighty's sake! – as Rachel Hurt here.'

'I don't want to listen to you.' That had been barely understandable for Toplis appeared to be losing his grip on his thinking. Rogers thought of him as a misfit Neanderthal man, about to react to his baiting with savagery.

'I want to ask how you and Mrs Arbitt came to a decision to kill her husband when, as I see it, you were supposed to be the victim. Had you persuaded her . . . ?'

Toplis had risen from his chair, giving Rogers a brief glimpse of mad eyes, a mouth opened pink and white-toothed in a senseless yell as he grabbed at the underside of the desk's surface, lifting it with a wild strength that slammed it solidly into the chairs occupied by Rogers and Kilpatrick. Rogers felt the pain of its contact with his legs, the collision of the falling desk lamp against the side of his head and then, even as he heard Kilpatrick cry out, the back of his head thumping into the carpet.

Dazed and confused and trapped beneath the heavy desk in the semi-darkness, he wanted to swear vilely in his terrible anger, then hearing a man's voice crying out, the banging of a heavy door and, he thought, the sound of running footfalls.

He turned his head to check on Kilpatrick. She was a virtual shadow looking at him, trapped with him, her face pale as though anguished at what had happened with, somewhere outside the office, the background of a loudly shouting voice.

He smiled an unseen smile at her to show that this was a nothing much. 'You're all right, Eva?' he asked.

'I think so.' She sounded shaken. 'Nothing broken, though it hurts. Does this happen often with you?'

'Only on Thursdays,' he grunted, trying to release himself, not helped by a small warm hand feeling for his, though incredibly uplifted by it. 'I'm sorry you've been caught up in it. The bloody man's mad.'

The room lights were suddenly switched on and the anxious face of Elkins, the PC guardian of the door, showing a bloody nose, appeared over the upturned desk. 'You're OK?' he asked, then, seemingly effortlessly except for a grunt, lifted and toppled the desk back on its legs.

Hauling himself to his feet, Rogers said, 'Where is he? Where's the mad sod gone?'

'I'm sorry, sir.' Elkins was wiping blood from his nose and face with a handkerchief already crimson with it. 'He smashed me in the face before I knew he was coming. The door . . .'

'Him,' Rogers cut him off. 'Where's he gone?'

'The corridor, sir. I think he was stopped there.'

'I damn well hope so,' he said as he limped out into the corridor, crocked, he thought, at the knee. 'That's what we're here for. Look after Miss Kilpatrick, will you.'

In a corridor empty of visible life but for an obviously distressed Mrs Seaforth-Major and her accompanying WPS, he had a rear view of PC Clement hanging out over the sill of one of the open windows, talking to somebody outside who had to be Toplis. There was nobody else – but bloody hell-fire, he swore in his fury, we must have aroused the whole goddamned building and he's done a jump on me. He thought that his swearing was doing his crocked knee some good, but nothing else.

He clapped a heavy hand on the massive Clement's shoulder, moving him aside and thrusting himself out to see what had happened to the man he could now happily throttle.

'He saw me coming and out he went,' Clement said, not too happily. 'There was nowhere else to go. I didn't think he was in the mood to do a jump, just mad at someone and wanting out.'

It was dark outside with not much reflected light but he could see, about twenty feet below, the bulk of Toplis standing with his face pressed sideways on to the wall, the fingers of one hand holding on to protruding stone ornamentation on the palely glimmering white wall. The toes of his shoes supported him on an extremely narrow ledge while his free arm was outstretched, his fingers appearing to be searching for a further hold. Below him, about two body-lengths from his feet, its glass reflecting starlight, was the roof of the entrance to the dome.

Rogers knew it was no time for talking to him even had he anything to say, he himself wanting to move in several different directions at once. He said to Clement, 'Get down below to cut him off. When you're there call Headquarters for half-a-dozen reinforcements on the double. I don't want him slipping the leash and our losing him.' He was worrying more, he thought, about Charles Jarvis and his own promises to him about being unobtrusive in effecting a peaceable arrest, than about the possibility, or impossibility, of losing the escaping Edward Seaforth-Major, alias Peter Toplis – a triple murderer if he could only prove it.

With Clement gone, Kilpatrick, calm and unflappable, took his place. 'You need me, George?' she asked, looking down at the agonizingly snail-slow movements of Toplis.

'Desperately,' he said, smiling at her, feeling her shoulder against his and hoping that she might really be meaning it.

'That's good and I'm glad.' She gave him a gentle affectionate smile which he thought had in it some sort of a future for him, then whispered, 'Shall I deal with Mrs Seaforth-Major? She's about to have a bad attack of the vapours.'

Rogers nodded, back to being a police officer on duty, his eyes on Toplis below him, doing blindly a very dangerous version of his rock climbing. Though the light wasn't very helpful, he could make out the desperate paleness of Toplis's face with his agonized eyes against the stark whiteness of the wall with its narrow, fingerhold ledges and embossed ornamentation. He felt no particular drama about it, for he couldn't see how Toplis could avoid arrest except by jumping, and he didn't think him desperate enough for that.

He could hear movement below him in the house and he again thought about the going-to-be-unhappy Charles Jarvis who would never again believe anything he might be promised by an over-optimistic Rogers. Then, as he watched Toplis with a growing frustration, wondering when he would see Clement arriving below, Toplis grabbed at a too-far ornamentation and missed it, falling sideways in slow motion and, in a seeming infinity of bated breath, crashed splinteringly through the glass roof into the passage below.

Leaving the corridor in a headlong rush, his knee promising to collapse on him with every stride, he made the stairs for the foyer, thrusting himself between two astonished late return members on his way, and then through the glazed door into the passage.

Clement was already there, squatting at the side of Toplis's body, standing on Rogers's approach. Looking doubtful and shaking his head, he said, 'He was choking, but I think he's had it.'

Rogers looked down at the bleeding and broken man lying on his back with one leg doubled beneath him. 'Dead men don't go on bleeding,' he said, then crouched over him, noting the shards of glass in his face and clothing, feeling for the pulse in his neck. It was there, not very excitable, but there. He thought he might yet occupy a prison cell.

Having radioed for a helicopter ambulance with paramedics, he left Clement with the unconscious Toplis to return to the upper corridor and Jarvis's office intending to collect Kilpatrick and Mrs Seaforth-Major *en route*.

He wasn't going to feel too sorry for Toplis until, or unless, he died, which he was only too likely to do if the paramedics didn't get here in time. The possibility didn't seem to him to be worth too much worrying about. A ruthless murderous Toplis had killed a dishonest and conniving Poukas who had certainly extorted large amounts of dishonestly obtained money from Kathrin Arbitt in her guise as Rachel Hurt. And, as certainly, Toplis had disposed of her, his criminal associate, as a probable menace to his future safety.

So far as the death of Chadwick Arbitt was concerned – and this would be Eva Kilpatrick's problem – it was originally planned, in Rogers's own opinion, that Seaforth-Major (as he was then) had been clearly marked out as a sacrificial victim by the two Arbitts, but had somehow managed to reverse his role, manipulating Kathrin Arbitt – probably from sheer greed – into joining him in treacherously killing her husband. To Rogers – who wasn't the all-seeing, and did not pretend to be – it seemed highly improbable, but it had happened; that was for certain.

None of it mattered very much now, for in his opinion, justice had never been more satisfactorily served. The two Arbitts and Poukas had been hoisted with their own individual petards, with Seaforth-Major, alias Peter Toplis – or was it the other way round – having a deservedly strong possibility of joining them.

The next hour or so wasn't, he guessed, going to be the most pleasant he could imagine and, as he trod the stairs, wondering where the devil everyone was, he tried to think of the appropriate words he could use on an inevitably irate Charles Jarvis. It wasn't going to be easy, for Charles would not yet have forgotten about him and Nancy Duval having been in a closer association than even his undoubted generosity had originally allowed for.

Life, Rogers thought, was a sod.